A SURVIVOR'S GUIDE TO ETERNITY

First Published in the UK 2014 by Mirador Publishing

First edition: 2014

Any reference to real names and places are purely fictional and are constructs of the author. Any offence the references produce is unintentional and in no way reflects the reality of any locations or people involved.

A copy of this work is available through the British Library.

ISBN: 978-1-910104-11-8

Mirador Publishing
Mirador
Wearne Lane
Langport
Somerset
TA10 9HB

A Survivor's Guide To Eternity

By

Pete Lockett

Table of Contents

Mystified, he continued on his way, none the wiser but slightly refreshed by the mysterious drink.

Bacon and eggs. I could really do with bacon and eggs and a Frappucino with caramel. Maybe even an almond croissant, he thought to himself.

Thoughts of proper refreshment triggered enthusiasm amongst the neurotransmitters in his heavy limbs, spurring him on, even though he felt more like a donkey pulling a freight train. The vegetation got thicker and harder to progress through, but reward was soon realised when he came across a mini-jet of water spilling over the crest of a small rocky area high up to his right.

Excitedly, he positioned himself under the flow until it hit him full in the face, steam coming off his hot, bubbling skin like beer evaporating from sauna coals. It was super-chilled and totally soothing, smacking into his closed eyes, compressing them from the front, combating the pressure from behind, that made them feel they were about to pop out from his head like pellets from a peashooter.

It ran down his face, over his gasping mouth, down his neck and across his overheated upper body. It felt like ice-cream on a cold sore, Bonjela on a mouth ulcer or ice on a burn; painful, but irresistible and vitally necessary. Eagerly, he moved his head in fast jolts in and out of the aggressive flow, his open mouth gulping at the cool liquid, impatiently sucking down mouthful after mouthful, his tongue panting like an excited puppy's. He tried to stretch his arms around to the cool flow but just couldn't reach. They felt heavy and onerous, difficult to lift or even move. He realised he couldn't feel his fingers or thumbs, which sharply focused his attention back from the watery salvation to his predicament. He had no idea where he was or why he felt so bad.

He continued on, awkwardly manoeuvring himself around the slippery mud slime, when – thud - he was smacked on the head by an ant the size of a mouse. It had been shot out the rapid flow of water, landing in front of him, startled, enormous, and unconditionally an ant.

It landed on its back and lay motionless for a split second in the small puddle before righting itself, struggling out of

4

Chapter 1
Through the looking grass

Ed Trew was no stranger to hangovers, but this was something else. His head throbbed like a Belisha beacon, his throat was arid like used sandpaper and he had a nausea that occupied him from the lowest depths of his stomach. Slowly, his heavy eyelids forged open one by one, like inflatable lilos dragged through quicksand. Desperately, he gasped at the air that dragged over his dry tongue like barbed wire across sand. This was going to be no ordinary day!

As his eyelids opened, the brutal light pierced to the centre of his brain with blinding incision. He frantically fumbled to cover his face from the powerful rays, confused as to his whereabouts.

The light was jetting in from a small arched opening just ahead of him. He reached forward and began to peer through the hole, moving his head further out into the brilliant sunlight. A merciless heat immediately began scorching the top of his head and arms as the light smothered him like a nuclear flash, intensifying the thumping inside his head and pushing his eyes from behind as if they were stuck in a rugby scrum.

Tortured, he momentarily retreated back into the semi-darkness not sure whether it was some sort of cave or hut that housed him. After a brief moment of respite he ventured out again, anxious for information and acutely aware of his crippling thirst.

His arms and legs felt strangely paralysed, cumbersome and heavy, his movement severely limited. A stiff and inflexible neck minimised his field of view, whilst his head continued to pulsate with tension, his eyelids fighting helplessly to defend against the brightness.

Unable to stand, face down on the floor, the only way he could move was to throw his arms and legs forward in pairs like a swimmer wading through wet cement. His momentum was slow and each movement kicked dusty soil up into his face, choking and irritating his dehydrated mouth turning it into a dried up, powdery hell.

As his eyes adjusted, he slowly became aware of his surroundings. It felt like a fairy tale setting where everything was too big to be believable. Strange, tall stalks and clumps of thick grass partially obscured his view as he struggled along as best he could. Desperately thirsty and hungry, he felt heavier than ever, exhausting himself with every cumbersome body movement, slowing his progress to a snail pace.

Maybe I should've stayed back under cover after all, he thought as he picked his heavy limbs up one after the other, trying to move forwards.

He continued up a small slope and into the respite of the shade. The parched grass was bigger and thicker than he had ever experienced before, looking as if it could be measured in feet rather than inches. Progress continued in minute increments as he continued on, launching unwieldy arm after unwieldy leg against the partially verdant resistance, way too heavy for any meaningful momentum.

His head continued to pound from within, his stomach churned and his eyes succumbed to the baking sun, even in the shade. The eyelids had loosened a little but were nothing more than a tissue in a thunderstorm.

Soon he ground to a halt on a flat piece of ground alongside a grass clump. His head was motionless on the dirt, impervious to the dust that crept deep into his mouth with each breath. Nervously, his arms pulsated in time with his breathing. This would normally have been a definite cause for concern, but in the circumstances it went largely unnoticed. This aside, he remained inanimate, fixed, frozen, immobile and stalled, wondering if it was a strange dream or a nasty reality.

The last thing he remembered was driving home to London from a business trip in Devon. It was just snap shots and flashes: getting in the car, whipping past vans and trucks, white lines firing past the vehicle, tedious news bulletins interwoven with unnecessary interjections from the sat nav, and annoying text alerts on his phone. How did all this lead him to where he was now?

Suddenly there was a powerful explosion and a great thud, as a gust of wind rushed past his motionless head, forcing him to flinch in panic and momentarily loose consciousness. Next thing he knew, he had woken back in the darkened hut.

"How can I have got back here? All that effort and struggle and I'm back where I started in this strange hut. What the hell's going on?" he said out loud to himself.

Disgruntled, he peered through the bright opening and pushed his weary head forwards. To his shock, he was not back at the start at all, but was right where the loud thud had startled him. Once again, with his face to the ground, he gestured with his big heavy arms and manoeuvred his body to the left to see the cause of the scare.

This must be some sort of stupid joke, he thought to himself as he took sight of the fallen object.

Great! A giant, scrunched-up Coke can! Have I landed a Panto set or what?

The half-crushed vessel rested not far from his head moved cautiously towards it to get a closer look. The reached around with his arms but was not able to exten far enough to get a hold of it.

Wow, I must be in a bad way. I'm going to need h mused. He nudged the can with his forehead, forcin spin over, causing a trickle of fluid from one of the the thin metal exterior. He smelt it as it leaked out a amazement, realised that it was Coca Cola.

Thirstily, he angled his head underneath and t tasted the flow of liquid. He opened his mou giving the sticky fizz a free passage over the de tongue, past his breeze block tonsils and down i throat. He'd never been a big Coke drinker, h heaven. The joy was short-lived, however, as tl ceased.

Gradually he manoeuvred his body around the mystery hut that seemed to be followin degrees, one hundred and eighty degrees, thr sixty degrees and full circle, only to see folia weary grass. No hut.

Uhmmghhh! What? Er!

Chapter 1
Through the looking grass

Ed Trew was no stranger to hangovers, but this was something else. His head throbbed like a Belisha beacon, his throat was arid like used sandpaper and he had a nausea that occupied him from the lowest depths of his stomach. Slowly, his heavy eyelids forged open one by one, like inflatable lilos dragged through quicksand. Desperately, he gasped at the air that dragged over his dry tongue like barbed wire across sand. This was going to be no ordinary day!

As his eyelids opened, the brutal light pierced to the centre of his brain with blinding incision. He frantically fumbled to cover his face from the powerful rays, confused as to his whereabouts.

The light was jetting in from a small arched opening just ahead of him. He reached forward and began to peer through the hole, moving his head further out into the brilliant sunlight. A merciless heat immediately began scorching the top of his head and arms as the light smothered him like a nuclear flash, intensifying the thumping inside his head and pushing his eyes from behind as if they were stuck in a rugby scrum.

Tortured, he momentarily retreated back into the semi-darkness not sure whether it was some sort of cave or hut that housed him. After a brief moment of respite he ventured out again, anxious for information and acutely aware of his crippling thirst.

His arms and legs felt strangely paralysed, cumbersome and heavy, his movement severely limited. A stiff and inflexible neck minimised his field of view, whilst his head continued to pulsate with tension, his eyelids fighting helplessly to defend against the brightness.

Unable to stand, face down on the floor, the only way he could move was to throw his arms and legs forward in pairs like a swimmer wading through wet cement. His momentum was slow and each movement kicked dusty soil up into his

face, choking and irritating his dehydrated mouth turning it into a dried up, powdery hell.

As his eyes adjusted, he slowly became aware of his surroundings. It felt like a fairy tale setting where everything was too big to be believable. Strange, tall stalks and clumps of thick grass partially obscured his view as he struggled along as best he could. Desperately thirsty and hungry, he felt heavier than ever, exhausting himself with every cumbersome body movement, slowing his progress to a snail pace.

Maybe I should've stayed back under cover after all, he thought as he picked his heavy limbs up one after the other, trying to move forwards.

He continued up a small slope and into the respite of the shade. The parched grass was bigger and thicker than he had ever experienced before, looking as if it could be measured in feet rather than inches. Progress continued in minute increments as he continued on, launching unwieldy arm after unwieldy leg against the partially verdant resistance, way too heavy for any meaningful momentum.

His head continued to pound from within, his stomach churned and his eyes succumbed to the baking sun, even in the shade. The eyelids had loosened a little but were nothing more than a tissue in a thunderstorm.

Soon he ground to a halt on a flat piece of ground alongside a grass clump. His head was motionless on the dirt, impervious to the dust that crept deep into his mouth with each breath. Nervously, his arms pulsated in time with his breathing. This would normally have been a definite cause for concern, but in the circumstances it went largely unnoticed. This aside, he remained inanimate, fixed, frozen, immobile and stalled, wondering if it was a strange dream or a nasty reality.

The last thing he remembered was driving home to London from a business trip in Devon. It was just snap shots and flashes: getting in the car, whipping past vans and trucks, white lines firing past the vehicle, tedious news bulletins interwoven with unnecessary interjections from the sat nav, and annoying text alerts on his phone. How did all this lead him to where he was now?

Suddenly there was a powerful explosion and a great thud, as a gust of wind rushed past his motionless head, forcing him to flinch in panic and momentarily loose consciousness. Next thing he knew, he had woken back in the darkened hut.

"How can I have got back here? All that effort and struggle and I'm back where I started in this strange hut. What the hell's going on?" he said out loud to himself.

Disgruntled, he peered through the bright opening and pushed his weary head forwards. To his shock, he was not back at the start at all, but was right where the loud thud had startled him. Once again, with his face to the ground, he gestured with his big heavy arms and manoeuvred his body to the left to see the cause of the scare.

This must be some sort of stupid joke, he thought to himself as he took sight of the fallen object.

Great! A giant, scrunched-up Coke can! Have I landed on a Panto set or what?

The half-crushed vessel rested not far from his head. He moved cautiously towards it to get a closer look. Then he reached around with his arms but was not able to extend out far enough to get a hold of it.

Wow, I must be in a bad way. I'm going to need help, he mused. He nudged the can with his forehead, forcing it to spin over, causing a trickle of fluid from one of the splits in the thin metal exterior. He smelt it as it leaked out and to his amazement, realised that it was Coca Cola.

Thirstily, he angled his head underneath and tentatively tasted the flow of liquid. He opened his mouth further, giving the sticky fizz a free passage over the desert of his tongue, past his breeze block tonsils and down into his arid throat. He'd never been a big Coke drinker, but this was heaven. The joy was short-lived, however, as the flow soon ceased.

Gradually he manoeuvred his body around to try and see the mystery hut that seemed to be following him. Ninety degrees, one hundred and eighty degrees, three hundred and sixty degrees and full circle, only to see foliage and the heat-weary grass. No hut.

Uhmmghhh! What? Er!

3

Mystified, he continued on his way, none the wiser but slightly refreshed by the mysterious drink.

Bacon and eggs. I could really do with bacon and eggs and a Frappucino with caramel. Maybe even an almond croissant, he thought to himself.

Thoughts of proper refreshment triggered enthusiasm amongst the neurotransmitters in his heavy limbs, spurring him on, even though he felt more like a donkey pulling a freight train. The vegetation got thicker and harder to progress through, but reward was soon realised when he came across a mini-jet of water spilling over the crest of a small rocky area high up to his right.

Excitedly, he positioned himself under the flow until it hit him full in the face, steam coming off his hot, bubbling skin like beer evaporating from sauna coals. It was super-chilled and totally soothing, smacking into his closed eyes, compressing them from the front, combating the pressure from behind, that made them feel they were about to pop out from his head like pellets from a peashooter.

It ran down his face, over his gasping mouth, down his neck and across his overheated upper body. It felt like ice-cream on a cold sore, Bonjela on a mouth ulcer or ice on a burn; painful, but irresistible and vitally necessary. Eagerly, he moved his head in fast jolts in and out of the aggressive flow, his open mouth gulping at the cool liquid, impatiently sucking down mouthful after mouthful, his tongue panting like an excited puppy's. He tried to stretch his arms around into the cool flow but just couldn't reach. They felt heavy and onerous, difficult to lift or even move. He realised he couldn't feel his fingers or thumbs, which sharply focused his attention back from the watery salvation to his predicament. He had no idea where he was or why he felt so bad.

He continued on, awkwardly manoeuvring himself around in the slippery mud slime, when – thud - he was smacked on the head by an ant the size of a mouse. It had been shot out by the rapid flow of water, landing in front of him, startled, enormous, and unconditionally an ant.

It landed on its back and lay motionless for a split second in the small puddle before righting itself, struggling out of

the water and disappearing into the undergrowth like a bullet into a cloud. Ed remained motionless and stared at the spot with disbelief. A massive Coke can, and now an ant that could easily be sold as a pet!

He decided it must be a dream. If he could have pinched himself then he would have, but without being able to feel his fingers, this was impossible. Besides, he had pinched himself numerous times in dreams only to find that he was still within the dream; a pointless intervention. Maybe instead he could play the dream at its own game, go to sleep and bypass the whole ridiculous fantasy and wake in his bed, not far from the kitchen, croissants, bacon, eggs and Frappucino. Sure, he was mighty hungry, but this must be a good option.

He patiently projected himself forwards through the muddy pool created by the water flow, his arms, legs and chin cooled further by the chilled churn. Exhausted and past caring, he lumbered on to a shady area hidden from view behind a large clump of super-sized grass.

Why on earth do I need to be hidden if it's a dream? he mused, as he resigned himself to the situation. With his arms and legs flat out, he lay face down on the arid land, the heat of the sun moderated by the shade from the stalks of lifeless grass. Soon he drifted off into a calm, but light sleep, the tall dry leaves whispering in the wind from side to side.

Flashes of memories shot by. Mini snapshots, almost too short to recognise. A car, a road, the inside of a room, a desk, a stabbing pain in the ear, diving into a pool, falling from skis at high speed, jumping from a moving train, a blow job in the Sahara, being in a nappy, a gun, running and running, more running. Then a lift, a balcony and a roof top terrace covered in Astro turf, a football match, a road, and then all was blank, black, empty, zero, vacant, absent, invisible, undetectable and anonymous. An all-encompassing darkness with hermetically sealed silence. Sensory deprivation was a night club compared to this.

Chapter 2
Into the light

A pinprick of light in the darkness, hardly detectable but piercing with intensity. A bright dart which soon focused, pulling him towards it with a monumental gravity, faster and faster as he approached, his body mass feeling heavier and heavier, a free-falling object gaining weight as the air resistance diminished and he sped like a jet into the expanding whiteness, blinding with its power, deafening with the noise of friction and finally with screaming panic, total silence and tranquillity.

The brightness still dazzled and overpowered, but the noise of the crazy supersonic free fall ceased. He began to wake to his surroundings, hoping for a bedroom rather than a bush. Soon, colour came into the equation, worryingly greeny-brown and not the warming yellow of his bedroom.

Everything came smoothly into view, like a camera zoom slowly realising its focal length. A green-brown haze soon became tall sun-bleached dusty grass, and Ed's spirits took a deeper dive into the black depths of misery. He hadn't given up hope it was a dream, but began to concede he had crossed paths once more with a vile reality.

He raised his head as best he could, took a deep breath and converted it to a despairing sigh before flopping back onto the floor, motionless and confused. His body felt drained. Where in God's name was he, and why was he there? The pangs of hunger rippled up from his stomach, through his neck and into his still-throbbing head, defined by emptiness and longing. It was a desperate feeling that completely drained him of energy.

Gradually, he mustered his dwindling powers and forced himself forwards. The terrain flattened out slightly and down a slight gradient as if towards a stream or water source. This slope at least helped conserve energy and made his progress slightly easier.

He then started to notice a very strong odour coming from

the surrounding plants. It was as if someone from Chanel had gone around with plant-flavoured perfume nectar, spraying without mercy. It was overwhelming, like sitting in the theatre next to a gigantic fragrant sponge. Even the semi-dusty, balding grass area he was pulling himself across was odorous with extremity.

As he progressed, his head brushed past large yellow and white flowers, proudly facing the glistening sun. He couldn't help but notice their evocative smell, as tempting as bacon and eggs.

How very strange, he thought as he started to feel angry and helpless over his predicament.

As he brushed past yet another 'bacon flower', he recalled a TV documentary, where people had survived in the wild by eating flowers and general vegetation. Could this be an idea? How dangerous was it? Would he get poisoned from such things? Most importantly of all, why did they smell as good as a roast dinner?

He ambled over to the next clump of flowers that crossed his path. The smell was Egon Ronay, haute cuisine and luxury dishes. This was as good as it got. He sniffed and sniffed, the smell resounding right down to the cramps in his stomach, igniting the hunger with even more desperation. He sniffed again and then began cautiously licking their colourful petals.

His unusually slimy tongue pushed up against the colourful, magnificent flowers, still warm from the rays of the sun. The taste was exquisite, nutty and wholesome with a sweet, but savoury tang. He licked again, moving in towards the centre, causing some of the pollen caplets to break away into his mouth. They exploded with flavour, a cross between Wasabi nuts and M&M's.

Instinct took over and he began dragging at the petals with his fumbling mandibles, slipping them into his mouth with the aid of his strange tongue. He ripped at them with eager and fanatical desire, savaging them from their stately elegance, transforming the flowers into miserable and lonely stalks. He gorged and gorged, going from clump to clump, acutely aware of the strange chewing sensation. It was as if he had no teeth and was chewing everything with his lips. It was an incredibly odd sensation, and not one he liked.

He ate and ate, like a crazed animal destroying a flower show. Bunch after bunch was decimated until he came to a bloated standstill a few minutes later. Stuffed full, his stomach could take no more and his mouth was sore from the chewing. In the near distance he could see a fresh water stream, just down the incline and decided to pull himself down towards it for another drink. He felt that just maybe the flowers might give him enough energy to stand upright and walk out of the strange wilderness.

The sun had long since turned past midday and from the speed it was going down he figured he had a few hours before darkness. At least it wasn't searing heat with deathly light rays any more. His head had calmed down and the Belisha beacon palpitations had become more of a pulsating jelly fish. He struggled down towards the water with slow, heavy movements, weary from the events of the day. It took some while and by the time he got there, the sun was beginning to disappear over the top of the oversized growth.

How can that have taken so long? he pondered, as he got to the water's edge in mystical twilight. He took some slurps from what he dearly hoped was a fresh water stream before resting beside its gently comforting rumble.

I'm so tired, but I don't really want to sleep out here in the open, he thought, as he mustered one more burst of energy to pull himself over towards the longer clumps of grass to his left. Once again he struggled with his heavy arms and legs to slink in behind some dense bushes and rest his weary body for the night. He was beginning to doubt if he would ever get out of this mysterious situation in one piece.

Hopefully I'll at least get some rest and get rid of this ache, pulsing away at the inside of my skull, he thought to himself, as he rested his head on a small grassy lump and started to nod off.

He slept like a log, straight through in a deep, motionless coma. This was eventually interrupted by a violent streak of early morning sun penetrating through the stalks of grass and

onto his inadequate eyelids. Consciousness began to arouse him as he cautiously opened his eyes, soon realising that the pains of the day before, had demised. He was clear, headache and hangover free. He started to consider the rest of his body. Seemingly no nausea, stomach cramps, physical pains or anything else that indicated he would either feel as bad as the previous day or else that he had been poisoned by the flowers or water.

Did I really eat flowers? he thought, as he became more lucid, almost resigned to the fact he was in the wild and not a bedroom. He tried to stand but his legs felt too heavy and awkward. His vision continued to be restricted, regardless of how much he tried to angle his head around.

Then, as he started to become aware of the chirpings, squeaks, squalls and murmurings of his surroundings, he noticed something far more sinister. It was a low-pitched, growling, snarling, dog-like sound that slowly got louder and louder, closer and closer. It started to rumble his eardrums and suddenly he felt an instinctive whole body nervous spasm of panic and in a flash he was back in the protective enclosure where he'd woken the previous morning.

What the hell! This is some mad stuff right here! This is one indelible dream. How did I get back in here? he wondered.

He thought back on the previous afternoon where he had flinched from the large coke can and ended back in the hut. As mysterious as that was, he thought that he'd moved on but here it was again, haunting his perceptions of any reasonable reality. He looked through the opening he was getting to know so well. In the short time it had taken him to wake, the day had started to take hold and the dawn was rapidly being erased by a scorching sun, full of intent to burn and bake.

He then noticed something even more menacing. Jets of steam started to gust past and into the opening, a musty, breathy steam, accompanied by low toned breaths that resounded in metronomic time with the exhalations. It was most certainly the breathing of some terrifyingly massive animal. It shook and resonated through his whole body as it rushed in past his head in short bursts.

That's it, this will be the end, thought Ed. He strangely hoped he would be a satisfying meal for the unknown beast, not just a mere hors d'oeuvre or snack. He retreated back into his protective cell as much as possible, feeling very restricted and tight for space.

This is tiny, he thought as he realised his back and sides were tight against the walls of the small claustrophobic space. Nervously, he peered through the opening in front of him and caught first sight of the fearsome animal. Light brown hairs started to appear, erect stalks, more like small ropes. Then a gigantic, wet, black-button nose, with two massive steaming nostrils with lizard like scaly texture. The odour of the steamy exhalations was strong and ominously dog-like, overpowering his senses as it filled the enclosure with a fearful presence.

He heard the animal pause before its large nose edged slightly into the opening. The nostrils were large, wide open, cavernous tunnels. He could see right down into them like looking into some sort of strange drainage pipe. Larger whiskers also became visible as the animal reached in further. Then the inevitable sniff, an inhalation that pulled the air away from the inside of the enclosure, pulling at Ed's face and making it hard to breathe for a millisecond. The protruding snout then retreated and there was a momentary lull in proceedings.

Maybe he didn't see me? Maybe if I keep still and quiet he'll go away. I mustn't move; I must keep dead still!

These thoughts of invisibility were short-lived as he peered out at the black button as it approached once more. Then in an instant, his world was turned upside down. The animal pushed its nose into the opening and with what felt like the force of a bulldozer, shifted him backwards, lifting his whole protective shelter back on itself and sideways. He spun like a teddy bear in a washing machine, over and over, completely losing orientation, perspective and direction. He could see the world whizzing by outside through the opening. It was if he was on a fast train hurtling through the countryside, spinning in a circle. As it slowed he could see he was upside down, although still inside the protective hut.

He was dazed and confused but before he had time to think, he was off again, tossed like a pancake, feeling like a billiard ball rattling around in an empty suitcase.

This time he came to an abrupt stop, upright and peering out from the opening down towards the stream. In his line of sight was a terrifying looking, colossal paw, black fur at the bottom, beautiful and glossily groomed with light brown and white highlights, symmetrically decorated with fearsome looking whitey-grey sharp claws. Another paw entered the field of vision and they began to get closer.

His head once again pulsated like a squeeze ball in a weight lifter's fist.

"All right, whatever. Big oaf of a hound, you can't understand a word I'm saying but I couldn't care less, you're doing me a favour. Eat me and just get me out of this ridiculous Alice in bloody arid-land, nightmare. I'm all yours!"

The paws stopped in their tracks, claws retracted and a silence ensued for what seemed like an age.

"You are one of us," said a voice from outside the enclosure.

Another silence. Ed was dumbfounded. A monstrous sized hound that could speak! It really must be a dream.

"Okay, I give in. I'm obviously asleep, and when I wake up I'll be in my bed. This is driving me nuts. It's the worst dream I have ever had!"

"You'll wake up exactly where you are. Besides that, you don't have much time. You need to listen to me. I've got some important information for you."

"Great. Two minutes ago I was about to be your dinner, and now you want to have a chat! This is ridiculous," spluttered Ed.

The hound paused for thought and moved closer, lying down on the ground so Ed could see more of him through the opening. Glossy light brown fur with white trim, moist black button and thick long protuberant black whiskers.

"That was before you spoke. It's been some while since I spoke to anyone. Come out and we can talk. Anyway, I wasn't going to eat you," said the creature.

"Come out so I can be eaten more like!"

"I won't eat you, just come out."

Ed was paralysed with bemusement.

"What the hell, if it's a dream and I get eaten then I'll wake up. If I get eaten and it's not a dream than I'll be out of this hell, and if I don't get eaten then I'll be having a conversation with a giant hound; worthwhile in its own right. It's a no-lose situation!"

Slowly, he began to move closer to the opening and move his head out of the hole, soon bringing into view the terrifying size of this oversized animal.

"Don't be scared, don't be scared," barked the hound. "We have far more in common than you could ever imagine."

Ed manoeuvred himself out into the open, cautiously but philosophically.

"Crikey, you're massive, a massive fox!" he gasped as he began to realise exactly what he was dealing with.

"Well, it's you that's small rather than me that's large. I am actually only a medium-sized fox," replied the fox.

"Well, if six foot two inches is small, then I guess I'm small. It's all relative, and doesn't change the fact that you're enormous," rebuked Ed.

"Listen, there's a lot for you to find out. How many days have you been awake? Is it your first time?"

"Well if you mean, 'is it the first time I have woken up in some sort of surreal arid landscape with oversized vegetation, nearly been killed by a Coke can, had flowers for supper, been put in a tumble dryer by an outsized hound and struck up a conversation with a fox ten times my size,' then I have to say yes, this is my first time!"

"Ah. Yes, it's your first time. That's obvious now. Good that you've eaten something though. They don't always do that. How long have you been in this state?"

"Well I guess it's around twenty-four hours or so."

"Have you seen what you look like?"

"Well if you mean do I carry a vanity mirror with me everywhere I go then I have to say no! Also, you might have noticed there are a lack of service stations and toilets with mirrors in the bushes!"

"Well toilets aren't my main concern. Didn't you drink from the stream at all? Didn't you see your reflection?"

"It was getting dark last night. I didn't notice my reflection. Do I look that bad?"

"No, not that bad, possibly even normal. Let's go down to the stream and have a drink and get you to see yourself."

"Is this some sort of trap? Why do you want me to see myself? I know what I look like."

"Yes, I'm sure you know what you *looked* like. Let's go down there."

"Okay. I'm not exactly feeling on top of the world. I can't stand up and have to crawl. I'm not exactly lining myself up for the Olympics."

"I noticed! I'll go over there and see you in half an hour."

"Half an hour; it's not that far!"

"See you there in half an hour. You are a bit of a slow mover."

The fox shot upright onto all fours, his fat upper thighs powering his powerful legs, so slender at the bottom. He bounded off down the slight incline, his big bushy brush tossing around behind him from side to side. He seemed to Ed to have the power of a stallion, galloping down to the water's edge in a matter of seconds.

Ed meanwhile threw his tired arms and legs forward in the motion of a broken fan running out of battery power.

"Oh, fuck," he groaned as he struggled to drag himself in the footsteps of the proud dog. "If this is not as surreal as you can get, then I'm a Baffin."

Breathless and some while later, he made the final languid motions to pull himself next to the fox, who was reclining beside the water with his head bent over his body snatching spasmodically at fleas with his sharp, white, shiny fangs. As his head moved sharply from side to side, he bit exploringly into his fur, dislodging the unwanted insects and launching them in Ed's direction.

"Great, thanks for that," said Ed, as an oversized flea smacked him on the head and bounced to his left side. Not fazed by the large insect, he glanced to where it landed and saw a procession of mouse-sized ants, each labouring with its own over sized item. Twigs, stones and bits of grass all passed by upon the never-ending parade of little soldiers going about their duties. Ed was mesmerised by their methodical organisation. It was as if each individual insect was being controlled by a central controller guiding them on their intricate un-conflicting path. They went around, over, under, across and through the others' routes with pinpoint precision, never faltering or losing control of the unwieldy objects that looked far too big to manage.

It looked incredible seeing them like this with such clarity. He thought about how organised and powerful humanity would be if people worked together with such common goals, never faltering from the task at hand, working towards the service of the whole community. He looked up at the fox, glistening brown in the light. Beside them the water sparkled calmly, reflecting laser-like sparkles from the tiny ripples towards the centre.

"Let's get on with it. You want me to see my reflection. Why should I care? It's all so very odd. I'm just going along with anything right now, conversations with a fox, humongous everyday objects, whatever, bring it on! Anyway, how come you can speak in the first place; you're a fox for heaven's sake?"

"Just look at yourself in the reflection and then we can talk. Keep calm though and don't be alarmed by what you see. It's perfectly normal. I'd advise you to sit down, but in the circumstances it would be rather pointless."

"What do you mean, pointless? What's your problem? Why should I sit down?" snapped Ed as he moved closer to the water's edge trying to reflect back on any incident which might have left marks on his face. His memory was sketchy, just tiny glimpses and flashes. He thought of his life and his modestly successful young business. He thought of his wife and home in London. He was a fairly contented man, not eaten away by over-ambition or under-achievement.

He continued down to the water, angled his head down, drank a satisfying gulp and half submerged his face to cool himself. He pulled his head from the stream, shook it like a soggy dog and looked upwards.

"I'm not looking. I don't know why you want me to look, but I'm not doing it."

The fox jumped up elegantly and bounded over to beside Ed.

"Okay, then look at my reflection; what do you see?"

"Erm, well, a fox obviously."

The fox snarled approvingly, revealing his tremendously sharp teeth in the process.

"Mate, you have teeth the size of my fridge freezer; can you not understand that makes me feel a tad uncomfortable?" Ed stammered nervously.

"Don't worry, you're safe with me. Take a look at your reflection, for goodness sake, what do you see?"

Ed bent his head to look at his reflected image, irritated by the ridiculous game.

"A tortoise! EHHHHMMM, a tortoise, a fucking tortoise! Christ, what sort of nasty joke is this? Wake up, wake up, wake up, wake up, bloody well wake up!"

The realisation was like an Exocet missile fired into his brain at top speed, in one ear and out the other. He felt it in his stomach as if a dance troupe was performing in his intestines. He stared at the reflection, stunned and disoriented.

"I was not the best looking fella at the best of times but this is simply ludicrous!" he reflected, wishing he could be reunited with his large bloodshot nose and balding head complete with fluffy wisp that gave an illusion of profusion as sustainable as the euro zone.

The fox sat quietly behind him, observing respectfully. "The first time is always the hardest."

"The first time? How many times exactly can you become a tortoise?" Ed barked back from his reptilian beak-like mouth, as a flat-nosed, stripy badger wandered into the scene.

"Great, you're taller than me as well. I suppose you've got something pertinent to add to all this?" he snapped at the furry animal.

The badger ignored him and emitted a strange, low-level growling noise before going around to sniff his behind. Ed could feel the breath of the animal as he tried to scurry around to dissuade him from the activity.

"Go on, have a good sniff. Is that all you want or what? Well?"

The badger silently moved over to the fox, who had turned round to assess the situation. They went nose to nose, doing a little Chinese nose rub before the badger turned tail and slid his stripy being off into the undergrowth.

"The badger doesn't understand you. It can't talk. I need to explain a lot of things to you right now. You need to listen very carefully."

"Well how come you can talk and he can't? What's the deal there?"

"It's not easy and there's no easy way to tell you. Basically, you've died and been reincarnated into a young animal, in this instance, most unfortunately for a first-timer, a tortoise."

"I've died? Are you completely crazy? How can I be talking if I've died? How can I have my consciousness and memories? How is it that I can still feel my arms and legs and still dream of bacon and eggs? How can I remember my car and physical appearance? There are so many other things. Besides, why do you keep saying, 'first timer?'"

A silence ensued but before the fox could reply, Ed continued.

"How can I not have been aware of dying? Surely that would have been something I might have noticed? How switched off from my environment would I need to have been to miss that?"

"You'll never really remember dying, or that much of the journey afterwards, but you will remember moments leading up to it. Things will become much clearer, trust me."

"What's the point in things getting clearer if I'm a tortoise with the memories of a human? From what I remember, they don't even have hands. Even with an iPhone, I wouldn't be any better equipped to get any help."

"Get help? Are you mad? There's no help for you now, other than from yourself, and you're already running out of time. Besides, even if you could 'instant message' someone

16

to say you'd somehow accidentally been transformed into a tortoise and you were down by the river with a fox, how do you think they'd deal with that?"

"Well they'd come down and I'd speak to them just like I'm speaking to you now. How difficult can that be?"

"Mmmm, I forgot to mention, only other transients can hear us speak. It's been absolutely ages since I last spoke to someone. Transients can hear one another, but any 'non transient' only hears normal animal noises, bleating, barking, squeaking etc. For a tortoise, I think they might find it hard to hear anything at all."

"What do you mean, a transient? What on earth are you talking about? What's a transient?" enquired Ed curiously.

"Well that's what's happened. You've been transitioned into the body of a tortoise."

"Is that a term you've just made up or something?"

"I wouldn't say that. It is common usage of the word, changeable, deciduous and emigrating in a fleeting and impermanent way."

"Fleeting and impermanent? So I won't stay like this forever then?" queried Ed.

"No, you won't stay like it forever. There are some issues we have choice over."

"What issues? What choice? This must be hell. A tortoise. Why a tortoise?" replied Ed with a growing feeling of angst.

"From what I understand, transience into an animal host seems to be arrived at randomly. It is not a reflection on your worth, dignity or morality. For you, it's just bloody unlucky that you've ended up as a tortoise."

"Great. I'd like to say I'll take this on the chin and move on, but I don't actually have one. Besides, how could you take 'being turned into a tortoise' on the chin anyway?"

"Erm, maybe not."

"Presupposing I believe you for a while, how long do you think I might have been dead?"

"Hard to say for the first time. Maybe a year or eighteen months before you get reincarnated the first time. I have no idea why, maybe a backlog? Time does seem to flow more predictably from the second time onwards."

Ed thought quietly for a moment, overwhelmed by the whole idea of being dead for over a year.

"I have no idea how to respond to all this. It's so far fetched. Maybe I've taken some very strong hallucinogenic drugs or something. This can't be happening? Besides, why do you keep saying first and second time? Does it keep happening over and over again?"

"Yes, unfortunately it happens again and again. There are some important things to know though," replied the fox gently.

"Important things? What do you mean?"

"What's your name?"

"Ed. Ed Trew"

"Well, Ed Trew, I'm Sam Edwards and like you, I have human consciousness and memories. Just like you, I had the whole jolt and shock of coming around to realise I was an animal with human memories. Also, just like you I was incredibly lucky to meet another like us, a 'Transient' who told me what I am about to tell you. Most Transients don't get this opportunity and before they know it, their minds are cabbage and they've lost their opportunity. Basically the deal is this. You keep your human consciousness for around four days. During this time your human memories will gradually fade. As this happens, the instincts of the host animal get stronger and stronger and you start to give yourself over to that creature."

"What do you mean, give yourself over?"

"You start to lose all your human awareness and basically your soul dissolves into the animal's basic consciousness."

"What about speaking and communication?"

"You lose all that."

"Memories?"

"All gone. You become a basic creature."

Ed sat motionless, in a state of shock and disbelief, listening to the fox's revelations.

"After the four days expire, all your human memories, habits, instincts, awareness and emotions disappear completely and you become the common or garden animal with no self-consciousness whatsoever. What happens with

18

these animals after death, I don't know, but I do know that if you die in the four-day period then you go back to the beginning, reincarnated into a new animal randomly, giving you a new, four-day period all over again. It could be any species from a rat to a poodle; it might be in the wild or a zoo or as a household pet. Anything is possible."

"But if you only have four days, and say you get born as a helpless cub or something, what happens then? What could you possibly do in that state?"

"You never come round as a newborn. It's always youthful, but never a vulnerable pup or anything like that. Maybe it's because we can jump into animals because they have no souls?"

"No souls? Are you sure?" queried Ed.

"What's the alternative, that an animal suddenly has two souls or that the first is banished in an instant? It's my belief that we're being tested. I don't know how or why but I think we need to solve some sort of puzzle or riddle or something to find out what all this is about and why we're here. There must be a reason this is happening, and so I keep going round the four-day cycles, trying to work out what it could be. Maybe there's a way one can release oneself from the cycle and be reincarnated back as a newborn human?"

Ed stared on, his beak-like mouth hung open, his senses oblivious to the re-entry of the badger into the scene, once more sniffing his bottom mercilessly. He turned towards the fox, trying hopelessly to bend his thick neck.

"So I've woken up as a tortoise, made friends with a rather large, talking fox, realised I have been reincarnated and now you're telling me I have to kill myself every four days?"

"In a word, yes, although I'm not large, it's you that's small. Also, for safety's sake I'd suggest suicide every three to three and a half days to be safe. As a tortoise this might take some research. I can just cross the road and get pummelled. I think the cars would just swerve around you."

"Fantastic, all that, and now I have to find out the best way for a tortoise to kill itself. Well, as I recall from my faint memory, I didn't have a lot of suicidal tortoise friends when I was a human."

"There's no rush, you still have a couple of days. I suggest you come over to my lair and I'll go and get some food. It's your first time, and you should relax. Talking will help."

The badger looked on without concern, as it came round to the front of Ed and started sniffing at his head.

"Whatever!! Let's go then. It's the first time I've been invited into a fox lair. How far is it? It might take me more than two days to get there," replied Ed sarcastically.

"It's just over here. Very close."

"Can you get this badger off my case? He's driving me nuts."

The fox gently manoeuvred the badger away with his snout, snarling with gentle authority. The badger sniffed back before slowly retreating up the dusty, parched incline.

"Just follow this path along and I'll go ahead and wait for you. It won't take you much longer than forty minutes."

Fox trotted off looking like two ballerinas in a pantomime costume, elegant but comical. The brush, as ever, trailed behind without a say in the matter. Ed mustered strength into what he now conceded were four fat legs, looked at his reflection once again and resigned himself to having to haul his shell through the scattered clumps of grass, onto the slightly trodden path and off after the fox as the wispy brush disappeared from view.

Chapter 3
Sliding deeper

Thoughts raced by as Ed began to digest the whole situation.

I looked miserable when I was a human; God knows how miserable I look now. Why couldn't they have erased my memory? I'm a tortoise; I don't need to know about iPads, relativity and pornography. It makes me suffer. Anyway, how can all those thoughts and memories fit into this tiny shrimp of a tortoise brain; it just doesn't add up? thought Ed, as he continued ambling in uncomfortable distress through the terrain.

If there's something up with your satellite TV box or a delivery hasn't arrived, there's someone you can call. When you've been reincarnated as a tortoise with the consciousness of a human, what are you meant to do then, what helpline is there for that? Even if I could get to a phone I wouldn't be able to pick it up. What would be the point anyway if all they could hear at the end was a tortoise in distress? Certainly not covered on my insurance plan, that's for sure.

As he progressed onwards, he was again overwhelmed by that delicious flowery food smell. He manoeuvred over to a small clump and began munching away hungrily.

At least it saves me going to the shops. Saves money as well I'll smell like a flower stall though when I have a crap, he thought ironically, before pulling himself from the colourful edible smorgasbord and on towards the fox lair.

Ed began to reflect on his unfortunate situation and the life he had lost. He thought of his wife Abella, a striking brunette, well out of his league but yet somehow attracted and committed to him. He reflected on how they'd met at a works party when he'd been stock controller and buyer for a small electronics firm in Petersfield. This was more than awkward, bearing in mind she was married to his boss. He remembered that evening as if it was yesterday. He recalled how he couldn't resist her gravitational pull and spent that evening courting her whilst her husband spent time with everyone else in the room. He loathed his arrogant swagger.

"Get me a bottle of Corona from the bar, Bella? Oh, and don't put that lime in the top, you know I hate that."

She hated being called 'Bella' and just as much loathed being used as a waitress on call. Their teenage romance had long since been transformed into middle-aged confusion, even though she was in her late twenties. She was five years younger than her husband Jonathan, and about the same age as Ed. The misery and sadness glinted in her eyes as she turned with resignation towards the bar to fulfil her marital duty.

"I'll give you a hand - we both need a top up anyway," announced Ed keenly, realising her anguish. He was not set on making advances at this point, but hated seeing someone so unhappy. Just a short while later she was heading obediently over to Jonathan whilst Ed looked after her drink.

"I told you not to get one of those bloody limes in the top. For Chrissake, take it out and put it in an ash tray," barked the large-foreheaded man in a light grey tweed sports coat and white flannel trousers. His friends in the group grinned, some with pleasure and others with wincing discomfort. Abella turned tail instinctually, embarrassed to the core and hoping for the ground to open and swallow her up. The heat flushed into her face, reddening it to a bright fireball as she discarded the lime and handed the bottle to her husband.

He neither looked at her nor acknowledged the gesture of servitude, and turned to resume the conversation with his associates, analysing the potential development of a smaller circuit board for their central heating controller.

Abella shuffled invisibly across the room and out into the cold night. No one noticed apart from Ed. He gave her a minute and then subtly followed her out, leaving his drink on the cigarette machine by the door.

He found her huddled and crying in a doorway on the far side of the car park.

"It was so good at first. I don't know what's happened to

him. He's a different person, so boring, so cold and so unaffectionate. I don't know how I can survive." The words struggled out through the lonely tears which intercepted their announcement as they fell to the floor like her mood.

"Don't worry, you'll find a way," said Ed, comforting her with his words before continuing. "Look, it's freezing out here. Come back inside."

"I can't. I just want to die. I know it sounds extreme but it can't be worse than this," replied Abella as she tossed her glorious curly brunette locks with a quick flick of her head to the left. She looked up and straight at Ed with her huge and gorgeous big brown eyes. They shimmered with flashes of light glinting with an enchanting teary reflection from the car park security lights.

Ed tentatively put his arm around her and handed her a clean white hanky, careful not to be overly intimate or misunderstood. He glanced down at her astounding hourglass body, short pleated patterned skirt, black seamed stockings and tasteful stilettos.

"Look, it's freezing. You don't have a coat - you'll freeze," pleaded Ed as she put her head down onto his shoulder, soaking his shirt with tears whilst her immaculate hair cascaded down over his shirt pocket. The hanky was held motionless in her hand. The car park was deserted and silent apart from the sound of her sobs. She lifted her head up and glanced at Ed once more, a lot closer than the last time.

"Do you have a car? We could sit in your car?"

"Er, yes but, well, that might be deemed inappropriate?" replied Ed slightly nervously.

"Well I'm not going back in there so the only other alternative is to freeze, I guess," uttered Abella, the tears calming slightly. She lifted the hanky up and began patting her eyes dry.

"Okay then, it's in the car park at the back. I got here late and missed all the good spaces," uttered Ed as he started to usher her towards the back of the building.

"It's over. I decided already before tonight. I just need to decide when. I can't take this shit anymore," declared the beautiful woman as they approached Ed's Toyota people carrier. He opened the back door and she got in, delicately manoeuvring her perfect stilettoed feet with dignity.

"I'll sit in the front," stated Ed as he began to pull the door shut.

"No," whispered Abella as she stopped him closing the door. "Sit in the back, I won't be able to hear you from the front."

Her tears had demised. She moved her hand forward as if to hand Ed the hanky. He reached out to take it from her and she clasped his hand.

"Please come and sit with me?"

Ed felt a blood surge across his whole body. It was like having a rush from an adrenalin injection. He started to shake slightly as he lifted himself up into the back of the car, pulling the door closed behind and sitting next to her. The hanky fell to the floor as she lifted his hand to her mouth and gave it a gentle kiss on the knuckles.

"Thanks for coming out after me," she whispered seductively into his ear as she moved her head closer to his, still clinging to his hand.

"That's fine, it's the least I…" Ed turned his head as he spoke and had not finished the sentence before their lips had met. He felt the texture of the slightly sticky red lip gloss as his tongue parted her lips and met hers. She lifted his hand up and over her right shoulder and behind her neck as the duo turned their heads slightly and began dancing with their tongues. She enveloped him with her arms and began stroking the back of his head affectionately, as they continued kissing.

He stroked her hair and then moved down over her shoulders, inspiring an excited arousal like never before, aching to be inside her. She reached down and manoeuvred her hand palm down around his inner thighs and up over his bulging enthusiasm. He began gently stroking over her breasts before pulling her sleeves down. She reached behind herself and unzipped her dress to assist.

The situation moved very fast and before he knew it she was on top of him. His hand reached around and slid along her stockings and up to the suspenders and then the beautiful smooth silky skin. Bodies interlocked, they fondled and cuddled, the sweat lubricating them as they manoeuvred together. It was too much for Ed as he climaxed quickly, clasping her firmly but affectionately with one hand, stroking her hair with the other whilst staring into her eyes. It was a moment of utter magic, sublime and all satisfying. It was a moment enough to satisfy him for life.

Soon they had cleaned up, tidied themselves and headed back to the event.

"This is the first time I've been intimate with someone straight away like this. It's not like me - please don't get the wrong idea. But I want to see you again, Ed," said Abella as she slid a small piece of paper into his pocket before adding,

"that's my mobile phone number. I expect to hear from you."

"You will, trust me on that. I'll text you my number." With this, Ed placed his hand on her shoulder, stopped walking, and turned her to face him.

"I tell you one thing from the bottom of my heart; I will never treat you like that animal treats you. You're like a goddess in my eyes. I would give everything for you. I'm going to resign on Monday. This will be a lot easier if I'm not working for your husband."

"Soon to be ex-husband, Ed."

"Sounds good to me," replied Ed as they skipped off back into the hall. Less than a year later they were married and Ed had started his own company.

He felt very sad reflecting back on his wife and that magical evening. He would never see her again and it filled him with such an overwhelming sadness. His thoughts turned back towards his current predicament as he continued his very slow passage towards the fox lair.

The sun was beginning to bake the ground and heat his shell like a little oven. He realised why he had felt so hot and dazed the previous day carrying all that weight around whilst being slowly cooked like a lobster in its own shell. He looked forward to getting underground in the fox den sheltered from the heat. The going was getting tough though, as he struggled on in the bright day.

"Get inside your shell," he heard from beside him as he saw the fox come into view.

"Get inside your shell," the fox repeated.

"Well, I don't know how to do that."

"RAFFF, RAFFF, RAFFF," the fox barked loudly, forcing Ed instinctually to shrivel up into the shell and out of sight.

"Thank you," gasped the fox as he got behind Ed and pushed him with his snout, speeding along the path like an out-of-control bobsleigh.

"AArrggghhhhhhh... Wheeeyyyyyyyyyyyyy, errrrrr," Ed cried out helpless, but excited at the new rapid mode of transport offered to him.

"This is too much, stop, stop! More like, how the hell are we gonna stop?"

Suddenly, the tortoise was propelled into a soft bush, tossed over and over until he landed in an upside down position, whirling around like a spinning top.

In no time, the panting fox was on the scene, having lost control of his projectile.

"Sorry about that. Lost control a little bit. Easier than you walking though," barked the fox as he flipped Ed upright like tossing a coin.

"Yes, easier for sure, but that's like saying that jumping off a high rise is quicker than using a lift. Thanks for the thought, though."

"Don't mention it. Anyway, we're here now, you can get in the shade. I suggest you pop behind that bush though and do a bit of natural stuff before you enter."

"Yes, I've been holding that one off. I don't know how it will be. I haven't been yet. Is it the same?"

"How do I know? I've never been a tortoise! Do you want me to have a look at what you have back there?"

"No I bloody well don't, thank you very much. I'll go and do it alone. I am sure nature's designed it so it's not pointing in my face."

Ed slinked off behind the bush and quickly did his thing

26

before heading back over to Sam. Exposing himself to the elements in such openness seemed strangely comforting, dropping off his parcels without any toilet paper or bidet to finish up with. It did little to hide the smell though, intriguingly scented and evocative.

"That's incredible, it did smell like flowers. That is one improvement on the human situation for sure."

"Yeah, but it's not always the case, trust me on that," said the fox shyly as he headed down into the lair, followed by the tortoise.

It wasn't all that deep, but was enough to give protection from the elements and any aggressive beasts that might fancy an impromptu vulpine snack. It was surprisingly spacious with twigs and leaves scattered around, adding a degree of comfort in spite of the circumstances. The fox lay down, slightly on his side, his head peering back over his body with the brush wrapped around preventing any nasty draughts.

"Don't suppose you have room service?" uttered Ed before taking up his position opposite the fox.

"I'll go and get something later for both of us. There are a couple of small shops through the bushes which are easy to raid."

"Where are we?"

"Definitely somewhere in the UK. Home Counties I'm guessing, but I've only been here a day longer than you."

"Right, that means you'll leave a day before me, presupposing everything you say is true."

"Well if it wasn't true it would be one amazing pointless story. Christ knows I wish it wasn't true. I've been through numerous transitions and it doesn't get any easier. Worst of all is not knowing what sort of revelation one is looking for, and beyond that, what would happen if I had it."

"Could it be some sort of eternal sin thing? I was a bit religious and loosely held some beliefs along those lines."

"I don't think so, although I wouldn't rule anything out. I was not religious at all. That's the difference between us right there. Maybe you were praying to the wrong one? Got to the gates of heaven and Shiva was there instead of St

Peter. That would be a shock if you'd spent your life believing in Christ," announced the fox.

"Yeah, wouldn't it be. In retrospect, it might have been more beneficial spending my time watching Animal Planet and National Geographic."

"Are you a Christian, a Muslim, Hindu? What did you believe in?"

"I was Christian, Church of England. Not fanatical, but a regular church goer."

"Was?" enquired the fox.

"Well I'm dead aren't I? Anyway, I honestly don't know. Church of the living tortoise? I don't think so. Turning me into a reptile wasn't the best way to ensure continued loyalty."

"I'm with you on that one. How religious were you?"

"Not massively but I was swayed by social pressure and conformity. I liked to have that comforting belief that there was something out there much bigger than me that I could hold out a hand to and ask for help. Now I can do that in reality, it turns out to be a fox ten times my size."

"I personally find it a little odd to worship something that's completely impossible to verify scientifically? Even if there had been proof, I wouldn't have been a follower."

"Even if it was proven? Why not?"

"Well, let's assume for argument's sake that there's a god. We then have to consider the possibility that its nature is either good or bad, or even a mix of good or bad just like the mortals on Earth."

"Why bad? How can there be a bad natured god?"

"It's just for the purpose of the argument. Would you agree that if it was a bad natured god then you wouldn't worship it?"

"For sure."

"Me too. How would you feel though, if it was a mix of good and bad and its actions one way or another, were dependent upon its moods or prejudices?"

"Well off the top of my head, I wouldn't feel comfortable about that either. What would make him, or her different from regular people?"

"The power and omnipotence, of course."

"Of course, power. Power which could be used for good or evil," replied Ed, getting more and more engaged in the conversation, almost forgetting he was talking to a large, brown fox in an underground lair.

"Exactly. I certainly wouldn't want to worship such a god. You could be praised one day yet scolded the next for the very same action."

"I guess you're right. But what if he was good, but without any powers?"

"Well maybe there'd be some people willing to entrust their hopes of wellbeing to an impotent god, but I wouldn't be one of them."

"Me neither."

"This leaves us with the ideal candidate for worship, an all-powerful and good-natured god."

"Indeed."

"I don't see any evidence of it though; did you in your lifetime?"

Ed paused for thought, the moist scales on his head catching some penetrating flecks of sunlight glinting down into the lair as the day slipped into night.

"Well, not especially, to be honest."

"Me neither. If there was such a god then how could he stand by and watch tsunamis and earthquakes destroy people's lives? Isn't that an argument that no such god exists?"

"Maybe."

"On the other hand, if he caused it to happen, then he'd be evil in nature. Or, if he observed it but was unable to stop it, then that's complete impotence. If he caused it and then chooses a select group of people to save then that's even worse. What other options are there? Maybe he didn't notice it at all?"

"Well, put like that, it's hard to think of any other scenarios."

"Exactly! I just can't see a counter argument against it, apart from one that requires brainwashing, emotional irrationality and enforced doctrines. Whichever angle you come at it from, I cannot personally see a reason to be a worshipper."

"Your argument makes total sense to me, Sam. However, proving it one way or the other isn't the only point. To my knowledge, the question of the existence of God doesn't even come up in the Buddhist doctrines."

"Well, for me the doctrines of any faith can create a direct conflict between personal morality and philosophy on the one hand, and a belief in an all-powerful master dictating a specific set of rules, on the other. With this we give up a degree of freedom and start to think of reward or punishment, guided more by fear and compliance than by a natural desire to be good and morally honest people. I prefer good for good's sake. It doesn't make me a Buddhist or a believer in god, but rather a belief in good. An extra 'O' and such a different meaning."

"Yeah, anyway, at least it's easier to become a Buddhist if you're a tortoise. You don't have any choice in the matter regarding clinging onto worldly possessions."

"There is that," replied Sam as he bent his head back around to nip at an unsuspecting flea on his side.

"What do you mean exactly by personal morality?" enquired Ed.

"I'm not an expert but I'd be inclined to say that it's the ability to imagine the consequences of actions upon another as if it were happening to oneself and then build a code of conduct based on this."

"But what about people who couldn't care less about this code?" asked Ed inquisitively.

"Maybe there's some sort of brain malfunction or short circuit?

"It's not only about not hurting or not inflicting suffering on others though? That's really just altruism isn't it?" enquired Ed.

"To a degree, but a whole load of stuff gets bundled in there with religion which doesn't come from any personal morality that could ever occur naturally. Don't masturbate, for example. Why not just make people with shorter arms and solve the problem at the design stage? The only person who could possibly benefit from that is the person that cleans the sheets. Beyond that, why come up with something like the seven deadly sins and then programme people to be tempted? Either have the sins and consider them as 'OK' or else remove any instinctual desires mankind might have in that direction."

"Ha ha! There's another angle though. Maybe these religious doctrines have the positive aspect of creating a better social structure and a degree of harmony in the community? If everyone believes in the same thing then they'll get along just fine."

"True enough. I guess I was more of a rebel than that. I didn't like having sets of rules and regulations imposed upon me."

"Do you see faith and belief as totally negative then?"

"No, I just don't see them as the bedrock of good they are made out to be. You can't have faith or belief without some degree of doubt. In my book, something is either a fact or it's not; you either know or you don't know. To me, having faith is no more than having hope, and belief is no more than hope, or passive acceptance of unproven speculation."

"Incredible really, Sam. I've never really thought deeply about this. You seem to have thought it all through," replied Ed, dragging his cumbersome body around to the left with his oversized chubby reptilian legs.

"A bit. I was quite interested in philosophy as a student, and since being in this whirlwind of a conundrum, I find it helpful to get a deeper understanding."

"I'm with you there. Like I said before though, my belief did give me some comfort, However, I was also confused as to how the world could get into such a state. It did cast some doubts for me."

"That's understandable."

With this Sam manoeuvred himself upright, stretched his front legs out in front of him, gave in to a massive yawn and stretched his lengthy body to the maximum. Ed looked on, marvelling at the size of the proud fox.

"You know, for a minute there I'd forgotten I was a tortoise."

Ed twisted his head and neck from side to side and moved forward slightly before continuing, "I'm assuming from my last movements that tortoises can't yawn?"

"Can't help you with that one, my friend," replied Sam as he settled back down into his comfortable recline, reaching his head down the side of his body to bite away at some fleas with his sharp, white teeth. They sat silently for a while, digesting their conversation.

"Anyway, there's only one important question right now, and that is how the hell did we end up in this mess? Is it something to do with our beliefs or is there something else at work here?"

Ed looked at Sam as inquisitively as a tortoise possibly could.

The fox's ears pricked up as his head came to attention on his brown furry neck, sprouting elegantly from his relaxed horizontal body.

"In all honestly, probably not. We both seem to have very different experiences and beliefs. I can't see anything in there to suggest that."

"I agree," replied Ed before continuing, "I might, however, have been 'praying to the wrong one', as you mentioned earlier. We can't exclude that.

The more I think about it, the less I consider religion as a possible factor. There are just too many factions and religions to choose from. There must be something else."

"I agree. Can you remember your last moments yet, Ed?"

"Well, to a point but not really. It's sketchy. I was driving back to London from a business trip. I owned a company that was doing quite well. I was a bit of a wacky inventor and some of my stuff started to get noticed."

"What sort of stuff?" enquired the fox, sitting upright.

"I had invented numerous things that hadn't really taken off, but then I invented a really clever unit that melted snow off your shoes before going indoors. It was basically a solar powered box that you would step into. The base was a pressure plate and the weight on it would turn it on, gently close the four sides above your ankles, and streams of hot air would be pumped onto the top, sides and backs of your feet.

There were also jets coming out from the footplate underneath to clean the soles. The snow would melt off and disperse through drainage pipes on one side of the device and the feet would be thoroughly warmed in the sixty second cycle. It would then open up, and after you got out it cleaned itself with high powered water jets coming out of all the pipes excluding the footplate. It was a big hit in Russia and Scandinavia but the real deal maker for me was the solar power system I used. With the use of mirrors, I devised a way to multiply tenfold the power generated by solar panels. That led to the development of my company, 'CubiZ', which developed this technology to the next level. It ended up with a translucent cube structure with multiple solar cells and mirrors inside. With the use of the mirrors, the light would be trapped going between the cells numerous times, magnifying the charge. I started doing little portable ones which had a cable and one, two or three plugs as an extension. Then they started to get bigger and bigger until I merged with another company specialising in power generators and we started to develop much more ambitious devices. We had got to the point where music festivals such as Glastonbury and Sonicville were using them for most of their onsite power."

"Fantastic ideas. You must have been worth a few quid then?"

"Well I'd ploughed the majority of it back into the company. Developing the larger units was very troublesome. They would sometimes overheat, even melt in some instances. I was comfortable for sure, but it would have been a few years until I could really have sat back with the mattress full of cash. Things were starting to go well though. As it happens, I became a tortoise instead."

"Well look on the bright side, at least you're still naturally powered," said the fox as he lay back down into reclined luxury on the twigs and leaves.

"Yes, that's some compensation. Better laughing than crying - that's if tortoises and foxes could laugh."

"Anyway, back to my previous question. What can you remember about that last trip?"

"Just flashes, like people holding up big cardboard backed

pictures for a second or so and then they're gone. Snippets and glimpses. I definitely remember getting in the car and driving the 303. I ended up on the M3 heading into London. I had numerous annoying texts coming in on my iPhone. That's all I can remember."

"In all likelihood you probably crashed your car because you were sending a bloody text. How idiotic can you be? What age were you?"

"I was in my late thirties. Yes, it's pointing towards something as ridiculous as that. To be honest, if it was a car crash then I'm really glad I can't remember it."

"I was in my early fifties. It's good having this opportunity to discuss things because you can rule certain things out. We were different ages, different religious beliefs and died in completely different ways. It's very important for us to discuss as much as we can in the next day or so. I realised how important this is after many rebirths. Until I met you, I hadn't met another Transient like I did on my first visit. You are also very lucky to have met me first time, Ed."

"I can see that."

"Each encounter is not to be taken for granted. Make the most of it, try and find out if there is any common ground, any rhyme and reason why this might be happening," replied Sam, twisting and turning in the twigs and leaves, trying to convince himself against the odds that the new position would be more comfortable than the old. A brief silence ensued, pristine and still.

"How did you meet your end then?" enquired Ed after a few minutes of watching the fox make minor adjustments to his recumbent position.

"Man, if you think sending a text whilst driving is stupid then you should hear my story."

"I'm listening," replied Ed wryly.

"Well, I had gone on holiday with my wife, Elise to Marrakech in Morocco. It was such a great place and so different from everywhere I'd been before. The souks and bustling markets with their colourful produce and beautiful carvings, the architecture, the busy crowded streets and

34

squares, it was something else. We went off for lunch to this incredible local restaurant in the depths of the little alleys and walkways. It was on top of a building in the most unlikely of scruffy little streets but was a really refined place with haute cuisine and fine wines. We stayed there for a couple of hours, eating, chatting and drinking, having a thoroughly fine time. My wife read through her guide book, planning where we would go next, and I played with my new camera that I had got especially for the trip.

"Once our food had gone down and we had rounded off everything with a nice Moroccan coffee, we left the restaurant. It was such a world apart that I had completely forgotten about the busy alleys outside. We went down the stairs and out into the mania, momentarily shocked having left the calmness of the restaurant. We started to walk out into the alley and started to wind our way back to the main market area for a bit more shopping. People's road manners there were a little lacking, and if you weren't careful you could easily get knocked by a speeding bike or cart. I looked up and saw one of these carts, pulled by a donkey heading towards me at quite a lick. It was a bizarre sight because the guy driving it looked like the grim reaper with a black hooded gown draped over his whole being. He stared down at the donkey's arse, not concerned at all with the people he was careering past. I immediately whipped out my new camera and started to snap away to get a picture. I thought I had plenty of time to grab the shot from the front and then jump sideways, even though Elise started to shout anxiously for me to get out of the way.

"I snapped two quick shots and just as I was putting the camera down and about to dive sideways, I felt her arm on my shoulder. At the exact same second, I saw that there was a huge scaffold pole poking out from the front of the wooden cart. It came out from the rear, beside the driver, over the top of the donkey and was protuberant by about two feet. Suddenly it was as though I was in front of Lancelot himself in full flow. Sadly for me, the new camera had made it seem as though it was much further away I didn't have time to react and got smacked in the head with the scaffold bar and then trampled to death and run over by the cart with its wobbly wooden wheels. Definitely not an impressive way to go, killed by a fucking donkey in Morocco."

"That's insane. It is almost an achievement."

"Yes, not one I am proud of though. It can't have been too pleasant for Elise either. God knows how she dealt with that mess. I suppose she must have had to get the body back to the UK and everything. A very nasty situation, and all because I was a fucking idiot."

"You can't blame yourself though, Sam. Not entirely."

"Well I'm afraid I do. I hope she's okay now, maybe with someone else in a new relationship and getting on with her life. It hurts not to know."

"I can see that would be hard. Did you remember the incident when you came round?" asked Ed.

"Not exactly, just fragments. It all gradually assembles itself though, like a magnetic jigsaw that explodes and then patiently reassembles in the right order. I'm just resigned to it now. There are too many other things to keep me distracted. I must keep moving forward," stated Sam with an air of sadness in his voice.

"Onward and upward as a Transient, jumping from animal to animal," he added.

"Indeed! I have a lot to learn about that, Sam."

"That's for sure. Anyway, are you hungry? I'm going to pop out and get some provisions. Before you ask, I'm not going to get any slugs or snails for you, so don't even think about it. I'm going to assume you require a vegetarian meal and will cater accordingly."

"Okay then. D'you want any help?"

"If by help you mean accompanying me and making me walk at 3 metres an hour then I have to decline. You stay here. You'll be fine. I'll be half an hour or so, max. Chill out and relax."

With this, the fox leapt up and sped from the lair, brush flapping excitedly behind. He knew just what he wanted for supper and where to get it. He headed out into the quickly darkening twilight and up along the path, away from the stream where he had met Ed earlier that day.

"I don't want bloody slugs or snails anyway," Ed barked petulantly, way too late for the fox to have heard.

Ed sat quietly in the lair, trying to come to terms with the situation.

"This is such a massively unlikely scenario. Maybe I'm really dreaming after all? Maybe I'll wake up in a cold sweat and realise it was all one big false alarm? How can it be possible, surviving with my consciousness and getting grafted into another creature? It's ridiculous. What would it mean to me, my ambitions, loves and desires? Would they all suddenly become completely meaningless? How could it possibly be worth living without those incentives, just eating, shitting and sleeping? It would be totally pointless. We're driven by our desires and ambitions and pulled into family circles with the gravity of love. I can't be me without that; more to the point, I don't want to live without that. This is horrible, the longest and nastiest dream I have ever had. Christ, if I had any hands, I would pinch myself," thought the tortoise, getting more despondent with every passing moment.

Time whittled by, with Ed alone in the lair. He started to worry the fox would never return. An empty nervous feeling brewed in his stomach as he decided to make his way out of the lair to see if Sam was anywhere near. It was dark outside with just the gentle light of a half moon.

Mmmm, is that waxing gibbous? he thought as he stared up at the stunning celestial body. Just at that moment there was a strange rustling noise down the path. In the half light he couldn't quite make it out but was sure it was the fox. Even so, he cautiously half retreated into his shell, slightly less nervous, bearing in mind he was planning suicide a day or so later.

The rustling got closer as he began to see a vague silhouette in the distance. It looked mysteriously like a cardboard box coming along the path.

Now that would be taking it one stage too far, thought Ed, resigned to his temporary reptilian form but keen not to become a cardboard box.

As it got closer Ed backed towards the entrance of the lair. It was indeed a cardboard box. However, he could clearly see that behind it was a proud, bustling brush, erect but flexible as it swooped from side to side.

"Biodegradable, don't worry, the box is biodegradable," he heard, barked out from behind the box. At that moment, the forward motion stopped a few yards short, and the fox appeared from around the side.

"It'll just break down into compost or something," he added before pushing the box over with his snout.

"I knew you'd be waiting outside. It's dangerous you know."

"Well how dangerous can it be for someone... er... for 'some*thing*' that's only got a day or so to live anyway?"

"Good point," replied the fox as one of the items tossed from the box rolled towards the tortoise.

"That's for you," uttered the fox, as a big green ball twice Ed's size rattled against his protective shell, forcing him instinctually to withdraw completely from sight.

"Great," he said, as he peered out from his shell, his head brushing the outside of the plastic wrapped sphere. He could see the label clearly: 'Iceberg lettuce.'

"Lovely - did you get dressing?" said Ed, as Sam nudged the lettuce down into the fox hole, sending it rolling down the opening like a cannon ball in a barrel.

"No, it was a quick in and out job," replied Sam as he went back to the box to retrieve another object.

"This is for me," he said, as he clasped his teeth around what looked like some sort of plastic pot.

"What's that?" asked Ed as the fox tossed the item into the hole behind the lettuce, knocking it from where it had got stuck and down all the way into the depths of the lair.

"Chicken pate, lovely stuff. Saves me killing a chicken, squirrel or anything like that. I try to avoid killing if I can. I'm upset enough about having to leave the plastic wrappers down here. Not biodegradable at all."

Sam headed back towards the box.

"Is there more as well? How on earth did you manage all this, and the box as well?"

"You need to be wily if you become a fox. Foxy schemes, cunning and crafty; I'll tell you about it when we get inside. Go on, you first."

The fox grabbed the final item from near the box before nudging it into the undergrowth with his snout. Ed meanwhile headed down the hole, nudging the chicken pate pot forwards with his head as he did so. It ended up beside the lettuce as he made his way into the chamber, followed by Sam with a double size Mars bar in his mouth.

"A Mars bar? Are you kidding me? How the hell did you manage all this? Do you have your visa card with you or something?"

Sam tossed the unopened chocolate bar next to the chicken pate and nudged the lettuce over towards Ed.

"Thanks, but how am I going to open this?" he bemoaned as the round green globe finally rested beside him.

"Don't worry. I'll take care of that for you. This will all last us until tomorrow. You can't have any chocolate though. It'll make you sick."

"Marvellous. You're my doctor now as well I suppose. It just so happens I don't particularly like chocolate so it's not an issue."

With this the fox moved over and started snarling and gnawing as his shiny, white teeth tried to rip open the plastic wrapping of the lettuce.

"Well, how on earth did you manage it? I can't imagine you waltzed into the shop and filled up the box."

"You're absolutely right. Truth is I went round the back and rummaged through all the stuff that had been thrown out. There's some good stuff in there normally, any shop, any town, any country. A lot of waste."

"Good idea! You're too clever."

"Whatever! Anyway, the most difficult thing is nuzzling the box all the way back without being seen."

"Yeah, I guess it would be. This is better than flowers for me though. I am grateful, thanks," said Ed, as the fox clasped the outside of the lettuce between his teeth and tossed it from left to right, unravelling the plastic and revealing the tortoise-friendly, tasty meal.

"I'll need to rip it apart for you. Otherwise you might have a bit of trouble eating it. Don't worry about catching anything from me. You'll be dead in a day or two anyway."

"Ever the optimist," replied Ed ironically as Sam chomped, dissected and sliced the lettuce with his razor sharp teeth into smaller and smaller pieces for Ed.

"I might as well do the whole thing and then that saves me a job tomorrow," he gasped, as he gathered the pile of cut lettuce next to Ed in the corner.

"Thanks. This smells really good. I don't think I ever ate lettuce when I was a human. I missed out on something there. Much better than processed tortoise food."

Ed turned around and started munching at the leaves. "I don't suppose you got any napkins did you?"

Sam ignored him as he began tearing at the cardboard cover on the large pot of chicken pate. That still left him the tough plastic shrink wrap to get through before he could get to his tasty meal.

"I'll have half today and the rest tomorrow," he said as he finally got into the container, covering his snout, whiskers and black button nose in the surrounding jelly. Eagerly, his long wet tongue came out and swiped around the whole area, nose and all, to clear up the oily mess.

"I love that bit. The jelly is the best. The pate itself is overrated," he blurted as he dug his teeth and tongue down into the soft mixture in the pot, covering himself once again.

Silence ensued as they respectively consumed their nourishment. Soon they were both in sleepy digestive mode and the evening became night, became day.

Chapter 4
The last supper

Slowly Ed came around, eyes still closed, taking in the soothing snoring sound resonating around the small space. He remained still and calm, scared to move in case he woke into his nightmare once more. How he longed to wake in his nicely decorated bedroom, with feather pillows and pretty wife, go downstairs for coffee and toast and jump out into his car and off to the office. The snoring continued. Maybe it *was* his wife, maybe everything would be okay. Nervously he engaged his eyelids, raising them like heavy external shutters outside a shop. Soon reality smashed him in the face and there he was staring at the large brown furry fox, the steaming black button vibrating ferociously with every loud snore.

"Oh fuck. Fuck! Fuck! This is too much," thought the tortoise, once more back in his new reality. The fox was unmoved, motionless apart from the loud expulsions of air that loudly ripped through the lair.

"As if things weren't bad enough, why does he have to fucking snore? Please help me someone," exclaimed Ed, looking upwards for divine providence. Sadly for him the fox slept on undisturbed, deafening Ed for what seemed like hours until suddenly coming around with a start.

"Ah good, you're still here," stated the fox as he got up onto all four feet, stretching his body out full length before ripping into an exhausted yawn. Ed stared in disbelief into his large mouth with its razor-like, offensive dentures and unpleasant looking tongue.

"Wow, those teeth look really sharp, Sam."

"I know, that's 'cos they are," replied the fox before adding, "Did you sleep through okay?"

"Yes, but I've been awake for hours watching and listening to you snoring. It wasn't a whole lot of fun, I can tell you that."

"Don't worry, I'm awake now. No more snoring, I promise," replied Sam reassuringly.

"That's good. Anyway, I've got to be honest with you, Sam. Sleeping on this hasn't made this whole scenario any more believable," said Ed, as Sam began to stir.

"I know. It wasn't easy for me either in the beginning. I'd wake every morning, hoping it had all gone away, and that when I opened my eyes, I'd be with my wife on holiday. It was really only after my first transition that I properly started to come to terms with it. If you can believe for now, then reality will take control once you have jumped. Don't despair, you're not the only one," said Sam trying to comfort the first-timer.

"Yes, I keep telling myself that, but comforting oneself with the notion that it's okay because you'll be killing yourself soon does have a few contradictions in it," replied Ed reflectively.

"Well at least you're killing a tortoise and not something you love."

"You're full of confidence-boosting insight, Sam," replied the hard-shelled animal ironically as he turned and began munching a lettuce leaf to his left. Sam did likewise with the pate before ripping open the Mars bar and scoffing the lot.

"Crikey, that lot went quick! You've got some on your snout, it looks weird. You're a very messy eater," observed Ed as Sam's tongue came out and swept the outside of his face, clearing up the mess, as he returned to his horizontal position, leaving his head bolt upright looking at Ed.

"You look like one of those pharaoh's statues outside a temple."

"They were cats weren't they?" replied Sam.

"Whatever. One thing's for sure, you can get up, stretch, yawn, move around, sit down, and stand up again. All I can do is sit in this same bloody position with my arms, legs and head all poking out like a bloody starfish. It's very annoying," barked Ed.

"I think they are all legs. I don't think any of those are arms. Just a small observation. It doesn't change anything really."

"So my head's a leg now is it?"

"No, not your head, just your arms. Well, they're not arms, they're legs. You know what I mean?"

"Very helpful once again, Sam. Thanks for that. At least I liked the lettuce though. I can't get over how much I like it."

"Yeah, there are lots of surprises like that as you go from animal to animal. On the positive side, you'll certainly get reincarnated into more agile animals than a tortoise, trust me."

"I'm sure. Anyway, changing the subject, I was wondering to myself last night what life is worth without ambitions, possessions, desires, success and all that. What do you think? Was that a problem for you?" enquired the tortoise with interest.

"For sure, but then it's all about being philosophical and trying to understand your own position in the scheme of things. Of course one feels sad about losing life as we knew it, but that would have to have ended at some point anyway," replied Sam.

"Yes, but it makes me sad to lose it before my time."

"Well don't get too despondent, Ed. Life as you knew it was temporary, fleeting and finite. There's nothing permanent at all, either about your existence, your species or even the planet or solar system that hosted it all."

"You are so comforting."

"I'm just stating fact. Becoming aware of that puts you in a much better position to become enlightened or liberated."

"I know. It's a shock though. I did think of things as permanent. That's what I built my ambitions and objectives around."

"That's no different than imagining a holiday camp is permanently yours, even though you would be fully aware that it was only a two-week holiday."

"Yes, but it feels like yours when you're there."

"That's as maybe but at the back of your mind you always know it'll end and you'll be back in your office, school or workplace at some point. The equivalent with human existence is the awareness of death. We all know it will happen but choose not to dwell on it. We notice it deeply when someone we know passes. That sadness is not just about the loss, it is also a realisation that it will definitely happen to us one day as well."

"That's very true. Luckily not many people I knew died. When they did, it was horrible though. A strange, dark absence, looking at the seats they sat in and the shoes they wore. It was hard to accept that they would never return."

"Yes, but we have a different perspective now, eh!"

"Well, if everything you say is true then we certainly do. Going back to my question at the beginning though, what is our life worth now without ambition, possessions, success, objectives and goals?"

"As long as we stay in the four-day periods and keep self-aware, we retain a semblance of that. By trying to understand our predicament we have objectives, goals and hope at least."

"You can't seriously compare that to what we would've had as humans? That's like saying a life prisoner lives a good life because he has an ambition to escape. The point of human ambitions is that they propel us forward to better states of existence and hopefully a more fulfilling life, not just to survive," replied Ed.

"That's very true. On the positive side some human traits won't be missed at all."

"Such as?"

"The desire for fame for example, or greed. The ridiculous tendency to compare ourselves negatively or arrogantly to those around us. The negativity of hoarding well beyond what would ever be necessarily required. There must be more," replied Sam.

"Good point. They're all negative, but for sure, comparison is by far the most painful for people personally. I can't say it didn't affect me. I remember sitting on the train as a boy feeling like a complete geek because I had the wrong jeans on, or something that wasn't too fashionable. It would lead me into a completely negative cycle and before I knew it, I hated how I looked and what my body was like. I would stare in the mirror with dismay wishing I was like some of the other boys. It was a really horrible feeling. Right up to the end I couldn't dance at parties because I felt so self-conscious."

"We've all been there, Ed. Bad dancing won't kill the ground though."

"Philosophical yet again, Sam."

"Truth is everyone probably felt the same way, comparing themselves to someone else, maybe the older boys or some young pin-up lad or whatever. The cycle never stops."

"I think girls and women were worse, don't you?" enquired Ed.

"It's not so much about better or worse, it was just different. The end result of self-loathing or arrogance would probably be the same."

"Very true. Well, we're agreed that we won't miss that. I can't imagine I'll be going around comparing my six-pack to that of a local tortoise do you?" said Ed ironically.

"Exactly my point."

"Greed as well, Sam - can't imagine any need to hoard stuff if we are only around for a few days."

"Yes, It never made any sense to me. I always thought there was enough money and resources in the world for everyone if it had just been shared out a bit," replied Sam.

"It's hard to say really, without having all the facts and figures. One thing is for sure though; the habitually greedy didn't do much to help the needy innocents. It's hardly surprising that there was so much conflict all the time."

"Sad but true, my reptile friend, sad but true…"

Sam and Ed continued talking throughout the afternoon, debating, musing and considering life, death, morals and reincarnation. The evening dusk began to advance upon them and soon crept down into the lair on a mild twilight dew. The previous night Sam had gone out around this time to get their impromptu meal. Tonight he was going to leave the lair for a very different reason and for the very last time.

"Don't come with me, Ed. I must be on my way now. You don't want to see me go to the next stage of my journey. It won't help you for tomorrow."

"But can't I at least come some of the way with you?"

Ed was distraught at the idea of losing his new friend. In

such a short time he had become his only link to sanity and reality.

"I could just come up to the top of the path with you?"

"No, stay here till morning and then go up to the stream. If you crawl in you'll get caught in the current and swept downstream. Try to turn yourself upside-down and it'll be quicker. You'll then have your next transience and start over."

He walked past Ed, stopping alongside and nuzzling his snout beside his scaly reptilian head.

"Just to say goodbye. You've been a real friend this last thirty-six hours. I'll not forget you. You'll give me strength for the next part of my journey. Don't worry about me. You'll learn once you've been through it a few times. It's really quick. There's a blinding light and then a thud like someone has punched you. Then it's all over, no pain or suffering."

Then he turned away and made his way up the small tunnel out of the lair. Ed turned his body around to see the brush departing out into the black dense night. A moment of fearful panic swept up from the depths from his stomach into his mouth as he clambered after him out of the small opening in the ground and into the evening.

"Sam, Sam," he yelped forlornly as he surfaced into the sinister night. Sadly, he had disappeared along the path, through the bushes and down towards the busy road. Beside him, the cardboard box from the previous night lay discarded. He knew he would never see Sam again. His body felt weak with misery as he turned around and headed back down the hole, slightly nauseous. The next day it was his turn and that if it went wrong, he would be stuck as a tortoise for the rest of his life.

The lair felt so empty without Sam. He gazed over to the empty spot where he'd been laying, a makeshift bed of twigs and leaves. He scrambled upon it, the scent of the fox still strong in the air, clumps of brown and white fur caught on the various bits of branch, the pate pot and Mars bar wrapper lying just to the left. It was a miserable and lonely moment, characterised by a strange absence and a horrible emptiness. He settled down and tried to sleep, fearful of the next day.

Chapter 5
Home county rapids

The morning was bleak as Ed surfaced from the lair, having consumed the remainder of the lettuce. Ironically it was the first day without a searing sun and sadly, he wouldn't benefit from the respite. His stomach still ached with misery and sadness at the loss of Sam and he began to wonder if a life as a reptile without self-awareness would be such a bad thing after all. He manoeuvred himself down along the path towards the water's edge, the same way Sam had gone the night before. He passed by the disturbed section of bushes that Sam had cut through towards the road. He stood motionless for a few seconds staring, oblivious to the fact that the badger was back, sniffing his rear end.

He carried on down towards the water, passing columns of marching ants going about their daily chores. Now they seemed to have bits of cardboard box to keep them busy. The badger came alongside and walked him towards his departure point as if it knew what was about to happen.

"Well, mate, maybe you had the same choice as me and opted out. Can it be that bad? You look happy enough, easily pleased as long as there's an arse to sniff. Well, regardless of all that, I don't want to be a shelled reptile, crawling around like a punctured football with chubby legs, eating flowers and doing Interflora poos. No, matey, I'm at least going to give this a shot at least once. Maybe I'll come back as a well cared-for poodle or a fearsome lion. Here I go."

After a quick slurp from the fresh water, Ed manoeuvred himself backwards into the stream, pushing with his fat legs against the shore to project himself away and into the powerful current. The badger looked on bemused, sniffing at his head before he started to drift out into the current like a wooden raft.

"I really honestly don't want to drown. It sounds like a hideous idea, but what choice do I have? This'll surely be the best and quickest way. Tortoises are certainly not renowned for their prowess in water sports."

At this point, Ed drifted into the main current and was whisked away like a white water raft, spinning round and round as he started to ride the cascades of water. Alas, none seeped into his shell and he floated perfectly. He was certain that tortoises sank. Why didn't he sink? Was he a new breed of buoyant tortoises, maybe related to a turtle?

He got faster and faster and remembered that Sam had told him to try and turn upside down. He squirmed with his body, trying to throw his weight to destabilise himself. All attempts were unsuccessful until suddenly there was a loud 'thwacking' sound and everything stopped dead in its tracks. The sound of the water was deafening as it rushed over his shell, hitting him full in the face and lifting him upwards, the white spray creating beautiful patterns of water in the air.

Then another loud noise, a slight movement and then he came to a sudden stop. The hydraulic and all-powerful gushing torrents battered him from every angle, around him, over him, under him, and across him. He had been turned around by the water flow and now faced landwards, caught on a fallen branch of a dead tree. Squirming nervously, he tried to swing his legs and manoeuvre himself free to continue in the stream. Alas it was fruitless. It was going to be a lot harder than he first assumed. He knew if he got stuck for the day, then that would be that. He would be condemned to live out his days as a reptile.

After what seemed like an age of struggling, he heard voices in the distance. They sounded mumbled, but became clearer as they got closer.

"Look, Daddy, it's a tortoise. We must help him, Daddy, please, Daddy."

"Fuck off, you little bastard, get the fuck away from me," barked Ed as the boy's father waded into the water for the rescue.

"I'm not going to become your fucking pet, you little ponce."

"Oh, Daddy, can you hear, he is bleating with little

tortoise noises crying for help, how sweet. He knows we're going to save him."

"Oh, for fuck sake, piss off, piss off and leave me alone, I'm trying to kill myself."

At this moment the father reached out his enormous hand towards Ed. He seemed like a giant, an absolute colossal monster. Even so, at full stretch he could barely reach him. Patiently moving closer, cautious of the fast currents, the man reached out to his full extension and got his fingers under the shell between his head and left leg. As he levered him from the branch, Ed saw his opportunity and with all the might and strength he could muster, he flicked his head around and bit his hand aggressively.

"Arrhhhh, you little reptile fucker. Did you see that, Billy?"

The man had responded exactly as Ed assumed, pulling out of the rescue attempt abruptly and freeing him from the branch and back into the vicious flow of water.

"You killed him, dad, you drowned the tortoise. He could have been our pet," the kid snarled at the bemused man as Ed sped off downstream like a sperm in a fallopian tube.

"Ha, ha, mother fucker," blurted Ed through the watery bubbles as he got tossed upside down in the depraved current. The water gushed in, dragging him to the bottom of the flow, crashing him against rocks and boulders and knocking him from consciousness. Ed had achieved his goal, a relatively painless end. The first suicidal tortoise in the history of the Home Counties had concluded his reptilian adventure, at least for the time being.

Chapter 6
Silicon Alley

Supersonic gusts tore at speed over Ed's body, forcing his flesh to ripple in fast moving waves of motion. Bewildered and muddled, he started to come round, unable to open his eyes in the whirling tornado. Thoughts flashed through his mind, the fox eating chocolate, the strange adventure in the lair and the dim recollection of eating flowers and lettuce in abundance. He screeched to a halt, decelerating to stillness like an instant sound effect in reverse.

He gradually became aware of a focused ray of light, burning into his eyelids with laser precision. Soon his squinting gave way to blurry vision as he realised he was floating helplessly in some sort of windswept tunnel.

He twisted and turned anxiously with zero gravity, spinning crazily in an anti-clockwise direction catching sight of the stationary laser light once every revolution. His body felt more familiar to him and sensation had come back into his limbs. He lifted his head slightly and glanced down towards his feet. To his amazement he was dressed in his own clothes, the last ones he could remember wearing. He wiggled his feet, crinkling the surface of the light tan Italian leather shoes, creased at the stress points. Above them he could see his light-blue designer jeans with frayed bottoms. He lifted his hands up revealing a large-faced, silver wrist-watch as it popped out from his long shirt and jacket sleeves. He wriggled his fingers, the thick gold wedding ring prominently visible.

"Maybe it was a dream after all?"

He bobbed gently up and down, continuing to spin in a high-powered stream of air which seemed to be battling against a strong counter flow from the side. He started to become aware of a loud gushing sound all around him, like a thousand trains in a single tunnel.

Suddenly, from nowhere, he felt an intense pain around

the side of his neck as he was jolted off sharply to his right. He had no idea what was going on.

"By thy leave, nice and easy, I prithee," he heard loudly in his right ear as he felt himself hurled to the floor with a sobering thud which made up for all the lack of gravity of his bobbling spin. He looked up to see a small wiry man removing a shepherd's crook from his neck. To his left he could see a large curved opening and what appeared to be some sort of fast-moving, gushing, misty flow, strangely dry but travelling at phenomenal speed from right to left.

"A thousand pardons. I would like to design a better method but really cannot see how it can be done any other way. Good morrow to you."

The man took the crook into the upright position and rested it on the floor, standing against a curved wall of black glistening rock. Ed remained on the uneven rocky floor, more than startled. He looked down at his hands and stretched them once more, his wedding ring glinting in the small, bright light beams that shone from thin-cut hollows in the arched ceiling. The granite-textured walls gleamed with perfection as the rays spread out over them like rivulets of light from a sculptor's candle.

He grabbed his legs with his hands and felt them from top to bottom, first the right one and then the left. He then wriggled his feet again before feeling his face, noticing a soft breeze dancing across it from the movement of the adjacent flow.

"Well that doesn't feel like a tortoise to me," he uttered as he pulled himself to his feet and moved cautiously away from the man across the awkwardly uneven rock underfoot.

"*Hey, I can stand up and move normally. Maybe I'm saved, and back to my old self.*"

He continued to back off from the man until he had moved a couple of feet towards the curved wall of what appeared to be a tunnel. The rock was the most evocative exotic-looking stone he had ever seen, subtly undulating with smooth wave-like forms with no jagged edges.

He noticed the man was a fair bit smaller than him and a little frail, not someone he would instinctually feel afraid of.

The man stared at him speechless, looking him up and down from head to toe and back again. He wore big black shoes with tight white stockings, light brown trousers that came down to the knee, rolling up into a little roll of gathered material at the bottom. On top there an extravagant white frilly-collared shirt covered by a slightly tight waist-jacket, black with gold trim, undone at the front. On his head was a wacky, brown suede beret with a medium-sized firm rim all the way round, crowned with a flamboyant-looking feather.

"You're looking at me like that; you might want to reflect on what you're wearing first - what is that?" queried Ed.

The man grinned, expanding to a muted chuckle.

"I meant not to gape. I apologise."

"That's fine."

"My raiment may surprise you. I daresay I should be better garbed. It's Tudor costume from Middle England I wear. You, on the other hand, are altogether more modern, my friend. I'm Thomas. What is your good name, sir?" said the diminutive character as he moved closer to Ed with an outstretched hand.

Ed looked him over a little more closely. His face had the complexion of a scrunched paper ball, determined to somehow unravel itself into a more pleasing texture. Years of anxious grimacing had taken its toll, leaving crevices and creases that may well have been better explained by the movement of glaciers. Defiantly, the freckled leathery skin did what it could to feign a complexion that wasn't more associated with the surface of Mars, his big, ambiguously coloured eyes, peering out like seals from holes in ice.

Ed approached closer, ready for the customary handshake.

"Erm, I'm Ed. Ed Trew," said Ed, unsurprisingly cautious as he accepted the gesture.

"You need not worry. I know you must be in a state of stupefaction. Just freshly deceased," replied the Tudor gentleman, sending shockwaves through the tired flesh on his face.

"How do you know I just died? Are you a mind reader or something? What's going on?"

Thomas sighed knowingly as their hands parted and each wondered what would come next.

"Why did you have to grab me round the neck with the big crook?" enquired Ed.

"Well I was pulling you from the Transience tunnel. You could not have tarried there, by my troth."

"The Transience tunnel? What the hell's that?" replied Ed, beginning to notice the quaint and outdated dialect.

"Shall we go inside and find somewhere to sit down? I can tell what I can, or at least what I know." Thomas gestured down into the dim tunnel, away from the hole that he had been pulled through with the long crook.

"Okay. Let's do that. You have to know though; it's been quite a couple of days already, so please excuse me if I'm a little short with you," replied Ed, wondering if a similar bombshell of revelation similar to Sam's was about to whack him like a great big rubber fist.

"Let us away then without further ado. I know what people have been through when they get here. I have experienced the same myself after all."

"What, were you a tortoise as well?" enquired Ed, as the couple moved off deeper into the tunnel.

"Not exactly. I will tell you everything, worry not."

"Okay then," replied Ed, marvelling at every step he made as a human, reflecting on the trials and tribulations of being a perpetually exhausted and less-than-agile reptile. During the short distance they'd walked, the floor texture had become much smoother and easier to navigate, in contrast to the awkward uneven surface near the entrance. Ed looked down and noticed the strange sand, black in colour and slightly firm, just as he imagined it would have been on a volcanic island. He stopped briefly and looked behind to see the footprints melting away, the holes filling in and gradually leaving a smooth surface. He bent down and ran his outstretched fingers through the perfect surface, causing four equidistant indentations.

"Have you seen this, Thomas?" queried Ed as he got back to his feet, only to see the lines gradually disappear.

"If I had not noticed that in all the time I've been here,

Ed, I would have been a little unobservant, is that not so?" replied Thomas without even looking round.

"I guess so," acknowledged Ed as he continued on his way, beginning to reflect on why he might have ended up in this strange scenario.

Maybe I had fewer moral misdemeanours after all, and have been transported back as a human. Maybe this won't turn out so bad after all and I might be able to get back home, thought Ed, trying to make sense of the rapidly changing situation.

"You mentioned you had been here a long time, Thomas. How long exactly?"

"Since the sixteenth century; I cannot recollect the exact date."

"Okay, not that that sounds a little far-fetched. You've kept well for someone hundreds of years old. Do you work out?" said Ed sarcastically, feeling he was being ridiculed by the small, well-worn man.

"Honestly, by my troth, give ear to me. There are plenty older than me here; we have quite a collection."

They continued further along the tunnel and came to an intersection which acted as a hub for numerous other tunnels, all dimly lit with beams of light jetting out from the ceiling. The tunnels shot off in every direction, all made up of the strange shiny black rock.

"Goodness, this is a big place. How big is it exactly?" asked Ed. He paused to gaze down the various tunnels, feeling slightly bothered that the fox had not mentioned them, but also aware that he might not have even known about them.

"Bigger than I ever verily discovered," replied Thomas as they turned left into one of the tunnels.

"Are they underground or in a mountain or something? Is there a way out?" enquired Ed.

"No one knows exactly where we are or even how far it stretches. It could be the size of a pin head and we are infinitely small or else it could be bigger than all the stars in the universe. It's all a mystery, by my troth."

"But is there a way out?" asked Ed once more.

"I need to resolve thee of this mystery later," replied Thomas.

"I've heard that one before, although not exactly in those words," reflected Ed ominously, whilst walking alongside the strange man, their feet making a gentle squelching noise as they disturbed the sandy surface. The temperature was bearably cool but the air was still, with no wind or draughts from the now distant entrance.

"Are there many people here?"

"There are not so many and they can be insular and private. You can pass many days without seeing anyone. Methinks they all like to keep themselves to themselves. T'is not a land of jangles or japes but we all have our friends and associates."

"Well how many are there here?"

"I know not, possibly a thousand or more, I think. T'is hard to say. You be the first new arrival in quite some time."

"Really? Well, what's it called down here? You must have a name for it?"

"T'is true. Some of the newer residents call it 'Silicon Alley' whilst us 'Olde timers' prefer 'Ancestors' Cove'. Much quainter, think you not?" replied the Tudor gentleman, glancing over at Ed to see him nodding in agreement.

Thomas drew to a sharp stop and pointed into a small opening in the rock. Ed could see there were dozens of similar openings along the walls, all with deep black silky curtains about a foot inside the curved doorways.

"This is yours, at least until you decide whether you wish to stay or move on. By your leave, please."

Thomas ushered him into the small enclosure, removing the feathered hat, causing tiny clumps of ginger hair to spring forth revealing what looked like a terrible gardening experiment with reddish bonsai bushes. He held the hat proudly by his side as he brushed the curtain aside. Inside was a small, private, cave-like room with one stream of brilliant light coming from the ceiling. There was a bed, pillow, stool and sink, all of which looked like they were made from rock. On the pillow was a pair of black cloth eye-shades. Ed bent down and picked them up, stretching the elasticated strap back and forth.

"Eye-shades. The lights cannot be extinguished, so you will need those if you favour the dark."

"Thanks. I won't need them," replied Ed as he put them back down.

"It's actually quite comfortable," remarked Thomas, pointing to the seemingly uninviting bed.

"Really," replied Ed as he sat down on the edge.

"You're right. It's not bad," he remarked as he lay down putting his head on the pillow.

"Better than the twigs and leaves I had last night," he joked ironically as he prodded the material, which appeared to be some sort of soft spongy rubber.

Thomas sat opposite him on the stool, a metre or so away.

"You are informed, I assume, of those we call Transients then?"

"Yes, to a point, although I'm still a little reluctant to believe in this whole scenario."

"You have plenty of time to help your belief. How many times have you been through?"

"Well, once I suppose. I was a tortoise and I just committed suicide."

"A tortoise? T'is a toilsome one indeed. Well, whether you die naturally or kill yourself, you still become transient and you either find yourself in the tunnels or else propelled into another creature. Your first time and only one completed cycle. We call this the death cycle."

"Fine! I'll remember that."

"Were you fortunate enough to be in contact with another Transient?"

"Yes, a guy called Sam. Well it would be more accurate to say, a fox that had been a guy called Sam, if you get my drift?"

"And he spoke English?"

"Yes, luckily. I hadn't thought about that. What if he was a Chinese fox? It might have been that much more surreal. Not sure really. After all, here I am, chatting with a four-hundred-year old man in Tudor clobber who appears to have been beamed up into the modern age. How is it that you're dressed like that?"

"T'is easily explained, Ed. Most people don't get the opportunity to stop off in here. Generally they get whisked straight past us through the windswept tunnels towards the light and on to their next transience. However, some seem to get swept to the side of the flow and become stranded towards the edge in the slower part. When you get paused there then your human form is temporarily restored and you're reunited with the very same garments you died in, no difference whatsoever. T'is fortunate indeed that any scars, cuts, bruises or the like, are not apparent, thus we appear in good health. Anne Boleyn herself is here – complete with her head. I know not how this was achieved."

"Christ, man, I don't know whether you are ridiculing me or not. It seems so absurd. How can you keep the same clothes on for ever? What about your underpants?"

"T'is true, by my troth. You must bethink we are not verily alive anymore, at least when we are here. We are like phantoms in a sense and have no bodily indulgences such as eating, drinking, sweating, pissing or farting. You name it, you have it not. We often feel tired though, and even succumb to the odd ache and pain."

"But what about when I was a tortoise. I ate and drank and... well... everything else..."

"Yes, t'was when you have completed a transient contract and rejoined the physical realm. At the moment, you are caught in the middle. A 'paused Transient', as we call it," stated Thomas, as he turned to his left, whilst crossing his left leg up onto his right.

"If we can't drink and don't need to wash, then why the sink and tap?"

"T'is well said. I am of the mind that people simply take pleasure in drenching their faces with water. I cannot forsooth imagine any other reason. If you try to drink it then it does not go down at all. Anyway, you will not suffer from thirst so it matters not. Give not yourself the trouble."

"I won't. Tell me again about being 'paused'. What do you mean exactly?"

"T'is not I fancy myself an oracle, but I will readily impart my small knowings to you. The place I pulled you from was the jet stream of light and time that one travels down as a Transient. T'is the doorway between lives and different physical forms. It is an exceedingly speedy highway for souls. However, once in a while, a person, spirit or soul is knocked off-course in the main flow, drifting out to the edges into the very slow flowing outer part of the stream. T'is then they pass the contrary air flow from tunnel systems such as these and are stuck. Paused. Floating helplessly. If you are fortunate enough to be spotted, you might get pulled in and saved from the purposeless floating. Some manage to clamber out themselves but otherwise you could just drift downstream forever. In truth, we know not."

"How long do you think I would've floated there for?"

"Tis hard to determine. I do know though, that one needs to be in the main central flow to be carried through into the next 'mortal' reincarnation. Floating down the edges all the way to the end is a path of great uncertainty, although you may have been rescued by one of the other communities along the way. We believe there may be many such."

"How could you know?"

"We can only surmise, but certainly some I have rescued have been subjected to failed rescue attempts further back along the tunnel. T'is suggesting to me that there may be more communities in both directions. Many Transients that are stranded here seem to be first-timers, so t'is hard to know too much."

"Stuck? Will I be here forever like you?" queried Ed nervously.

"Verily the choices presented to you are many, even though they not reveal themselves with haste. Of course, you could tarry here. Ageless and timeless. A strange idea indeed, but t'is truly a very peaceful and calm place, with no particular demands or rivalries. Everyone is relaxed and reflective. Some state it resembles a large sensory deprivation tank of existence - not that I have ever seen such a tank."

"Mmm, not sure I would want to live like that. I need hope and objectives."

"Alternatively, you could get back into the flow and become Transient again."

"Really! How would that work?"

"Well, there is a small stairway which cuts through the rock around and above the main tunnel. There is an opening and you can jump down and get abruptly swept into the flow."

"Really? Does it work?"

"Not always, in truth. There are occasions when 'jumpers' plummet all the way through the main flow into the lesser flow at the bottom of the tunnel. They drift off downstream, as when you were floating."

"Well if there are further communities along the way, wouldn't they get rescued by them?"

"There is not really any way to reach them at the bottom of the tunnel. Your good self was floating along at the side of the stream at the same height as the entrance. That was just lucky. Many more float past on the other side or too low or too high. T'is random. Maybe they get into a better position to be rescued further along."

"Heavy duty. I wonder what happens to all those souls?"

"I too. Another thing you need to bear in mind is that your choice is limited by time. Just like as a Transient you have just a few days to die, once you are here, you have a similar limitation. You have four days to decide. I can tell thee, after that, t'is final. You either attempt to continue onto your next transience or else stay here peacefully forever."

"Really? That's intense. Why only four days?" replied Ed, as they made their way past the hub and back along the adjoining tunnel to the opening.

"Goodness knows. They say God works in mysterious ways but it seems that everything works in mysterious ways."

"What's to stop me jumping back into the stream after the four days have expired?"

"Nothing at all, the only thing is you will end up here again. Do you not imagine that people would have tried it already?"

"I suppose so. Can we go back and see the stream again please? What did you call it? The Transience tunnel? I'm intrigued and I want to know a little more."

"Most certainly, whatever you wish," replied Thomas as they got up, separated the silky curtain and moved out into the tunnel and back towards the place they first met. It was only a short distance back through the tunnels and the two men walked at a calm but assured pace, proceeding past the complex intersection and onwards to the tunnel of souls.

As they approached the opening they came across a third man dressed in an American football kit, brightly coloured and complete with shoulder pads. In one hand was a long crook similar to the one used to save Ed whilst the other clutched onto his enormous cage like helmet. American footballers looked ridiculous to Ed at the best of times. The huge brightly coloured padded costumes, crazy knee pads, testicle protectors and eye makeup that made them look like they'd sold their cheeks as advertising spaces. This gent was no less ridiculous, his fat head and crew-cut hair looking more like a thin layer of Astroturf.

"Yo, Bro," he drawled, looking at the approaching duo before adding, "Yaw scooped one from the tunnel, Dude?"

"Greetings, Bob, yes, this morning. Bob, meet Ed, Ed, meet Bob."

Bob put his caged helmet down onto the ground at the side of the tunnel, and after a round of customary handshakes, rested the crook against the wall and headed back into the tunnels towards the rooms.

"Yeah, Man, thought I saw one myself but then lost sight of 'em. Maybe they'll get them further down," bemoaned the sportsman as he continued on his way.

"We shall readily continue our endeavours though, Bob, think you not?"

"For sure, Bro, locked and loaded," replied Bob over his shoulder as he walked into the distance.

"Most certainly, lock and loadeth with haste."

Ed couldn't help a smirk, entertained by the clash of modern America with Shakespeare's Britain. Thomas turned to impart more detail on the individual as he disappeared into the distance, encumbered by the large shoulder reinforcements and excessive padding.

"He broke his neck in a football match."

"That's gotta hurt, Thomas."

"I assume it might well involve a degree of discomfort. Anyway, he is a permanent resident now. Have you ever seen it? Football, I mean."

"Yeah, ridiculous game. Like a load of over-testosteroned apes chasing an ostrich egg around. You didn't miss anything there, Thomas."

By this time, the duo had reached the opening and stared into the fast rushing motion of the stream.

"Where's the opening?" queried Ed.

"You cannot behold from here, t'is above the flow."

The tunnel looked like a fast-gushing river of air, an undefined blur in the middle which got clearer, closer to the edges. It looked ferocious and fearsome; a mighty power to be approached with utmost caution.

"It's phenomenal! You must stare at it in awe every day, Thomas?"

"By my troth, t'is a miracle. I find myself often here, at the ready with the crook just in case. T'is worst when someone floats by, too low or high to be saved."

"I can imagine. Anyway, how many times were you transient?"

"Not many, just two or three. So long ago, I cannot recall much about it. I was a dog twice and a hen once. T'was not easy to be a dog in those days. Each time I got transported directly from animal to animal and never met another Transient to tell me what was happening. With a fair degree of fortune, I died within the allotted time on both occasions before ending up here. T'was my choice to stay - an easy decision to make."

"I can see that, Thomas. Are you happy here though? Doesn't it get boring?"

"Well, I know not whether I be truly happy, but I feel settled. I'm certain I'm not the only one whose need for security dominates their need for freedom."

"I hear that. There must be stuff you miss though from the old days, ambitions for example?"

"In truth, Ed, when I was alive, all we had time to focus on was survival. We had a basic lifestyle with few creature comforts, continual exposure to disease, lack of hygiene and the constant threat of some sort of violent death. Sumptuary laws dictated our cloth and people were bled for their humours. I don't really miss anything about it, although I do sometimes dream of a fine jug of mead," replied Thomas.

"Yeah, doesn't sound too good when you put it like that. Didn't you have any ambitions though?"

"Ambition to survive, t'was all we had."

"Doesn't sound like it was that easy either. I'm not sure I would've taken too well to that lifestyle at all. Maybe ambition and bettering oneself is an idea of the modern age. I bet you regret not living in a more liberal age?"

"What you've never had you can't really miss, Ed. I do wish I'd lived in a time when I could have witnessed those big flying metal birds though."

"You mean planes I assume?"

"Yes, I think that's what they're called. The ones that carried people and products. Is it really true that their wings didn't flap?"

"Yeah, that's right, their wings didn't flap, Thomas," replied Ed, breaking out into a smirk.

"How can they possible have flown in that case? I am sure that I am the victim of some sort of joke here?"

"They have engines that propel them forward. Birds don't have engines."

"I never witnessed such a thing as an engine. It's all as strange and unfathomable as the whole Transient situation."

"Put like that, I guess you are right, the vast metal birds are indeed hard to believe, especially when you consider they could carry hundreds of people at once."

"Really, that many? I hadn't heard that. Are you certain, have you seen it for yourself?"

"Yes, Thomas, I've even been on one. It was an unforgettable experience, staring down at the earth from above the clouds."

"Indeed, if it is true, then it would certainly have been a majestic experience," marvelled Thomas as they continued on their way. Ed was soon enquiring further into how his new friend dealt with his environment.

"Was it easy to adjust to being here then?"

"By comparison, t'was like being in heaven."

"There must have been some things you had to adjust to though?" enquired Ed with an awareness that he might have to make that decision one day.

"It took me a little time to realise that I was not living in an environment where people's anger and lust was totally out of control. That I need not cast glances over my shoulder every time someone was behind me. That was liberating indeed."

"I can imagine. Things did get a bit better down there over the last few centuries though. I guess one of the objectives of civilisation was restraining those primitive instincts and making people think more about their actions," replied Ed with insight before adding, "What sort of life did you have out there? What was your profession, where were you born?"

"I was born in the countryside but do not recall much about my childhood. I think I repressed it. I do remember being beaten by my father numerous times but not much more than that. I left home, moved to London and did a cooking apprenticeship before moving on to one of the larger London bakeries. T'was nothing special. I never got married, had children or anything of the sort. Most importantly I managed to avoid getting press-ganged into the navy or army. That would truly have been a miserable fate. Anyway, I am content here now."

"I can see that. I'm not sure it's for me though."

"Everyone feels differently. Verily, you have time to decide. T'is my advice to stay a while and rest. The quality of slumber here is truly wondrous, the finest you will ever have. There is a calmness that soothes in this place."

"Really?" replied Ed as they turned tail and headed back into the tunnels.

"Oh look, Bob's forgotten his helmet," he exclaimed, as he picked it up and carried it along with them.

"Even if he lost it, he would wake up with it beside him come the morn. These are permanently part of our existence; we can never get be free of them. If you were to leave your jacket here and see what may befall it, it would forsooth be beside you in the morrow."

"It goes against all my instincts. Besides, I was dreaming of dressing in it again when I was marooned as a tortoise."

"I understand. Are you of a mind to meet some of the others, Ed? They are a little shy but I am certain you would receive a hearty welcome. We do not see a new face every day."

"Maybe tomorrow, if that's okay? I'm more than a bit fazed out by everything that's gone on over the last few days. It's all moving by so fast, it's very disorienting and hard to come to terms with."

"I understand your meaning. If t'is any help, that is something to which you become accustomed. The four-day transient window most certainly gives a feeling of time speeding by."

"I'm sure. I still can't come to terms with the idea that I'm actually dead though. I feel it just happened with so much unfinished and left to complete. Strangely it's the little things that stay in my mind, the shower gel left in the bottle, the half-finished biscuits and the dentist appointment I always meant to make. I don't want to leave it there, Thomas," replied Ed, feeling a wave of despondency engulfing him.

A long considered silence ensued, Thomas not sure what he could say to comfort the individual as they continued their hike. It was Ed that broke the hush some two or three minutes later.

"Anyway, what language does everyone speak down here? Is it all English? Do they all have a 'Tudor bent' like you?"

"Not at all. English is the most common, but we have every language you can imagine here. It can be more than strange at first if we cannot communicate, but we usually muddle by or have someone translate. Having said that, we have so much time on our hands, many become multilingual. Forsooth, I thought I had already lost my 'Tudor bent', as you call it."

"Same with Transients out there as well I guess, speaking the language they did when they were alive?"

"Exactly. T'is why you were fortunate indeed to meet an English speaker on your first encounter."

"You're right there, Thomas."

"If you do decide to continue your journey, Ed, I would suggest you try and take your time at certain destinations. Take rest and sleep for a few days if you're somewhere safe. You are at the beginning now but after a while, Transients really need to take stock."

"I'll bear that in mind, Thomas, thanks," replied Ed, as they continued on their way. Ed began to reflect on what chance he might have to get his old life back. All these stories and far-fetched goings-on could easily be a dream, albeit a very nasty and realistic one. Maybe he'd had an accident and was in a coma in hospital, waiting for his brain power to propel him back to consciousness.

His mind churned away exhaustively at different scenarios. Tiredness was beginning to get the better of him and his walking had become heavy and weary. The whole episode had worn him down, being pulled from the flow with the crook and then all the journeying back and forth in the tunnels whilst being bombarded by unbelievable revelations. Ed knew he needed to sleep and gather his psychological powers to grasp the situation and get a little more empowered. Thomas was aware of Ed's state and slowed his pace accordingly.

Some while later they arrived back at the cave-like pod.

"You can tell me something more of yourself on the morrow, Ed. You must be tired now and t'would be good for you to rest."

"Thanks. See you tomorrow," replied Ed as he handed the football helmet to Thomas and brushed past the curtain into the enclosure. He removed his jacket and jeans, perched down onto the edge of spongy bed, flicked off his shoes and laid down, exhausted. If every day was going to be like the last few then he was in for a very eventful time.

Chapter 7
Hotline back to the living

"Are you decent?"

    "Are you decent?"

        "Are you decent?"

The voice started to penetrate Ed's consciousness.

That was one fantastic night's sleep, he thought as he pulled the thin black silky sheet from over him and reached down to get his jeans, just as Thomas entered the space.

"Oops! I beg pardon, I mean to cause no offence, but you have not yet donned your trousers."

"Don't worry, I will have soon," replied Ed as he pulled them on awkwardly, still sitting on the bed. He leant a little further forward, grabbed his shoes and put them on hurriedly.

"It does cause me much mirth – we are the only creatures bar mankind that do garb ourselves, even after we are dead," exclaimed Thomas as he pulled his oversized hat from his head to reveal his scraggly reddish hair.

"Whatever. That hair's timeless as well. If you have any scissors, I can trim it for you."

"Leave thy jesting. T'is little point. Cut it off and it returns exactly as it was on your last day. T'is same with fingernails and all else that once grew from our noble bodies. T'is convenient indeed and might have been a good idea when we were alive, would you not agree, Ed?" bemoaned Thomas, as he came and sat on the adjacent stool.

"Well it would certainly have saved on hairdressing bills," replied Ed with a smirk.

"Another thing, when I mentioned bodily functions yesterday, that includes intimate relations. Nought doing down below. No rumblings in the pantaloons or frolicking with Anne Boleyn. Shame, for she is comely forsooth, beauteous beyond compare."

"You are always the bringer of brightness, light and sensitivity into my world. Saves me thirty minutes trying to get a Roger on to sort myself out anyway."

"Is that how long it took you to become aroused?"

"Of course not, I'm being ironic, understated, and disingenuous. I was like a god in bed."

"Did you listen to prayers all night then?" replied Thomas with a smirk.

"Shall we talk about something useful?" said Ed, as he glanced at his watch.

"Is it working?"

"What?"

"The timepiece, is it working?"

"Strangely, yes, but how would I know if it's the right time?"

"The right time; who cares? There's little concern for time in here, no mealtimes or workplace, no jousting, bear baiting or mead making. T'is no 'right time' as such that your clock can display. If it functions though, you can accurately tell when your four-day limit is due from the moment you arrive. Of course, you have not the benefit of such a timepiece when you are transient in an animal, but you could refer to wall clocks, church bells or the turns of day and night to guide you."

"That's true. Anyway, I've decided I'll leave shortly, try and get back into the flow and move on. I'll take the risk."

"I understand. T'is no surprise to me. People rarely stay on their maiden visit. It's only on the second or third times that the tranquillity becomes seductive. Not many people are given those second and third chances though."

"I hear what you say but I'll try my luck. I like you, Thomas but I'll get bored here with nothing to do."

"Tis not a problem. We will take you to where you need to be, and you will be ready to jump not long from now. There's one other thing we need to discuss though."

"What's that then?"

"Do you recall I mentioned before that you had several choices?"

"Yes, go on," Ed replied, enquiringly.

"T'is but rumour in truth. A long, long way down the tunnels, far away from here, t'is said an ancient Viking resides, that has been there for centuries. He is, so they say, a man of great veritable wisdom, and knows of some much more dangerous, but potentially rewarding transient streams."

"Rewarding? How?" replied Ed inquisitively.

"From what I have been led to understand, he can influence where you arrive on each transience."

"What, the location?"

"Not just that, apparently the time or even what animal you become."

"Really?"

"Honestly, I know not for certain, t'is rumour from people travelling through."

"Well, if it's true that I'm dead and this isn't a dream, could he transport me back in time for me to change events? Maybe I could….." Ed was sharply interrupted.

"You have big ambitions, even in death. Be careful for what you wish. Tampering with the design of things is not our place. Much has been rumoured and exaggerated. I would suggest you accept your fate a little more humbly."

"Shouldn't we at least try and find out the truth, Thomas, to see what potential choices we have, and make our decisions based on that? If there's a way I can get back and at least see what happened and what mistakes I made, that might help me in this environment. It couldn't change the fact that I'm caught in this transient cycle and will continue to go round and round, one way or another," enquired Ed.

"T'is true."

"Well let's go and see him then."

"It is not so easy. It takes between two and three days to get there. That's why your timepiece will be most useful. Then, if he can be persuaded to share his information, we do not know how long it would take to get from there to the other streams - if they even exist. T'is a big befuddle. If they did not, then you would lose your chance to jump, as it would be past the four-day point of no return. He is also, so I hear, very fussy about first-time Transients. He prefers to be consulted only by the experienced, apparently."

"Oh. That's a conundrum."

"Tis my wise observation to suggest it is too late to

embark on this journey now. My feeling is that you should risk another transience and see if you can perhaps be paused in the next jump back. Apparently, t'is possible: if you concentrate really hard at the time of death, you can partially cause a pause. I know not if this be true, but it will be something to bear in mind."

Ed sat thoughtfully listening to Thomas, who continued.

"Another thing is that if you are paused and rescued, it is very likely you would not find yourself in this community. You may end up further along in a different community which might not have access to the area where the Viking lives. Maybe there would not be any speakers of English there. Tis a 'conundrum' as you call it."

"At least I have my watch to identify a timeframe. Lucky I had that on."

"Well there is always something positive in death," joked Thomas as he departed into the tunnel.

"I will return in an hour or so. Then we will awake you for your jump."

"Okay. See you then, and thanks again for all your help."

Ed lay back down on the bed, discarding the silk sheet beside him. The silence was beautiful, crystal and pure, perfect and impenetrable. It gave such a marvellous platform for calm thoughts. He reflected on the past few days: Sam, the tortoise experiences, Thomas and the whole array of totally psychologically shocking things that had been revealed to him. He was somewhat surprised at how rational he had remained and how well he had adjusted to the fast changing situation. It was not an easy time and it really called for a calm head.

Soon a mumbling in the doorway pierced the silence. He couldn't make it out but sat up and shouted, "Come in, come in," expecting there to be a curious guest outside.

"Oh, hi, hello, hi. My name is George, George, ehm, George George," exclaimed a nervous looking small man dressed in a cord dressing gown and tweed slippers. His thinning hair was heavily greased back over his head, desperate to hide a barren scalp. Thin matted yarns stuck steadfastly to the skin, revealing open patches of baldness underneath. Apart from that, he was clean-shaven, neat and tidy and Ed guessed him to be in his early fifties.

"George, or George George?" enquired Ed.

"George George I'm afraid. Very cruel of my parents," explained George, as he ventured into the room.

"I think it is pretty unique. I like it," said Ed reassuringly before adding, "I'm Ed, Ed Trew. It's good to be talking normally without all that 'Thou behest my Lord, for thou art the angel of perplexity' stuff."

"Pardon? Oh, you mean Thomas? Can take a bit of getting used to but he's a sweet fella, don't you think?" replied George as they shook hands before Ed moved back on the bed and sat cross-legged.

"Yes, he's lovely. I didn't mean anything nasty. I really meant to say I was glad to see you're a more modern guy, with a more common tongue, George."

"Common?" queried George as he perched delicately on the small stool opposite the bed.

"Common as in, 'in common', not common as in 'commoner' or common as 'in or on Clapham Common.'"

"Oh, I see. Anyway, being a commoner ain't so bad."

"I know, I certainly am not landed gentry but I really didn't mean 'common' in that sense."

"It's not a problem. Anyway, in answer to your question, I'm indeed a little more recent than Thomas. Popped my clogs in the late eighties. Slipped up in the kitchen in the middle of the night and hit my head on the stove. I should have turned the light on really. There are a lot more stupid ways to die though I suppose."

"Yes, but they all end in death."

"They certainly do. Anyway, I'm going to help you with Thomas. We'll see you get off safely. It's easy really, nothing much to worry about."

"Thanks, George."

"Not a problem. I've never jumped myself but I understand it usually goes fine, apart from, well, you know, the ones that fall all the way through the stream and get stuck out of reach of anyone who can help them from the doorways. That very rarely happens though."

"Yes, Thomas told me about that."

"I understand he told you about the Viking as well?"

"Yes, indeed. I'm interested in that. I want to do a couple more trips and then try to hunt him down if I can get paused again. Looks like I have time on my side for that anyway."

"You certainly do and there's a lot to find out. I don't know if you realise yet, but in an animal transience you pretty much always end up somewhere within the locality of your death."

"Well I didn't know that."

"Well take it as a fact. You do. However, time is flowing forward at about the same rate as we experienced on earth, so with each transience, you are four days further on from when you died, or if your transience was shorter, then an approximate equivalent."

"Really? Carry on," uttered Ed, as he uncrossed his legs and moved to the front of the bed with his feet down on the floor.

"Yes, yes. Anyway, as I understand it, the Viking knows of tunnels which present different options."

"What sorts of options?"

"Well it's very dangerous apparently, but time options, changing the time periods, even going backwards through time."

"Backwards? As if it's not complicated enough already, being propelled from animal to animal like a bouncing ball. I asked Thomas about that but he seemed a little reluctant, even scared to dabble with things. It would really be good to have some control over the transience destinations. Maybe I could go back, who knows, maybe even influence what happened and change things for the better. Are you sure all this gossip is true?"

"I don't know. Anyway, that's there as a possible choice. I don't know what you want, but there are alternatives. Everyone needs to know that when they come here."

"Okay. Thanks, George," exclaimed Ed, as Thomas returned to the room.

"Ah, t'is but a man hard to locate. I was looking for you," said Thomas, gazing over at George.

"Good to see you've met Ed, anyway. We should get going. The flow is stronger at the moment, so that gives you a better chance of a successful transience."

"Why's it stronger now?"

"Not sure really, it just is. Maybe the amount of soul traffic in there. If there are more people in transit then maybe it's slower. It seems to have a few days every now and then when it's stronger."

"One thing puzzles me, Thomas. You mention 'days' but there are no clocks or hours of daylight to judge the exact time. How do you do it?" asked Ed inquisitively.

"It's guess work really. We have a rough idea of what a twenty-four hour period feels like and we all seem to naturally sleep twice in that period, albeit at different times. It's these sleep patterns that we go on."

"Oh! Pretty vague then?"

"Tis indeed," replied Thomas.

With this the three of them left the small room, Thomas followed by George and then Ed. He glanced around and looked back at the room for one final time, before skipping to catch up with the other two heading down the tunnel.

"Well at least I don't need to take suitcases with me and check them in. No security to go through or passport to forget. Not even any spare underwear. It redefines 'travelling light'," Ed mused, as he caught them up.

"We didn't have suitcases back in the Tudor days. T'is a most excellent notion though," replied Thomas, as they reached the intersection and turned down towards the opening.

"All these tunnels and intersections and sleeping rooms, they must have been designed and built by someone. It can't all be by chance, don't you think, guys?"

"It's a conversation we've had many times, Ed," replied George before continuing, "The stairwell we're going to now is rumoured to have been carved out by the Viking but we can't see how it could have been possible. The rock's so hard that he'd have needed proper tools. The tunnels and all that's linked to them does on the surface seem to be of human design, but we really have no way to verify it."

"Mystery upon mystery eh," replied Ed, noticing the tunnels were getting a little gusty.

"It sounds a bit more fearsome today," remarked George as he paused to tie his shoelace.

"T'is indeed," replied Thomas before adding, "T'is a good day to turn and step into the tunnel."

Ed also began to notice the strong breeze that weaved through the tunnels, dancing across his face with a very slight chill. The small beams of light seemed slightly more sinister than the day before and Ed started to feel nerves in the depth of his stomach as if there was a very tiny spin-dryer on the go. He marvelled again at the black sand, mesmerised by the disappearance of the footprints behind them. The breeze increased in power as they grew closer to their destination, making the whole scene even more menacing. The fears of jumping began to eat away at Ed but he knew he had no choice if he was to continue his quest and find a possible solution for his predicament.

They walked further through the tunnels and over to the opening where the firm sand gave way to an uneven rocky floor. Their pace slowed and they tiptoed delicately for the last few yards, the wind positively howling through the entrance, giving off a low resonant tone. All three stared in at the all-encompassing flow, mesmerised by its power. Thomas stepped back and pointed Ed towards a smaller opening to his right which led to a claustrophobic hand-cut stairway.

"You need to go up there. George will go with you and give you a helping push if you lose your nerve. I will keep watch from here with the crook just in case it goes wrong and you drift over to this side out of the main flow. T'is unlikely though because the force would take you all the way through the flow to the bottom," stated Thomas, as George put his arm around Ed's shoulder and led him over to the opening. Ed was more than concerned that this might go horribly wrong and he might become aimlessly caught in the weaker parts of the current. He had no idea what would happen in such a circumstance but felt obliged to proceed regardless, anxious to become more empowered.

"One more thing, Ed, give ear to me," added Thomas loudly as the wind howled.

"What's that then?"

"Can you leave all your raiments for us, what say you?"

"Why? Why would you want my clothes?" barked Ed, slightly put out.

"Forsooth, the timepiece also, that would be of great use. Worry not - if you return and stop off in one of these places, then you will for sure find yourself garbed in the same vestments. You are inseparably bound with them. They are part of you now and if you find yourself here again, you will appear fully clothed. Your old garments from this visit are useful to us though. We can use them to make ropes and suchlike. We do not have sufficient yet, but I pray in time we can help rescue paused Transients in the bottom of the tunnel."

"Oh bloody hell, alright then!" exclaimed Ed as he slipped off his shoes and stripped down to his underwear, surprised not to feel cold in the gusts that brushed over his goose-bumped skin and on into the tunnels.

"Keep your shoes on though, Ed, you'll be more comfortable going up the rocky stairs in those," shouted George, almost drowned out by the noise.

"Okay. Elegance is out of the window here then," Ed retorted, as he bent down and put his shoes back on.

"I'll tell you something for nothing though, George, you can forget the arm around my shoulders now I'm half naked."

"Understood. No problem. Let's go," chuckled George before he headed into the stairwell, swiftly followed by Ed.

"Bye, Thomas, thanks for everything. Hope to see you again someday," Ed shouted back out through the doorway as they turned the corner and started to ascend the black stone stairs. The gusts of wind completely demised in the stairwell, leaving them in a calm and serene atmosphere.

"There won't be much wind in here, Ed, it's much calmer. Not sure why."

"That's good, it was getting a bit much," replied Ed, thankful that the stairs were smooth and not slippery.

"There are six hundred and twenty-four stairs altogether. Should take us twenty minutes or so."

"Now that's a lot of stairs. Will you be okay in slippers?" enquired Ed, aware that it was going to be a tiring climb."

"Yes, it'll be fine."

The walls of the stairwell were surprisingly smooth and as glisteningly miraculous as those in the main tunnels. Visibility was good and every twenty or so steps there was a tiny recess in the ceiling with a bright piercing light shining down. Each time the pair passed through the beams they cast a ghost-like, eerie shadow, melting back down over the steps with an amorphous freedom, getting longer and longer as Ed quickly fell behind George's pace.

"Hold on, George," panted Ed, as he pulled them to a halt after a hundred or so steps.

"No probs."

"Where do these lights get powered from, George? I can't see any cables or switches."

"As far as we can tell, it's all natural light. It is not electric or gas or anything. If you reach into the holes there's nothing there, they're just empty. Very strange, but when you land here after hopping from mammal to reptile to sea creature, anything seems possible."

"Sea creature? Tell me no, not a fish? How would a fish kill itself? What about a prawn?"

"I don't know. It's rare anyway, don't worry."

"Mmmm! There's quite a few things I shouldn't worry about, eh?" replied Ed ironically as they continued on their way, George slowing slightly to Ed's pace and allowing him to catch up.

Ed began musing on his next transience, wondering where and what he would end up with. He thought about the strange 'other world' running alongside the physical one and began to question George.

"Have there been any other ways that people have made contact with these communities down here?"

"How do you mean?"

"Well, if we know that some other physical world is going along parallel to this, isn't it possible that somehow we can make a connection from here, some sort of contact or message? Maybe that would save me having to make the jump."

"What, like a telephone hotline back to the living?"

"I don't know. What about Ouija boards, séances, mediums and all that stuff? I never believed in it but by the same token I never thought I'd end up here."

"Well as far as I am aware, there has never been any sort of contact made like that, at least not from this portal. We think it was all human hype, a myth. Pseudo contact with the spirits and all that. We have had a few fortune tellers and mediums in the past but they've never been able to do anything. They try for a while, sometimes over a prolonged period of time, but they always give up. One of them had the idea that it was the souls trapped around the outer edges of the flow that communicated with the other side, the physical side. They even held some 'events' down near the entrance, but all to no avail."

"That's interesting. Maybe getting trapped is like being half in and half out, caught between worlds. A distant and faint voice of misery. Maybe that's Hell itself. I hope that doesn't happen to me," replied Ed as they continued up the stairs.

There was a very faint chemical odour and as they got higher Ed could see a series of small cracks in the rock with minimal amounts of what looked like a black fluid leaking out. He stopped on a stair, spent a while to gather his breath again and poked at the substance with the first finger of his right hand.

"What's this?" he enquired, realising its spongy foam-like texture.

"I don't know. We've only ever found it here on this stairwell. It looks like it's leaking out but really, it never changes. In all the years I've been coming up here, it just remains exactly like that, no more and no less. Very odd, eh!"

"Yeah, very odd, along with everything else. Do we have much further to go?"

"No. We're nearly there now but come and look at this,"

replied George, pointing to something just ahead of him on the wall. As Ed got closer he could see it was a single vine growing from one of the steps and meandering up the curved wall, disappearing into the ceiling. Above it one of the jets of light bathed its entire length, casting evocative shadows across the wall and onto part of the stairs. Ed drew closer still and caught sight of a series of tiny bright blue flowers like tiny buttercups.

"It's the only one we've ever found anywhere in the tunnels. Amazing isn't it?" stated George.

"Certainly is. Why hasn't it spread? How long has it been here?"

"As far back as we know. It appears to be growing at a very slow rate. Touch the flowers in the centre, Ed."

Ed went even closer and put his little finger out towards the centre of one of the tiny flowers. It immediately and instantaneously curled up into a tight ball, leaving Ed aghast. He removed his hand away and was shocked to see it open up as quickly as it closed.

"We call them Tumpleberries. Odourless, harmless and altogether a mystery. Anyway, let's crack on," said George, continuing up the stairs, promptly followed by a bemused Ed. The mysterious flowers had certainly taken his mind off the task at hand and relieved his increasing anxiety of what was to come. The climb became steeper and steeper, causing Ed to become more and more breathless with every step.

"Not far now, come on, keep up."

"Alright then," sighed Ed begrudgingly as he followed suit, ascending higher and out of the grasp of the odour.

"Strange really, we don't know anything about each other, George. I didn't even tell Thomas much about myself. Truth is, it's still all a bit sketchy," reflected Ed with concern.

"Don't worry, maybe you'll come back. Anyway, it's too late now. We've arrived," exclaimed George, as they finally reached the top of the stairwell and a small entrance, through which the gushing wind noise could be heard. A light breeze manoeuvred across them, chilling Ed's bare chest. George directed his guest over towards the entrance and the point of departure.

"This is it, my friend. Take off your shoes and sit on the edge with your feet dangling down. I'll need a shoe to throw down the stairs to alert Thomas that you've jumped and to get ready with the staff. I'll count to three and on three, you jump and I'll push. That's it; job done. It's been pleasant meeting you."

"Thanks, George. Nice meeting you as well," replied Ed, as he bent down, removed his shoes and sat with his feet over the edge. As he looked into the hole, he could see the windy torrent below gushing from left to right. He was directly above it and starting to feel anxious about the jump. Would there be any impact or pain? Would he become nauseous or disorientated? What other horrors might await him?

"I know what you're feeling, Ed. Don't worry, just get on with it."

"Okay. Thanks again for all your support. It's only been a short time but I'll miss you both," replied Ed nervously.

"Maybe we'll meet again one day. We'll still be here, the keepers of the flame eternal. Anyway, are you ready?"

"Ready as I will ever be," replied Ed tensely.

"What if I land on one of the people, souls or whatever they are in the current?"

"Maybe it'll help you if anything. Perhaps it would cut the risk of going right through. I don't know, to be honest."

Ed stared down motionless into the gushing torrent. George could see the tension building and felt he needed to lighten the atmosphere a little.

"What do you call a flea on the moon, no, a crazy flea on the moon?"

Ed stared back round at the dressing-gown-clad individual, slippers looking even more ridiculous in this setting.

"What?"

"What do you call a...." Ed interrupted,

"I know; I just can't believe this is the right time for a joke. Anyway, what do you call a crazy flea on the moon, George?"

"A Lunar-Tic, a Lunar-Tic, get it?" announced George proudly, bursting out into an uncontrolled giggle.

"Whatever. Now you've really made me want to jump," replied Ed wryly as he glanced up at George's grinning face before turning to face the abyss once more.

"Good. Shall we go then, Ed?"

"Yeah, yeah. Let's do it," replied Ed apprehensively.

"Good. I'll throw the shoe down, give it a few seconds to get to the bottom and for Thomas to be prepared, and then we go. Are you clear? One, two and then we push on three."

"Yes, good as gold. I'm still full of hope though that this is all nothing more than a dream and I'm about to wake up to a big mug of coffee."

"Don't bank on it."

"I won't. Anyway, let's do it and stop talking."

George hurled the shoe down the stairs. It clattered in increasingly distant thuds as it descended to the bottom. The few seconds' delay felt like an hour to Ed. He was more than reluctant to jump into the ferocious flow.

"I would think of a prayer right now, but I'm having serious doubts about God," interjected Ed ironically as George began to count.

"ONE."

"TWO."

Then before he got to three, he gave Ed a sturdy push in his back, projecting him speedily out and down into the speeding flow of souls.

"Arrhhhhhhhhh," exclaimed Ed helplessly, before being tossed, turned, pummelled, aggressed and finally caught fully in the merciless central flow. Whoosshhhhh and there it was again, the fiery laser-like bright light, this time moving like a bullet train towards him. It got louder and louder, brighter and brighter until, zzaappp. Nothing. Sensory deprivation. No sound. No light. No feelings. No cares. No sensations. Nothing and nothing. A darkness that soon overcame all his consciousness. He disappeared.

Chapter 8
Get Smunky

"Dad, what's a Coalition?"

"Basically it's when a man without a head is rushed bleeding to the hospital, and they sew an arse on top to block up the hole in his neck."

"Wow, that's horrible; he'd crap from both ends."

"Yep, that's about the long and the short of it, Ali," concluded the plump middle-aged man, entrenched in a comfortable-looking, but cheap leather reclining chair. The TV blurted out the news, focused on the new dual party alliance that had been the disappointing outcome of an election full of hope.

"Sweeping legislation, big society, massive shake up, positive reforms, more changes than since 1832. A load of baloney if you ask me. They'll be just like the last lot, fraudulent and sleazy."

"I couldn't care less, dad. They're so old and boring. Why do politicians have to be boring old farts? They're about as exciting as a slug under a paving slab," interjected young Ali, a quickly growing thirteen-year-old teenager, riveted to his laptop and ever-expanding social network.

Similar as Ali was to his father, the pair weren't great lookers by any means. Slightly fat-headed, though not in a thuggish way, their heads sat upon their chunky necks like medicine balls on tree trunks. Their voluntarily short cropped hair gave them slightly more of an aerodynamic feel but that was combated by protuberant ears that jutted out gracelessly in a way not too dissimilar to a hippo. Their rounded features made their heads look even more spherical, as though they had been sanded into shape by someone who simply forgot to stop. It was like seeing a baby elephant with its parent, identical in everything apart from size.

He sported an ill fitting and extrovertly multicoloured stripy tracksuit top, whilst his dad was equally casual with jeans and an anonymous white tee shirt. They were the perfect pair.

"Is that computer still playing up?" queried Frank, his single-parent father, a bricklayer from South London.

"Yeah," replied Ali as he swivelled round in the bargain computer chair and gave a disgruntled face-scrunch in his father's direction.

"Well I don't know anything about them. Can't see why you bloody well bother with it anyway. Games and instant messages. Why don't you just call someone and go and play in the park? In my day you just needed a ball and a patch of grass and that was it for the week. That's why we have football geniuses like Rooney and Messi, because they had a ball in the street and not a nose in a faulty laptop."

Frank cranked the recliner back fully, perched a pillow under his head, and went quiet.

"It's not a faulty laptop. There's some temporary glitch. Anyway, at least you'll shut up now," replied Ali as he span back round to the computer.

"Oh no, it's frozen up again. I can't do anything," he exclaimed as he tapped furiously at every key of the QWERTY keyboard, furiously wiggling the mouse.

"It's now 6.30 and time for the news where you are," sounded from the TV, followed by the characteristic BBC news theme tune inter-spliced with: "Coming up on tonight's programme…"

"A man has been arrested in Hoxton after being caught carrying two holdalls full of guns and ammunition, along with a large amount of cash and class A drugs hidden in condoms."

"The clergy has announced it will be investigating the molestation of more than a dozen choir boys in one of their Islington churches. Two priests have already been charged for alleged offences in the early nineties."

"The mayor of London has criticised transport workers for going on strike, claiming they have been offered a fair 0.5% pay rise. The union for the workers has replied, criticising plans to completely scrap all pension schemes."

"Tottenham Hotspur football club are contesting the rule

to close their ground temporarily for excavation after the discovery of an ancient Roman burial site under the centre circle."

Ed was just starting to come round and could hear the voices getting closer and closer, clearer and clearer until his eyelids, seemingly spring-loaded, suddenly shot open. No pain, no dehydration or thirst and no headache. Truth be told, he was quite comfortably placed on a sofa. Could he have been reborn as a human?

As things came into focus, he could see he was in some sort of large residential room, tatty but bright. The velvet wallpaper was well past its sell-by date with corners peeling away and bubbles forming at the bottom, invaded by damp. The yellowish, stained skirting board was chipped and dented, probably by a Hoover, and the central dining table and chairs were a dulled and tattered pine. The saving grace was the big three-paned window at the front which let in gushes of light, even with the grey overcast conditions outside.

Ed started to feel his arms and legs, twisted his head from side to side to loosen his neck, and cautiously looked down to what the lottery of the transience had dished up for him.

Glossy deep black fur with white super-fluffy paws. He stretched them out and began a yawn with a stretch that rippled through his whole body. He looked down to see a set of four legs, each with outstretched retractable claws. They were impressive and aggressive, ready for scratching and piercing, and jet black in contrast to the brilliant white paws. He twitched his facial muscles in a way he had never done before and became aware of an intense sensitivity which seemed to give him what felt like a new sense.

It must be whiskers, he thought, as he stood up and arched his back upwards before slumping down into a comfortable ball once more.

This is a whole lot better than a tortoise, he mused, as he bathed in the comfort of the moment, feeling the odourless air pressure of a slight but barely noticeable draught across his face and whiskers.

"Oh for Chrissake, what is going on?" cried the boy, losing his cool at the frozen PC laptop.

"Control, alt, delete. Control, alt, delete. Then close down the offending program in the Windows task manager. Not rocket science, dude," exclaimed Ed, omitting only a wide range of audible cat purrs and growls in the process.

"Shut up, moggie," shouted Ali angrily before resuming his unscientific endeavours to get the computer functioning. Continued random tapping on the keyboard and jerky mouse movements did nothing to resolve the situation as his anger started to rise like steam in a pressure cooker.

"Oh, fuck it," exclaimed the teenager as he bent down to pull the plug from the wall.

"Don't swear," shouted Frank, not disturbing his reclined position or closed eyes.

"Oh no, not at the wall. Don't pull the plug out at the wall, use the reset button you moron," yowled Ed, as the young man did exactly the opposite.

Ali span round, pissed off at the animal noises coming from the cat, and seething from the powerlessness evoked by the faulty computer.

"I've told you before, don't get on the sofa. Are you thick or something?"

With that he leapt out of his computer chair and proceeded with haste over towards Ed, grabbing his fur coat behind his head and carrying him swinging like a six-pack into the kitchen. Once inside, he tossed him from waist-high onto the kitchen floor. Instinct kicked in immediately and Ed's legs splayed out to cushion the blow, large feline paw pads acting to reduce any impact from the landing.

It was a sensational feeling: the large pad and four satellite pads under each paw landed on the floor as he cascaded down into a crouched position and then back upright, arching his back in an upwards curve. His whiskers were super-sensitive, almost like a second set of eyes feeling out the location of objects around him whilst his tail counterbalanced him with delicate and subtle movements. He felt like he was gimbal mounted.

"Do something useful and eat your food. It's been there all day. What's up with you?"

Ali slammed the door and retreated back to the living

room, leaving Ed in the kitchen alone. Lo and behold, there in the corner was a bowl of cat food and a saucer of milk. He looked around the small room. There were white artificial looking cabinets, washing machine, oven and virtually everything one would expect in a low budget kitchen. The beige patterned lino on the floor was slightly padded but wearing thin and torn in places. The kitchen was in urgent need of an overhaul.

Next to the sink he could see piles of dirty washing-up and a solitary marigold glove hanging over the side with under-whelmed limpness. He ambled over towards the food, his legs instinctually following the walking pattern; back left, front left, back right, front right, back left, front left, back right, front right and so on, like an elegant four-legged centipede feeling proud of itself.

Mysteriously mathematical, but very satisfying, mused Ed, as he neared the food wondering how he would get on with it. It had not been a favourite for him as a human. It smelt good though as he moved his head over the small bowl. He started licking it, piece by piece before biting the bullet and getting his feline fangs involved in the extraction of the first whole lump. It was slightly oily, covered in flecks of semi-translucent jelly, but felt like proper cuts of meat. He tossed it up and down in a kind of juggling motion between his teeth before getting it into the optimum position for consumption. The flavour exploded as he took it fully into his mouth and sliced it apart with his sharp, white teeth.

It might not be too bad here for a few days, he thought, as he finished the first piece and went about clearing out the rest of the bowl, finishing up with a refreshing drink of milk, just like when he was a little boy.

I seriously hope they don't have a dog, he thought, as he began to explore the kitchen, a quick process due to the size. To the left of the food bowl was a comfortable-looking cat basket, complete with blanket and small furry pillow. *Excellent*, he thought, as he looked forward to a few nights' safe and comfortable sleep. Around the corner from the washing machine and sandwiched between it and the fridge was the door to the garden, a cheap plastic door, glazed at the top with pseudo Georgian inserts, partly falling away at the sides.

The bottom of the door intrigued Ed the most. A plastic cat flap about seven inches square led out into the garden. This would be vital for him to get out when the time came for the next transience. He butted his head against the flap and out into the small alleyway which led down into the main garden, leaving the flap swinging back and forth in his absence. The garden was small, probably about twenty-five feet long and as wide as the semi-detached two-storey house. At the back there was a small patio door which led out to the garden from another small room.

I would've knocked that through into the living room, thought Ed, as he made his way into the overgrown mess of the garden, reflecting that his new guardians were obviously not the green-fingered sort. He danced into the un-mown grass, keen to test his jumping and climbing skills. It was such a welcome contrast to being a tortoise. His whiskers were ever aware, jetting out like flexible laser beams of hair from his snout. It was an extreme sensation.

Eagerly, with his agile, feline legs, he jumped up and down out of the grass on the spot, over and over again, up and down like a jack-in-the-box.

"Dad, come and look at this, Smunky has gone mad in the garden. He's just jumping up and down like a lunatic," shouted Ali from behind the thin glass conservatory door.

"Whatever," replied Frank, uninterested in the whole situation.

Great, so I'm called Smunky! Why, why Smunky? What the hell does it mean?

Ed stopped his acrobatics and used his legs to jump up onto the fence. However, being new to the cat kingdom he had no idea of his own strength and completely misjudged it, clearing the fence to land in the bush next door.

"Dad, Dad, you'll never believe what he's done now."

"Shut up for Chrissake, I'm trying to get some rest," barked Frank, as Ali went back into the living room to see his computer giving him the dreaded 'frozen blue screen' treatment once more.

Meanwhile, Ed had landed upside down in a prickly thorny bush and was wriggling and twisting his body to get free. With a yank and a jerk, he suddenly spun out and fell three or so feet to the ground, uprighting himself in flight and landing on a soft mown lawn, legs splayed out.

Mmm, that's a cool design, thought the cat, as he shook himself down and began casually strolling across the garden.

"You scummy little bastard, what have you done to my bush?" suddenly rang out from Ed's left. He glanced round with surprise to see a red-faced and very angry old man proceeding towards him, clutching with angst to his Zimmer frame as he made very slow progress. He looked as though years of poverty had worn away at his body, whilst years of misery had slowly eroded his character. Tatty grey tweed trousers, baggy and torn, hung from his thin hips, a brown leather belt ambitiously trying to retain enough tension to avoid embarrassment. This was crowned with a grubby white shirt adorned with thin blue stripes and a purple synthetic tank top with numerous small holes and tears.

His gnarled and twisted hands clung to the top of the metal walking frame, knobbed and twisted as the protuberant joints seemed to be visibly growing like a complex of inconvenient ginger root. He struggled on, fuelled by anger and resentment, his wispy, overgrown, thin grey hair blowing randomly in the breeze.

"You really think you're going to catch a cat, you Muppet? Save it, or you'll have a heart attack," announced Ed, omitting a strange array of cat noises in the direction of the man as he grappled with the frame, lifting it one side then the other, trying to get to the cat. His vile rage showed in his frothing, bulging, red face and was evidence of a lifetime's frustration. The long grey tufts on either side of his mainly bald head flicked impotently from side to side as he shuffled further.

"You fool, what d'you think you're doing?" meowed Ed, as he calmly skipped onto a small wall and then up onto a cheaply constructed and tatty wooden garden shed. He looked down from the roof, at the door hanging on one hinge from a badly rotting door frame. The man came to rest just in front and grabbed his walking stick from the side of the silvery metal frame, lifting it skywards, shaking it in Ed's direction, banging on the bottom part of the gable roof.

"You bastard, you bastard," he shouted as he smacked away at the roof with the stick, causing bits of the unkempt structure to fly off into the garden.

"Chrissake man, were you on the losing side in a war or something? You're causing more damage than I ever could have in the bush," screeched Ed, as he backed off to the rear of the roof and up onto a tall thin wooden fence. It was hardly wide enough, but his fine-tuned balancing skills made walking along the slender and narrow wooden structure mere child's play. He skipped along, leaving the spouting buffoon behind, exhaling his rage like an impotent volcano.

The fence ran along the back of a number of gardens and was going to be a very useful through-route for getting around the area. He stopped for a moment and looked back to get his bearings and a visual landmark so he could easily return to the house.

They have food and a comfortable warm place to sleep so I'd be a fool not to go back and stay a few days. Besides, maybe I could try and browse the internet on the kid's laptop when they're out. That's not going to be easy with these fat paws though, thought Ed, noticing a rusting red swing in the garden where he had had the altercation with the old man. Next to it, the bush had indeed been left in disarray with wooden supports and bits of thin wire mesh left in a bundle on the lawn. The old man just stared motionless at the damage.

I don't recall making that much of an impact on it. Oh well, onward and upward, thought Ed.

With this, he resumed his journey along the fence, down into a small alley and along into a small park and pond, marvelling at his newfound agility. It was as though every time he jumped or landed he was Zebedee or some other spring-based jumping novelty toy. Excitedly, he pounced up onto walls, sheds and fences and back down again onto the tarmac walkway, his paws splaying out whilst his legs took all the pressure of each jump with a satisfying springiness.

His whole body felt so flexible, like a big slab of very soft, flexible rubber.

He ambled out into the main road, keeping on the pavement and slinking along close to the sides of the parked cars, ducking in and out from under them between the wheels. He powered himself skywards again with his strong back legs and jumped up onto the roof of a blue Honda Jazz car, walking along its roof, down onto the bonnet and then down onto the floor to continue on his way. He came to rest on the small front wall next to a finely pruned and arranged rose bush. The smell was almost overpowering for the cat, leaving him intrigued by the depth of its odour. Finally it got too much to bear and he jumped down and back along the way he'd come. The intensity of all the smells around him was altogether overwhelming. Even the car tyres gave out an incredibly strong rubber smell as he strolled along the street. Worst above all, were the piles of dog poo at every possible tree location along the way, sometimes even just dropped off in the middle of the pavement.

What must owners be thinking, letting them do that? If they could smell what I could smell they would certainly rethink the strategy of their dog's toilet habits, thought Ed, as he slinked past yet another mess, careful to keep his pristine furry paws away from any of it. Soon he was on his way back to his new home and back along the fence past the old man's house. He skipped down from the fence onto the brick and breeze block enclosure that formed a barbeque area at the end of his new garden and proceeded home.

Back into my Smunky shack, he thought, as he trotted along the small alley and flicked his way through the cat flap, leading with his head. Frank was in the kitchen making tea and toast for himself and his son. Ed snuck through the open kitchen door and slid into the living room. Ali was still at the computer, his right hand flicking through options with the mouse whilst the left hand held his mobile phone to his ear.

"What do you mean leave it on 24/7? Isn't that dangerous? Dad will go bananas about the electricity bill."

Meanwhile Ed had spotted another cat basket in the corner of the living room, smaller than the one in the kitchen but equally comfortably lined with a warm, thick furry blanket. He slinked over and skipped in, avoiding the saucer of milk alongside.

Great, looks like I'm going to be spoiled for a few days, he thought, as he lay down in the basket on his side, his legs straight out flat on the blanket. His head perched proudly upwards as he craned to see what Ali was up to.

"Well, it's okay now. It's all working fine, I think. Let me put you on speaker phone so I can use both hands."

Ali propped the phone up against the screen of the laptop and pressed the small icon on the screen for the speaker.

"Can you hear me?" shouted Ali.

"Yes, I can, you don't need to shout," replied the thin, tinny micro voice at the other end of the line.

"Great. What was it you said, Control, Alt what?" queried Ali.

"Control, Alt, Delete, hold down the first two at the same time and press delete."

"Won't that delete something?"

"Oh, for Pete's sake, you really are a beginner. No, it won't delete anything, just do it," replied his friend with more than a degree of irritation.

"Ehm? Which one is 'control'?"

"My god, are you kidding me? It says C-T-R-L on it. How thick can you be?"

"All right, all right! Keep yer hair on. This is the first time it's gone wrong. I knew we shouldn't have got a laptop. See, I told you Dad, we should have got a proper desktop computer," announced Ali as he turned round to his dad who had just entered the room with tea and toast.

"How the hell would I know? You decided, not me. If it was a kettle or toaster then I might have had an opinion. A bloody computer though, I don't know why you waste your time with that muck. Anyway, here's your tea and toast; come over to the table and eat it now," replied Frank as he deposited the two plates and cups on a small table by the window, carelessly slopping the tea over the edges of the cups.

"Carter, I'm going to have to go, sorry."

"Don't worry, I can come over tomorrow night and fix it up. Leave it on until then," replied his helpful friend.

"Did you hear that, Dad? We have to leave it on overnight. Then Carter'll come and fix it tomorrow."

"Okay, anything, if you just come over and eat your bloody toast. Get a cloth from the kitchen as well to mop this up," exclaimed Frank, less than bothered about the situation.

"Listen, I'll see you later, Carter. Thanks, man," exclaimed Ali as he hung up before heading to the kitchen for a cloth and back over to the table.

"Thanks, Dad. He'll sort it all out. He's brilliant with all this stuff. He knows more than the teacher about computers in our computer class. I should get a bit more knowledgeable about it myself really. I feel so helpless when something goes wrong," exclaimed Ali, as he tucked into his thickly sliced toast, covered in much too much butter.

"Whatever! Eat that and then we should leave to go to the match or we'll be late. A win tonight and we go five points clear at the top of the table," declared Frank, for the first time displaying a degree of enthusiasm in his voice.

"Hey, Basingstoke Town rule the world, 'Vestigia Nulla Retrorsum'. Come on you Dragons," exclaimed Ali excitedly before opening a drawer under the table, pulling out a blue and yellow scarf and tying it around his neck.

"What does that mean anyway, Dad? Why does everyone sing that?" queried the boy.

"Christ knows. Italian I think. Must be something to do with that bloody operatic twaddle they used as a theme tune for the World Cup. What a load of crap."

With that, Frank pulled down a strikingly unattractive, Basingstoke FC bobble hat and forced it over his slightly fat head, down to, but not over the ears.

"We really need to leave it on do we, Ali? Are you sure it's okay?" queried Frank, gesticulating towards the computer.

"It'll be fine, Dad, and it takes hardly any juice. Let's go to the match or we'll be late. I'll pop these into the kitchen," proclaimed Ali confidently as he scooped up the cups and plates and made tracks towards the kitchen.

As if the hat and scarf were not enough, they soon both had garish bright and lurid yellow and blue jackets and were heading out of the front door.

"See you later, Smunky. Take it easy, furry fellow," shouted the boy back into the living room before slamming the front door shut. He tinkered with numerous locks before heading down the garden path and out onto the pavement. Ed jumped up from his basket and onto the window ledge to see them both heading sluggishly along the road and away from the house.

Chapter 9
Vestigia Nulla Retrorsum

Right. This is my opportunity. Let's see if I can do anything on the computer with these ridiculous paws, thought Ed, as he jumped down onto the frayed and tatty carpet, up onto the computer chair, and onto the desktop. Ed had never been much of a football fan, but knew that if they were at a match then he would have a two or three hour window to explore online and gather some deeper information about the circumstances around his death.

He stared at the glittering ocean screensaver splashing over the laptop screen, keen to entertain whoever would be bored enough to stare at it. He looked closer and could see it was certainly not state of the art, without a brand name or any logos anywhere on the black and silver plastic body.

Right, I need to twist it round sideways so I can get better access to the keyboard, thought Ed, as he jerked cautiously at the front left edge of the machine, gently turning it sideways, careful that none of the cables became detached.

If I yank any of these cables out I'll never get them back in again, considered the cat whilst realising how lucky it was that the device had a touch pad controller rather than a mouse.

Thank God for that. Besides the fact that I wouldn't be able to control it with these paws, I might eat it.

With this, he turned the machine a good ninety degrees, realising how difficult it was going to be to do anything meaningful with it. Sitting in front of the machine with his body erect he stroked across the touch pad, disengaging the screen saver and switching the view over to the desktop and a commonly generic Microsoft image of flowing sandy dunes and an impressive blue sky. From the icons at the bottom of the screen he could see that it was still connected to the internet. The obstacles were falling one by one.

"So far so good. Let's try and open up a document and see if I can type anything meaningful."

Ed extended out his claws as far as they would go and with the far left claw of his right paw dragged down and across the touchpad, moving the cursor erratically all over the desktop. His left paw meanwhile rested on the left corner of the laptop casing keeping it steady. Up, down, across, left and right, back and forth, in and out and round and round. He slowly mastered the cursor movement and got fairly comfortable moving it around the screen.

Next he tried clicking a few things. He dragged the cursor over a program icon and moved his paw down to the click buttons to try and open it. It hurt his claw as he unsuccessfully clicked but he persevered and after a few attempts managed to master the technique. He then scrolled up to the 'close program' icon in the upper right corner of the screen and closed it, then opened it and closed it again. Time after time he opened and closed programs before switching his attentions to his typing skills, opening Microsoft word and trying to type.

'8ii anm a cat whyy m iu sa caat... I don@t lknow why I anm as xcat aanb I wwamt too so;lvee thwe riddfle on the ointewernet ifg ii vcan'

"This is hopeless. How will I ever be able to type a URL or navigate anywhere like this?"

Distraught, Ed pulled away from the computer and stared disconsolately at the screen, bewildered and disillusioned. After a few minutes the waves of the screen saver began splashing their optimistic wateriness in his face once more.

"Fuck it! I've already wasted something like an hour. I can do this. Pull yourself together, sort this shit out right now."

Ed gave himself a stern inspirational poke and got back into position at the keyboard.

"I can do this. I will do this. I am doing this and soon I will have done this. It might be the only opportunity I ever get."

With this he launched back into the word document, tapping, tickling, poking and prodding the keys until he mastered some semblance of control.

'I amm a Cat. My nsme is Ed, not friking Smunky. Whst is a Smmnky anyway? I am niot daftt or stuupid sndwould like to sit omn th sofa 3very now aand theen. I like th foopd you give me but I wa,mt more pleawse. Abnother thimg, you hsve comput3r problems b3cause you don''tt hsve a proper anti virus instslled. If I hav3 time tomight, I will do thst for you. Llove. Ed'

Save as; 'A massage frim your cat.doc'
Location; Desktop

"That will be funny when he finds it," smirked Ed as he clicked on the Mozilla Firefox browser icon and opened up an internet browser.

"Where shall I start? I don't even know the date I died."

Ed sat, confused about how to begin his search. He figured he had at least ninety minutes until Ali and Frank came home and he didn't want to waste time. Firefox had opened up on the Google search page and so he began typing in random search requests.

Motor accident on M3.

Car crash and death on A303 / M3.

Car accidents near Basingstoke.

Nothing significant came up at all, at least not anything that seemed linked to him in any way whatsoever. Was his death that insignificant that it had not received any attention whatsoever in the media? Was he such a nobody that he just disappeared with a whimper rather than a bang? He felt disillusioned once more.

"What am I hoping to achieve? Even if I do find any meaningful facts, what use will it be? I'm dead and in a perpetual cycle of being reincarnated into different animals. What's the point?" Ed slumped down again feeling sorry for himself.

"Christ all mighty! Give me some help here, dude. If you are bloody well there, which I now seriously doubt, give me a clue." He started to feel angry at the situation, the adrenalin pumping into his little feline veins and reigniting him once more as he stared up for divine intervention.

"Just one more go, one more go. Why don't I look at some of my company's online sites? I'll start with Cubiz."

Soon he was tapping away at the keyboard once more, typing into the address bar: www dot CubiZ dot Com. Lo and behold, the site sprang up and in the bottom right hand corner of the screen was a picture of him and a big fluorescent glowing announcement in a box.

Sad news. Ed Trew, creator and owner of CubiZ Ltd has been taken from us in a tragically fatal car accident. Click here for details.

He sat overwhelmed, miserable, confused and shattered. He thought he would read some headlines in his time but one regarding his own death was really pushing the boat out. Looking at his picture and seeing the announcement, it penetrated to his inner core with a painful permanence and forlorn solitary loneliness. For the first time in his existence, he was in mourning about his own death whilst asking himself a very important question: Do I exist?

I used to feel my existence was so permanent, or at least long lasting. Now I feel anything but. Does that mean I don't exist or is each new transience a new existence? Maybe my consciousness constitutes existence but even that is not exactly long lasting because it changes slightly with my tastes, desires and habits of each animal. What a conundrum, thought Ed, as he clicked on the link to the story about his passing.

Ed Trew 1970 – 2009

Ed Trew, the designer and owner of CubiZ was sadly killed in a road accident on **September 22nd 2009 at approx 17.00.** *He was thirty-nine years of age and was the pioneer in the design of all CubiZ solar power units and the 'RuZZia snow cleaner' which has done so well in Eastern Europe, Siberia and the Far East. He was posthumously awarded the ICBDF Designer of the Decade award for his stunning solar power inventions which will be such a vital ingredient of a greener lifestyle for the world.*

The cause of the crash is unknown but mobile phone records have shown a busy period of texts and calls just before the tragedy. He was alone in his silver Volvo estate at the time of the accident, and the only casualty. It was reported that a car near the scene had a tyre blow-out at around the same time on the same stretch of road and could have been the cause. The driver reported seeing Ed's car swerve into the central reservation before veering across the three lanes and into a ditch beside the carriageway where it appears to have overturned, probably twice. No other cars were involved in the accident on the M3 northbound half a mile or so from the junction with the A303 near Dummer.

Ed leaves a wife, Abella, but no children. His legacy will live on as his company CubiZ continues to grow from strength to strength. Abella Trew has taken over the chairman's role of the company and has appointed a strong team of experts from the field to work with her to take the company to the next level. Since Ed's death, numerous lucrative orders have come in from Siberia for the RuZZia cleaner and five local councils in the UK have committed to supply at least fifty percent of their street lighting with the CubiZ solar system. Consequently the company has expanded and is currently developing three large factory areas in the Midlands and expects to employ a work force of around 4,250 in the new facilities within twelve months.

Mr Trew is sadly missed by all his colleagues, friends and relatives but his legacy lives on and CubiZ Ltd continues to push towards being the world's leading solar power developer.

Ed stared emotionally at the screen. Everything he had dreamed of for the company was coming true but he was not going to witness it.

"Christ, all that success and I am becoming aware of it as a bloody cat living with two Basingstoke Town fans. How bad can it get?"

With this, Ed realised he could look at the date on the computer and work out how long he had been away. He dragged his paw across the touchpad and manoeuvred the cursor down and over the bottom right hand corner of the screen. It displayed the time, 21.03. As he moved the cursor over this section it displayed the date: November 07 2011.

Sam was right - looks like I've been dead for over two years. Whatever happened to me during that time? Was I just floating in nothingness? How bizarre. At least I know the truth now and can be sure it's not a dream. I don't know how useful it'll all be, or even if this Viking guy can help, but at least I know. That's got to be something, reflected the cat, catching his reflection in the glass of a small framed photo above the computer. It was Ali and Frank sitting beside a sun-drenched grey / green swimming pool, both clutching enormous ice creams. They looked so happy in that moment, as if their destiny was condensed there and then. An indelible moment of joy, love and companionship that must certainly be etched on both their memories.

It made Ed miss Abella even more and dragged his mood into a sudden forlorn misery. He sat motionless for a while before picking himself up to reflect on the positives. He felt reassured that Abella had become so committed to the company and seemed to be taking it all forward. He was glad she had found the energy and motivation to continue, but deep down he still couldn't help feeling bereft that she was living her life without him. It felt like they'd lived for each other and that anything else was out of the question.

The thoughts rushed through his head like fireworks in an empty gas tank. He wondered what to do. Could he contact her? How he would love to log onto his email and send her an email. How would she ever believe him though? He reflected on what he would say;

-----Original Message-----
From: Ed Trew [mailto:edtrew @ CubiZ dot biz]
Sent: 07 November 2011 21.09
To: ABELLA TREW
Subject: Re: I am a cat and was previously a tortoise
Dear Abella,

You do not need to worry. I am currently a cat in Basingstoke and was previously a tortoise in, well somewhere near Basingstoke I guess. I am not in pain and I am hoping to find a way to get back to you. I am sorry I died and although I would like to say that I won't do it again, that would be a white lie because sadly I have to kill myself every four days. Annoying but sometimes you need to go with the flow.

Trust me when I tell you that this is not easy to explain.
I love you so much and miss you even more.
Love. Ed

No. I can't send anything like this. It would just open up the wound again and she'd just think it was some digital prankster and be angry.

Ed sat back a little from the computer and slumped with misery, not knowing what to do.

"I'm dead but I have an opportunity to contact her. This would be redefining Ouija boards and séances. Speaking to the dead in the twenty-first century. Just hit send and you and your loved one will be digitally connected with our 100% authentic Ouija app," joked Ed to himself. He loved her so deeply though. Of all the things to lose with his passing, his relationship with her was undisputedly top of the list. However, he knew he could not send her an email. It would be so cruel and destructive. He sat quietly with his sadness for a moment before sitting bolt upright again, looking at his reflection in the computer screen. A proud Egyptian-looking cat browsing online. How modern can you get? Soon he was focused back on the laptop and navigated to the home page of the CubiZ website and on to the products page.

It listed a number of new products that he had not seen before. Solar powered shoes with thermal feet warmers, tents with solar panel material that powered little LED bulbs in the roof, solar powered flasks that would keep coffee warm for days and even a solar powered crash helmet that could blow either hot or cold air inside. The list went on and on as Ed scrolled through, amazed at how everything had come together. He glanced down again at the bottom of the screen to check the time. It had crept on to 21.19. He figured he had half an hour left before Ali and Frank arrived back home from the match.

He navigated back to Google and typed in; free anti virus download.

Soon he was on the site of 'Zap a spam MO-FO' and was downloading and installing the program. He was getting comfortable with the paw and claw motions on the touch pad, speeding through the process of putting the product on the laptop and updating the anti virus definitions. In no time he had clicked on the scan option and the computer was having its hard drive trawled through for nasty, unnecessary and downright bloody annoying infiltrations from some spotty anaemic computer hacker in Eastern Europe or the Far East.

Why do they even bother in the first place? They can't see when they have zapped someone. What's the point? thought Ed, as the scan completed itself.

1246 problems found. Do you want to quarantine and delete these problems.

YES? NO?

Ed happily clicked on 'YES' and watched the anti virus strut its funky stuff as it zapped each and every one of the invaders, proudly showing a bloody scene of a computer hacker being shot in the head at point blank range each time. That amounted to 1246 re-runs of the gruesome scene and took over fifteen minutes.

Right then. Turn on automatic updates, close down the internet browser and brush my paw marks off the touch pad, thought Ed, as he tidied up the scene and tried to get the computer back into position on the table before jumping down onto the chair and then onto the floor.

He meandered out into the kitchen and lapped hungrily from his saucer of milk before returning to the living room and the comfort of his basket. He got back into his now familiar recline with his legs poking out and his head resting over the edge of the cut out at the front. Soon he had nodded off, only to be abruptly awoken by a slam at the door and loud footsteps approaching along the passageway and bursting into the living room.

"What is this new bloody offside rule anyway? Not offside if the player is not interfering with play. How much is he bloody well interfering with play when he scores a goal? Can't bloody well interfere with play more than that. Morons, the lot of 'em," ranted Frank, completely disillusioned with the law makers and referees of the glorious game.

"Miserable, eh? Anyway, we were undone with a Kipper blow," replied Ali.

"It's not Kipper blow, stupid, it's a killer blow."

"Whatever. We're still top though, Dad; Scummers lost."

"Don't call them scummers. They are just another football team, or town or whatever you want to call them."

Together they headed into the kitchen, tossing their jackets at the sofa behind them. They disappeared from sight before Frank momentarily reappeared and tossed his hat towards the jackets, missing totally and landing on Ed's head.

Oh, for fuck's sake, thought Ed, as he tossed it off, whilst beginning to notice the alluring smell of fish and chips.

"Sorry, Smunky," said Frank as Ed followed him and the smell into the kitchen.

"We've got to give Smunky some, Dad, just a bit."

"Okay then, a bit of fish and a few chips and that's it," replied his father.

"Great, he'll love that," said Ali as he unwrapped his portion and broke some fish off. He placed this together with seven chips onto a clean cat bowl and placed in on the floor before putting his own, much larger portion on a blue and white patterned plate, lashing it with salt and vinegar.

"Oh please, salt and vinegar for me, salt and vinegar please," mewled Ed, standing on his back legs with his front clawing up the cupboard doors towards the seasonings.

"Is it my imagination or is he getting fussier and fussier? He surely can't be asking for salt and vinegar, can he?" said Frank disbelievingly as cat noises blurted with desperation from Ed's mouth.

"Wow, that's strange. I'll put some on and see," replied Ali, before grabbing both pots and bending down to the bowl on the floor. Ed jumped down, setting all four paws on the floor simultaneously like a moon mobile. He followed him over, nudging his hand when he had the right amount of salt and just enough vinegar.

"That is unbelievable, Dad. Either I am imagining it or this is the most clever cat in the world."

"Yeah, whatever. Let's go and eat this. Then it'll be time

for bed," replied Frank, heading into the living room with both plates in hand.

Brilliant, fish and chips. This has got to be better than being a tortoise any day of the week, thought Ed, as he began tearing at the food in true cat-like fashion, tossing it from side to side whilst trying to gnash at it with his jaws.

Once his treat of a meal was over he headed back into the living room. Ali and Frank had finished and Frank was bringing the plates back into the kitchen.

"It's late, time for bed, young man," said the father as he returned to the living room.

"All right, Dad."

Ali got up, and they both left the room, Frank switching the light off as he walked through the door, his arm trailing behind him. Squeaks and moans came from the stairs as the loose thin floorboards of each step felt the force of the heavy footsteps. Soon the sounds had demised, leaving only the odd squeak as father and son went about their duties in their respective rooms.

Ed returned to the comfort of his basket and tried to get some sleep. He was restless with all the discoveries of the evening and soon decided on a bit of adventure instead.

Right, a bit of night life for me I think. It will be very interesting to check out these 'night vision' eye balls," thought Ed, as he jumped out of his basket and strolled elegantly over towards the kitchen.

Might even find myself a little feminine feline companion. I wonder what that would be like. I wonder if I'd fancy her. thought Ed, marvelling at the prospect.

I definitely won't suggest 'Doggie' position though. That might go down very badly, smirked the cat to himself as he pushed his way through the cat flap and into the mellow night.

He proceeded down the thin path and into the main overgrown garden. The bright fluorescent street lamp at the front threw a reasonable amount of orange light onto the scene but as soon as he got into the main part of the garden his whole focus started to change and he began to see the benefits of feline vision. It was as if the view was being filtered through some sort of strange photographic ISO machine, making it much brighter and whiter than it really was. Then, when he looked around back at the brighter path area it compensated so that everything seemed pretty evenly illuminated. Meanwhile his whiskers sensed everything in the locality with GPS accuracy, like the sensors in a modern car sounding when something's too close.

I thought it would be strangely green or infra red, like a bizarre night time action commando movie," thought the cat, glad that the whole night scene was not like one big green and black inverted photographic image. He made his way down to the barbeque area, jumped up onto the wall, onto the small fence and finally leapt to the heights of the big long fence that ran along the back of all the gardens. He was astonished at how his feet just instantly found their footing, even on the top of the thin fences and in the evening light. It was so instinctual that it felt like someone was doing it for him without having to worry himself. His tail counterbalanced him from behind, compensating with incredible effectiveness every time his body twisted, turned or jumped. He really felt like the perfect night creature, superbly balanced and intricately aware of his environment. He skipped along confidently, wondering at how marvellous the gardens looked with this new cat vision. He was silently enjoying being a cat.

He proceeded along the fence, dancing one paw in front of the other in a satisfying quarternity of movement, past the strange old man's garden and those of his neighbours. At the end, there was a tall wooden post crowned with a small, flat, piece of wood. He jumped up onto it, the area being just big enough for all four paws to arrange themselves and balance him proudly on top. He looked around and saw down to the right a small pond surrounded by tiny bushes and shrubs. He jumped down and sat beside the water's edge, next to a small solar powered lantern flickering on and off as if the batteries were on their last legs.

Why can't they get it right? he thought, as he sat alert, mesmerised by the beautiful calm silence all around. He stared up at the clear starry sky and the sharply focused three quarters moon. It was indeed a thoroughly beautiful night.

Maybe this is the lesson right here. What's wrong with this? No ambition, no obligations, no worries, no stress, no bills, no arguments and no anxieties. Maybe this is enough. Why should I change anything? I get fed, have a warm place to sleep, gardens to roam in, extreme agility, night vision and ridiculously good balance. This ticks a whole load of boxes that are definitely not ticked for a lot of humans. Why should I want to go back to that?

Ed mused on his position, slightly surprised how quickly he had adjusted to the whole thing and how he had come to terms with being dead.

Sure, I miss how things were, but if I move on from this incarnation, there would probably be elements of it I would miss.

Ed moved over to the water's edge. He could see his reflection clearly as he moved his head over the calm water, stretching out his right forward paw and disturbing the mirror water surface. It erupted into a thousand ripples, moving outwards from the point of impact, breaking his reflection into a million quivering segments.

That sums it up. The reflection is as temporary as me. One little point of aggression and the whole thing shatters.

He stood up and moved around the small pond, mesmerised to see how one tiny point of impact caused so many ripples. His mood swung left and then right, one minute marvelling at being a cat and the next being distraught at not being his old self. As he moved around the pond, the surface underfoot changed from a soft mown grass to a loose shingle made up of tiny stones. Each paw sank smoothly into the shallow shingle as he moved forward creating a mesmerising sound, reminding him of the seashore and the stony beaches of the south coast. He continued reflecting on his situation, his tail adding to the soothing sound by brushing to and fro in the pebbles.

It's all well and good enjoying these animal attributes at the moment but what will they be worth if I stay around and lose any self awareness? Would there be any value in it or would I be merely surviving? What would looking up at the sky mean? How would I be able to appreciate night vision or different foods, even the warmth of the blanket? How vital is the 'I' in all this to have a fulfilling existence?

Ed pondered pond side for a few more minutes before moving on through some loose bushes and into an open area of ground. Just then he began to notice an evocative smell, romantic, alluring and lust worthy. He stopped in his tracks, looked around and caught sight of a bush just twenty or so meters away shaking slightly, as if an animal was entangled in it. He immediately wandered over and could hear a small whimpering noise, attractively feline. His whiskers got more sensitive than ever, almost throbbing with intensity, willing him towards his objective.

As he got closer he could see a beautiful, white, furry moggie, about the same size as him. It stared out of the bush cautiously with its tempting vulnerable eyes, longing for help. He moved in closer still and realised it was caught on some thorns. He moved around to the side and gave the cat a firm push with his strong front paws. Out it popped, like a pea from a pod landing gently on the short grass to the side. It immediately jumped up, shook itself down, went over to Ed and began nuzzling him. The cat smelt wondrous, Chanel and Dior all in one. The fur was super fluffy and brilliant white with the black nose standing out prominently like a big button.

That answers that question. I definitely fancy cats, thought Ed, realising that it was indeed a female feline.

The two cats circled one another with curiosity and intrigue. Ed was mesmerised and enchanted. She smelt irresistible and held herself with such grace and pride. She gave off an odour that penetrated deep into his instincts, stirring up a primeval archetypal lust, full of instinctual longing.

"Well I'm guessing that you are not a Transient, you young feline goddess," breathed Ed as he sniffed and nuzzled in her fur as she gave him the once-over.

"Meooowww, meoowww," replied the cat.

That rules conversation out then. Well many a

relationship has worked on scant communication anyway so I don't see why this one can't. Besides, what would we be doing wasting time talking anyway, he reflected, losing his breath with desire but letting his thoughts run away with him.

I wonder if this constitutes unfaithfulness with Abella? After all, I am dead and a completely different species. It hardly bodes well for our future together. Oh well, onward and upward. I'm beginning to realise more than ever with this whole situation that I have to go with the flow. Jump in at the deep end and experience everything I can as an animal, thought Ed, as the female cat gave him a perfect view of her behind.

"What shall I call you, Miss?" queried Ed.

"I know, I'll call you Kinky because I'm sure it's kinky for me to be having my wicked way with a cat."

Kinky shook and ruffled her body, put her head down and gave a very clear signal to Ed regarding her objectives. She started grunting sweetly and moved backwards towards him provocatively.

I don't think I'm going to need an instruction manual here, thought Ed, as he looked down startled to see he had a slightly barbed member.

"Here we go," he exclaimed as he mounted her from behind, instinctually biting her gently but firmly on the back of her neck before taking a more predictable course of action. It was a passionate but brief process involving a lot of screaming and yelling, especially once the job was complete. Before he could consider what had just happened Kinky was off into the bushes and away on her own into the distance.

"I suppose a cuddle is out of the question then?" exclaimed Ed ironically as her white fluffy tail bounced out of sight. The whole process completely drained him and he headed back to the house, shaky legs and all.

"That was absolutely one of the best orgasms ever. Forget tantric foreplay, this was the real deal. Sex in the wild. I'm learning more and more every day."

Ed zapped back past the pond, up onto the fence, past the gardens, along the path and back through the plastic cat flap into Frank and Ali's. The kitchen felt warm after being outside as he popped himself into his basket and onto the soft blanket. Soon the morning had come but Ed just slept right through. Even the noises and murmurings of father and son preparing their breakfasts and heading out into the day did little to stir him and he slept on into the afternoon. The previous evening had been exhausting, the information about his death, wild sex with a white furry pussy and everything else that had gone on. He really was in a strange dreamland.

When he finally woke, he wandered from the kitchen, through the living room and up the wooden stairs, partly covered with a strip of maroon carpet with three or four inch gaps either side, revealing an old stained wood. It felt very unsettling being in someone else's house, getting a glimpse of their most private activities, lifestyles and habits.

I shouldn't be too nosey, thought the cat, as he cantered and danced up the stairs, around two ninety degree bends and up to the landing where the carpet changed to a clashing grey colour with small beige diamonds. It looked hideous, all the more so because of the threadbare texture around the most used parts. Frank was obviously not a millionaire.

The landing at the top was tiny with off-white painted wood chip wallpaper and three scruffy painted doors, two of which were closed. He soon steered a course towards the only open door and through into a small room. It was well lived-in and scantily furnished, square with one medium-sized bay window with half-closed green and gold curtains tentatively hanging on fewer curtain rings than they should. They cast an eerie light across the room, which combined with the grey wallpaper made it feel quite dismal and despairing. The double bed had one set of pillows which were ruffled and disturbed on one side only. The blankets and sheets lay discarded on the unused side, tossed over by an individual obviously in a hurry to get up and out.

He jumped up onto the bed, skipped over the crumpled cloth and over to the neater side. A small framed picture was all that adorned the bedside table, a thin gold coloured frame and a picture of a plain but pleasant looking young lady.

Above the photo in simple and plain handwritten text were the words;

RIP Sammy. We will love you as wife and mother forever. Frank and Ali.

Ed sat looking at the picture, at the sweet blue eyes, the straight brown hair, the slightly pug nose and less than perfect skin. Not a stunner, but there was something charming and kind about her, an innocence and purity. Not an ounce of nastiness in the face, an uncut diamond.

He sprang down off the bed, through onto the landing and down the stairs with the speed of a kingfisher.

It's too sad. Frank and Ali seem so sweet. It must be terrible for them, thought Ed, as he came to rest in the middle of the living room.

The lock on the front door rattled and clunked as if a fat-fingered fool was trying hopelessly to find the hole. Finally there was a satisfying, 'clunk' and the door creaked open on its tired hinges. The cluttering of coats being arranged on an overcrowded rack in the hallway ensued, and then Frank entered with another man, small, wiry and completely bald. Ed jumped into his basket and sat upright with his front paws hanging over the raised side.

"Fucking hell, man, three and a half thousand pounds for insurance. That's crazy. That's ten pounds a day, plus twenty pounds a day to the cab company, petrol, MOT and tyres. They're having a laugh. How can I even afford to do that job? I want to work but it is just not cost effective. I would lose money if anything, even working a six-day week."

"Yeah, but you can't be on benefits for ever, Joe. That's just soul destroying."

"I know, I don't want to but what can I do? It doesn't make sense. You would think that there would be an improvement in lifestyle for those that want to work, not a step down. Billy was telling me as well that he gets at least two traffic tickets a week; that's a hundred and forty quid on top right there. That would wipe out any potential profit in the first place."

The couple moved through into the kitchen, followed by Ed who took up residence in basket number two.

"Do you want a cuppa?"

"All right then, a quick one. I have to go in a minute."

Frank took the kettle, spun the hinged lid open with his thumb and ran it under the tap, filling it and then placing it on the protuberant power receptacle for boiling. It soon started to chunter away in a manner that could relax even the most stressed in need of tea.

"Well he should park in the proper places."

"It's not like that. How can you pick up a passenger who lives on a street with a yellow line restriction? They order the car for their house, not two hundred yards up the road. Those fucking black cabs get away with it. They have their union and powerful lobbyists. Mini cabs have nothing. It's ridiculous. Not even a fucking union. Why should I subject myself to that pain?"

"Why is the insurance so high?" queried Frank.

"She said I haven't got a no-claims history. I told her don't be stupid, I haven't had a car or insurance for three years and therefore I have no claims. That must count as no-claims, doesn't it?"

"Erm, it doesn't work like that," replied Frank as he poured the water into the teabag-laden cups. Soon he had squeezed all their juices out and added a minimal amount of milk into the cups before they headed into the living room and slumped into the sofa.

"How does it work then?"

"Listen, Joe, if you're not going to do it, then let's not waste time talking about it," replied Frank, bored by his friend's lack of intelligence.

"Yeah, fuck it. I'll keep signing on for a while and do something else anyway. It's just that I got the offer of that car for two hundred squids and thought it might be a good idea. I didn't realise what a fucking nightmare it'd be."

With this, the man greedily gulped down his tea and placed the completely empty cup on the carpet.

"Listen, Frank, sorry mate, but I have to go. Lizzy will fucking kill me if I'm late," said Joe as he rose and headed towards the door.

"See ya," said Frank, remaining seated.

"Yeah, see ya," replied Joe as he pulled the front door open just as Ali arrived with outstretched key.

"Oh, hi, Ali. I'm off. Nice to see ya."

"Yeah, nice to see you, Uncle Joe," replied Ali as they passed each other and switched places, the door slamming shut between them more from carelessness than ignorance.

"Hi, Dad."

"Hi, Ali; the kettle's boiled. I'll have another cup," exclaimed Frank as he polished off his last mouthful of liquid, just as there was a knock at the door.

"That'll be Carter. Let him in, Dad, he's going to mend the computer," exclaimed Ali.

"Chrissake. Okay then," replied his father begrudgingly before getting up and going to the front door to let in his friend.

"All right, mate. Come in. He's in the kitchen," said Frank as he let in the young track-suited hoodie.

Soon all three were tea in hand and Carter was at the computer clicking and scrolling.

"No problems here, mate. It's running fine. Good to see you've put an anti virus on here last night. That will have solved a lot of it," exclaimed the youngster.

"Antivirus? I didn't put anything on there. I wouldn't know how," replied Ali, slightly confused.

"According to the history log on the computer you installed the software last evening at around 21.19, then you updated the virus definitions and deleted or quarantined 1246 viruses. Quite a handy bit of work. It was exactly what I was about to do. Why are you wasting my time getting me here to do it, for Chrissake?"

Carter was more than a bit pissed off as he spun round in the second-hand office chair.

"I didn't. We were at the football then last night, weren't we, Dad?" exclaimed Ali looking round at his dad.

"Yeah, we were, Carter. We went to the match. Maybe that damn machine is broken more than we first thought, bloody thing," grunted Frank before getting back into his committed tea swigging.

"Well that's what it says here and it does not lie. The

system clock and date are correct. It definitely happened last night."

"Maybe the anti virus is itself a virus. We left the computer on last night like you asked."

"Antivirus? More like bloody antichrist if you ask me," blurted his father.

"Whatever, dad! It's important to me and I do lots on it so it needs to be right," exclaimed Ali, getting only a grunt from his father in response.

"Well unless the cat suddenly started becoming computer literate then there's no other explanation," uttered Carter as he closed the application and went back to the desktop screen.

"Oh look, speaking of which, here's a note from your cat."

Carter had seen the word document Ed had typed the night before and saved to the desktop. He clicked on it and started reading it out as best he could with the typos, much to Ali's amazement.

'I amm aCat. My nsme is Ed, not friking Smunky. Whst is a Smmnky anyway? I am niot daftt or stuupid sndwould like to sit omn th sofa 3very now aand theen. I like th foopd you give me but I wa,mt more pleawse. Abnother thimg, you hsve comput3r problems b3cause you don''tt hsve a proper anti virus instslled. If I hav3 time tomight, I will do thst for you. Llove. Ed'

Carter got more and more annoyed. "Right, this is a piss take. I can see that this document was created last night. I guess you've filmed making a fool of me for Facebook. Wanker! I'm off, and don't ask for help again."

Carter jumped up, leaving the cheap swivel chair spinning, and departed with haste through the room, down the corridor and out the front door, slamming it behind him. Ali was stunned and sat speechless whilst his dad looked on nonplussed.

"I don't know what's got into him, Dad. Why would he freak out like that? We told him we weren't here last night. Did you muck about on the computer and mess anything up?"

"What do you think? I don't even know how to use it. How would I start doing things on it all of a sudden? More to the point; why? I think it's up the Swanee and you need to get a new one. Let's see how work is over the next few months and see if I have any extra money. I'm not promising anything mind," said Frank, trying to comfort Ali amidst the strange goings on.

"But if you didn't do it and I didn't do it, how could the document have the cat's name in it? I'm very confused."

"I didn't touch the bloody thing, Ali, button it for Christ's sake," replied Frank assertively raising his voice.

Ali shut down the word document and computer, closing its upper surface into alignment with the lower and pulling out the plug at the wall.

"Whatever. I've had enough of that for one day anyway. Bloody thing," exclaimed Ali disgruntled, before turning tail, leaving the room and heading upstairs, leaving his father ensconced in the sofa, remote in hand and ready for some light TV entertainment. The last thing Ed wanted was to listen to some hideous soap or comedy show and so he zipped into the kitchen and his secondary basket.

He slumped into recline and began reflecting disappointedly regarding the events of the evening and how his interference had turned out. It was not how he imagined it would be. He just wanted it to be a bit of fun. He also started to feel a little guilty about having to disappear from the duo's life and give them another loss to deal with. It was a new twist of emotions that he had not foreseen.

I need to move on soon. I'm no clearer as to why I'm embroiled in this cycle of events and I really need to dig deeper, thought Ed, slightly regretful to move on but mindful he couldn't get caught up in any relationship commitments at this point. He settled down in his basket, still tired even after a sleepy day. He decided to devise a plan in the morning and move on towards the next transience. Maybe he could be 'paused' again, and this time try and visit the mythical Viking warrior?

The morning came round in a flash and the kitchen rustlings of the duo woke Ed from his slumber, coming round just as Frank topped up his bowl of food and saucer of milk. He jumped up from his basket and went through to the living room to find Ali on the sofa staring without interest at the twenty-four hour news channel, volume muted. In the bottom right hand corner of the screen a small superimposed man danced and juggled sign language with his hands and arms, turning round to stare back up at the broadcaster whenever there was a pause, as if they were actually behind them.

Ed jumped up onto the sofa and onto Ali's lap and sat bolt upright facing him.

"What's gotten into you, Smunky?" uttered the boy as Ed changed positions and settled down into a curled up ball.

"You don't know it yet, but this is our goodbye. I'd like to stay with you and honestly feel terrible about leaving, but I have to continue on my journey. I hope you understand."

"Meeaaooww, Meeaaooww, Meeaaooww! I wish I spoke cat language, little fella. You are a cute little thing," replied Ali, stretching out his right hand to ruffle the cat behind the back of the head and stroke him down his body.

"I'm sorry, mate, I feel really bad," meowed Ed before settling into a low rumbling purr, revelling in the stroking for a few minutes.

Soon the silence was broken.

"Dad, I've got to go. I have to pick up a spare battery for my phone from Bobby's."

With this Ed wrapped both hands underneath Ed and scooped him down onto the floor.

"See ya later, Smunky," he said, as the cat ambled miserably into the kitchen towards his basket. Soon father and son had gone through their whole morning ceremony and had left the house, leaving Ed alone, lonely and tearful. It was as heartbreaking as seeing Sam disappear into the night just a few days back. The last thing he wanted was a repeating list of lonely farewells. He munched away at his breakfast and slurped up his milk before zipping through the cat flap, along the garden and off into the grey damp day.

He proceeded along the tall fence, past the pond and off through the shrubs and bushes, further than he had been before. His sense of direction felt amazing and he was continually aware of where he was relative to Frank and Ali's house. It was though he had his own internal GPS system, making it easy for him to move further and further away from his temporary home. He really didn't want to have them finding his dead body anywhere near and so decided to walk for the day as far away as he could get. Then he would take a decision on what to do next. Time was still on his side, although he could feel some of his human awareness and memories gradually slipping away.

He padded from street to street past the council houses, post boxes and bus stops. He noticed the myriad of strange street names as he proceeded: Winklebury Way, Ludlow Close, Bury Road, Brunel Street, South Ham Way and St Peter's Close. No rhyme or reason, just strange and disassociated names. He pondered on the American style of naming roads on a number system, north to south and east to west. It gained points in logic but lost them in emotion. It was too machine-like. He preferred the random scatterbrain approach of the British.

He wandered up through the cemetery, stopping to look at the gravestones and their inscriptions, wondering if he would ever meet any of these people on his travels. He wondered if he had a gravestone, what it was like and where he was buried. Had a lot of people attended his funeral and was there an abundance of flowers and greetings? Most importantly, was he missed? He passed from the cemetery into a fenced allotment area, ambling over towards a small plot of land being attended by a hunch-backed elderly woman, grey straight hair, bony features and plain supermarket clothes. He watched her from a distance as she dug at the soft earth, putting in small wooden posts and arranging the greenery with delicate care amidst the grey, dreary and depressing day.

He moved on silently and hopped over the small hedgerow out from the allotment. All the excitement about the spring of his back legs had drained from him as he continued to feel guilty about leaving Ali. He jumped onto a small wall and then further up onto a ramshackle wooden shed. He sat on the top of the pointed roof with his paws and head hanging over the centre divider looking back across the allotment and the busy bee of a green fingered lady.

He felt like he was at an airport waiting for a flight to a far and distant land. Exciting and enthralling when you get off at the other end but boring and uneventful sitting in a departure lounge trying to dissolve time considering pointless duty free purchases. He gazed at the woman going about her activities with methodical determination. He looked back over towards the cemetery and the row upon row of glorified head stones telling of noble deeds and loved personalities. He began to wonder what he was, amidst all this. What was his role and purpose? Why was he being given the chance to look at the world in this unique yet disorientating way?

Slowly he could feel his human consciousness drifting away from him bit by bit, making it harder to focus his thoughts and be sure of his memories. He didn't know exactly how long he had left, but he was determined to do the needful by the end of the day.

I must stay awake and keep focused, he thought, as he twisted round and sat upright on the roof.

What is this consciousness anyway? Maybe understanding that, is the key? 'I think therefore I am'. Who said that? As soon as I'm not aware of that awareness, would I stop existing? Is doubting my existence proof I exist? What if this is really a dream and all this is existence in a dream state? What if I am in a coma and dreaming, would I exist then? Would I stop existing if I ceased being aware of myself in the body of this cat; surely the cat would still exist?

Ed meandered through a matrix of unclear philosophical debate, wishing that questions carried as much influence as answers. He watched the little old lady as she wound up her gardening duties and left with her little bag of gloves and tools, only to be replaced by another OAP working a different plot with equal diligence. He mused and mused, tossing and turning between his upright seated position and the reclined regal position which gave him neck ache. Soon his thoughts turned to suicide and transition, setting him on his way down from the roof. The sun was getting low in the sky and the late afternoon was being lured into the embrace of evening. He danced off alongside the allotment, through the cemetery and back towards the small area of shops in the centre of the village. He thought long and hard about how he could kill himself this time around.

Once at the shops he wandered over to the small *provisimart* supermarket and slipped stealthily through the open door. He darted around behind the tills and into the main body of the shop. It was a quiet store and there were just a handful of customers and only one open checkout. He peered up at the packed shelves, row upon row, pile upon pile of various coloured cans delicately organised neatly along the thin walkways. He went to the corner, snuck a peek and darted round and along the aisle to the next corner, giving himself a better view of the signs hanging above the corridors.

Bakery, Dairy, Tinned, Vegtables, Meat / Poultry, Frozen, Fish and Household goods. All the choices one would expect.

Ed was looking for the freezer department. He had a bright idea of a chilly but pain-free suicide if he could work out how to get into one of the super chilled compartments. Then he saw the sign; FROZEN FOOD 15. He tiptoed along invisibly, keeping his arched back held high whilst his path hugged the sides of the shelves.

He proceeded along past fresh meat and dairy and finally got to aisle 15 without bumping into a single soul. He skipped up onto the flat topped transparent lids and sped along, hiding behind a large sign that read; *Jumbo Arctic rolls, 2 for 1 special offer.* Now it was just a matter of waiting his moment and taking his chance.

He was there for what seemed like an eternity. The shop seemed deserted and very few people came past. He began to get despondent and not overly confident that anyone would shop in one of these freezers. He glanced up at the glowing clock and saw it flashing 5.54. He had seen the sign outside on the door and knew that the store closed at 6.00 so he didn't have a whole lot of time to play with. He began musing as to possible ways he could prize the freezers open once the store was closed but knew how hard that would be in reality. Even for a human, those doors had a very strong seal. He wasn't overly optimistic.

The clock continued on its inevitable path, 5.55, 5.56, 5.57. He felt increasingly confused as to how long he had before his deadline. His human consciousness was continuing to dissolve and he was getting worried about being locked in the store, unable to kill himself. The anxiety grew as the clock chimed ever closer to the decisive hour. Then, out of the blue, a small elderly lady, complete with Zimmer frame and pink rinse turned the corner and caught sight of the sign Ed was hiding behind. She got closer and looked enquiringly at it. Ed was sure he had been spotted, as he did not fit behind it entirely, the tail poking out and along the back surface of the freezer.

Eyesight fading, she turned away momentarily before giving a rip roaring sigh and returning to the freezer.

"Ah, that's one offer I can't refuse," she exclaimed delightedly, as she opened a compartment just along from where Ed hid. She reached in and grabbed one Arctic roll, followed by another which landed in the small basket attached to her wheeled silver Zimmer frame. Her hand clasped the lid of the freezer in the open position, as from behind her a voice bellowed ignorantly,

"We're closing the store; sorry, you'll have to go to checkout now."

She turned to confront the young man, long black hair, small black bobble hat and a blue shop assistant's coat.

"It's not 6.00 yet. Look, I have one more minute," she replied assertively looking past him at the clock as she flicked the lid closed behind her. Ed took his chance and in the nick of time skidded across the transparent glass surface and slid into the freezer just before the door came crashing shut.

"Whatever. We're closing. Anyway, look, it has just gone 6.00," replied the young man petulantly as they both went their separate ways.

Ed slid along to the end of the cabinet, over the Arctic rolls and Haagen-Dazs vanilla and settled on the cheese cakes and frozen profiteroles. The bitter chill stung away at his soft paws like millions of tiny darts fired from a huge pistol, penetrating through his fur like he was being shot blasted. His breath virtually froze into little steamy clouds as it was expelled into the chamber. He settled down and stretched out as if he was lying on a bed of nails. He rested his head on his front paws whilst the chill crept into his brain, making it ache like a fireball of agony behind his eyes. He thought of Ali and Frank and his transitions, the tortoise, Sam and everything that had been going on in his busy schedule over the last few days.

He soon started to drift in and out of consciousness, the thoughts and reflections becoming more and more abstract and unrelated. Then suddenly, a tornado of a wind, the coldness disappeared in an instant and his journey into a supersonic kaleidoscope tunnel began, like a bullet being fired into a never-ending gun barrel. Gravity ceased to exist. One second he was up, the next down, forwards and then backwards, sideways to the left and then over to the right, all at such a speed that the transitions were hardly noticeable. Then he saw the light, the laser pinprick beam at the end of the tunnel that pulled him with unstoppable power. The noise and wind was deafening as he sped onwards, the light getting bigger and bigger. Then just like before, total darkness and absolute silence. If a pin dropped, it would just fall silently for ever. He had made the shift from deceased to Transient.

Chapter 10
The red leather saddle

Ed awoke to a loud squelching, slapping sound, staccato, like a powerful wet flipper on a marble floor. He was drowsily unaware of his surroundings but vaguely heard a stern voice yelling at him, piercing his dulled senses.

"There'll be plenty of that for you after, boys; this is just to give you the taste."

He felt disoriented and unsettled, like he'd been spun into a whole new dimension, blinded by a light and an intensity of sound and smell that overwhelmed him. He raised his eyelids languidly, like the heavy sails on an old clipper ship. Fierce rays scorched through, tazering his brain, reminding him of how he set fire to newspapers with a magnifying glass as a child. Soon, shapes and colours began to assemble into a vaguely comprehensible panorama, gradually focussing and sharpening his perception and confirming once more that he had not awoken in his bed at home with Abella. He also began to realise he hadn't arrived back in the labyrinth of tunnels and reluctantly began to prepare himself for the next unknown and strange adventure in the animal world.

The pain of the glare soon abated and in front of him he could see a small piece of uncooked steak splayed out on the stone floor, stains of blood splattered around its edges as if thrown from a height. His nostrils sniffed at the offering with a sensitivity he'd never experienced. It was as though he could taste every detailed aspect of it.

Just at that moment he saw two enormous feet in shiny black leather boots come towards his face. He was lying flat on the stone and started to wonder exactly what sort of animal he had become. He quickly stood upright before instinctually leaning over and tearing into the piece of steak, instantly devouring it. He had never felt so painfully hungry, as if he'd been starved or something.

"It's just you two this time," yelped the man as he bent down to Ed and started rubbing a fox brush in his face.

It's fox fur; it smells just like Sam but it can't be?

The man continued to rub the brown fur in his face, causing him to splutter on little bits that came loose. Ed then watched on as the individual wandered over to his left and over to a large, vicious and muscular hunting hound. Light and dark brown patches covered the body apart from a glorious white front and underbelly. The facial expressions went from intensely forlorn with a closed mouth to absolutely terrifying with it open. Ed was shocked with the realisation that he too must be a hunting hound and that they were no doubt being readied for a hunt.

He could feel a tight collar restraint around his neck and soon began to bark violently in tune with the other hound. He glanced down at his powerful front legs and paws, pulling forwards at the restraint so much that the front part of his body lifted off the ground upwards, straining against the leash which pulled his head backwards and up leaving him half upright on his rear legs. Meanwhile the man with the boots moved over towards a fine horse, dark brown all over with a strange white patch underneath a pristine red leather saddle. Steam oozed from the animal as the metallic hooves on his jet black legs scraped at the stone floor, its tail dancing from side to side excitedly as the individual scrambled up and into the saddle.

He looked ridiculous on the animal, his effeminate red jacket, white stockings and dainty looking black soup bowl hat clashing with the beauty and elegance of the beast.

Ed glanced to his left and watched as the other hound was let free by a young boy in tweeds. He raced off like a firework, shooting from the restraint as soon as it was released, catching the boy's hand slightly in the process.

"I've told you a dozen times how to do that, you stupid fool. You only have two dogs to release today and you even get that wrong," shouted the man angrily from the horse, his face red with overreaction.

"Sorry, Pop," replied the boy timidly as he reached around and released Ed into an equally jet propelled departure, hastily followed by the mounted clown.

I thought I had a strong sense of smell when I was a cat

but this is incredible, thought Ed, realising the sense was so strong he could actually see a red mist trail of the hound that raced in front. Soon a faint yellow trail accompanied it in the distance, gradually getting stronger and stronger, luring both dogs in that direction. Ed was well aware that the powerful muscular legs that propelled him with such haste were the strongest he had experienced so far, even stronger than the spring coiled power of the cat's hind legs. His feet tore at the ground, tossing up small clumps of dirt and grass as he sped violently across the countryside, steam coming off his body like a boiling kettle covered in a tea towel.

Behind him he could hear the loud, but pathetic horn of the huntsman. Ahead he could see the distinct red trail of the other hound and ahead of that, the less fervent yellow trail of what he assumed was a fox. He tried to power himself forward with determination, faster and faster and catch up with the other dog. It felt sensational to be so strong and move at such speed so close to the ground. He was urgently aware that he had no desire to kill a fox though. He liked foxes, their big brushes, soft brown fur and fine chiselled looks. They represented elegance to him and as he got closer to the second hound he couldn't help but attribute only negative features to it.

I feel like I've got Stalin as a mate and we're out hunting together. It's very strange and I wish I'd at least had a few hours to adjust. It's a very confusing instant transition," thought Ed, as the other hound tired slightly, pulling back the pace a tad. With the slight relaxation he began to take more note of the countryside around. It was very English, with flowing open fields dotted with trees and hedgerows. One thing that struck him more than anything was how everything had a coloured aura equating to its smell. Ed could see this around trees, bushes, mounds of earth and virtually everything. It was like having a clever smart phone app for smells, one that could be held up for a snapshot of the environment to reveal street names, famous buildings and directions. The only difference was that his displayed smells and trails of odour. It was overpowering and incredibly rich, like being in the barrel room of a fine vineyard.

Soon he had caught up with the other hound and was side by side. They galloped, raced, jumped and sped through the countryside following the scent of the fox. The strong yellow trail indicated they were catching up with the animal fast.

Ed was not happy with the fox hunting scenario at all. His bond with Sam sat heavily on his conscience. He recalled how his friend had eaten pate in preference to killing a chicken, advocating abstinence from slaughter whenever possible. It made the current predicament seem even more immoral. How could he overcome these new instincts and if so, how could he find a way to get the other hound off the scent to avoid killing the fox?

Behind him, the mounted hunter followed, eagerly blowing on his inadequate toy trumpet. The dogs ploughed on relentlessly in pursuit of the terrified victim who most certainly would have been in a state of intense panic.

Quickly, Ed shot off to the right, away from the prominent trail, hoping to lure them in the wrong direction and give the fox a little more time to escape. However, they had none of it. After pausing for thought and looking at Ed's alternative route, the other dog simply turned tail and carried on in the right direction. The scent was so strong that it would be virtually impossible to deceive in this way so he changed his tack and veered back onto the original path, catching up with the second hound and rapidly running through possible scenarios.

I can't let this happen. I've got to do something, thought the dog, sweating profusely and running out of energy to keep up. *Even if I do stop it, they'll just do it again anyway. I have to make a statement as well, a big statement.*

They got to the top of a small grassy crest and looked down to see the exhausted fox taking refuge in a bush, the brush poking out of one end and the whiffling snout from the other. He was defeated, helpless and panting furiously. Both hounds slowed down from their full speed run into a gentle jog. Behind them the hunter and his horse slowed to a canter as they knew the game was up. He puffed on his trumpet for all he was worth, trying to prove to the world that against all the odds, he could still get a hard on.

Ed immediately accelerated from his jog into a full pace advance towards the fox.

"That's my boy, you are eager today," exclaimed the man from the horse as the fox cowered trembling in the bush.

Just at the last minute and just a few feet from the bush he turned and faced the oncoming assailants, growling angrily. They mistook this for eagerness and a desire to finish the job as a team, not knowing that the hound had switched sides.

"We're coming, we're coming," shouted the man as they both got closer. Ed got louder and louder, barking ferociously for all he was worth.

The second hound accelerated as he closed in and was about to run past Ed to devour the fox. Ed however had other ideas and leapt out with his growling salivating mouth opened to its widest. He grabbed the hound around the neck, pushing him over sideways, tearing through fur and skin deep into tissue. Blood spurted from the dog as it fought with panic to regain its balance and fight back.

"What the hell are you doing?" yelled the man as he saw the exhausted fox run from the bush safely into the distance.

Ed bit deeper, tearing into the violent animal knowing that this was one fox hound that would not be repeating his ugly deeds.

"That's my best hound, you stupid mutt," exclaimed the hunter as he reached for his shotgun from the neat holster attached to the red leather saddle. He undid the popper stud and started to withdraw the weapon just as Ed withdrew his teeth from the limp and now lifeless hound. The man jumped down from the horse and came towards Ed, lifting the shotgun in his direction and pulling off a round. Ed ducked down and ran around to his right through the small clumps of grass before he could re-aim the gun. Then Ed pounced across and was upon the hunter in a flash, leaping up and onto the forearm, forcing him to drop the shot gun on the ground. He tore into his arm right down through the flesh and could feel his teeth grinding on the bone.

This is what the fox would have felt whilst you watched, laughed and blew your fucking trumpet, mother fucker," thought Ed, as he began to gouge a deep hole into the guy's arm, causing a waterfall of blood to squirt out in every direction. Nervously, the man fumbled with a holster of his other hip trying to free his pistol whilst the teeth dug deeper into the bone. Soon there was a loud bang and Ed felt a massive thud throughout his whole head. He saw the end of the steaming pistol and realised he'd been shot at point blank range by the thuggish pig. Smoothly he fell back in slow motion downwards, thudding into the ground dramatically. It was as if when he landed he went right through it and into the soil, like a diver into water. He was transported through a myriad of rainbow colours shining at him from every side, spectrums of light, kaleidoscopes, mirrored halls and bands of multi coloured effects.

Slow down, stay aware, I need to get paused this time. Focus, think of pausing, slow your thoughts down, remain aware. Thought Ed.

He desperately tried to cling to some sort of strand of consciousness, anything. He knew if he blacked out, he would lessen his chances of getting paused and meeting the Viking. He had plans and was anxious to try and make them a reality.

"Stay awake, stay awake," he gasped, as he could see the bright light ahead of him once more.

"I am Ed Trew, I am Ed Trew and I am staying conscious. I am slowing down, stopping. I am not going to the next transience. I am Ed Trew, Ed Treeew…"

Ed soon phased out of consciousness into the now familiar blank and empty darkness.

Chapter 11
The Koan Dome

A dream state began to take hold with a myriad of textured colours and a distant harmonic drone like a thousand people running moist fingers around different sized wine glasses. Ed started to come around, gradually becoming aware of a jabbing pain in his side. Barely conscious, he began to realise he was being prodded with some sort of stick. He noticed an extreme gushing wind noise, a deafening and continuous powerful flow causing a breeze to leak up his trouser legs and across his body. He felt another jab in his side and looked round to realise he was being poked with the butt end of some sort of rifle.

Maybe I'm still alive as a bloody hound, thought Ed, as he was jolted again, falling down around a short curved incline to the bottom of what felt like a tunnel. The wind pushed him more fervently and soon he felt bits of cloth pulling at every part of his body. It jerked his limbs into contorted and pained extremities with his right leg bent up to his stomach and his knee at a right angle. His head was twisted around slightly to the left and he could see his arm and hand caught up in a weird texture of homemade netting.

Thank goodness I'm not that hound still, he mused, as he began to realise he was once again in the tunnels.

What was that rifle butt though? And what am I doing caught up in this makeshift net?

Ed could hear someone calling out to him.

"Эй, не волнуйтесь. Я выступаю в другом. Я буду у вас, то и безопасными в нет времени. Я Donald, выпущен ваше имя?"

"Er???"

"Dag, bare rolig. Jeg er ven. Jeg vil have dem der og sikker i nogen tid. Jeg er donald, whats dit navn?"

"Erm," uttered Ed as he felt a sharp jerk on the netting which closed violently in all around him, wrapping him up in a little ball like a captured orang-utan.

"Dag, bare rolig. Jeg er ven. Jeg vil have dem der og sikker i nogen tid. Jeg er donald, whats dit navn?"

"Hé, ne vous inquiétez pas. Je suis un ami. Je vous aurai de là dans aucun temps. Je suis Donald, quel est votre nom?"

"Arrghh!!" yelped Ed as he was yanked and tugged upwards.

"Nem, ne aggódj. Én vagyok barátja. Nekem te meg az ott és biztonságos rögtön. Én vagyok, Donald módosított név?"

"What the fuck!"

"Hey, don't worry, I'm a friend. I'll have you out of there and safe in no time. I'm Donald. What's your name?"

"Thank Christ for that, you speak English. Don't I look a bit English? Couldn't you have tried that first?" yelped Ed as he was humped up the side of the curved tunnel and over a flat ledge. The wind noise immediately lessened to a hush and from where he had landed he could see back through into a side passageway. He was relieved to realise that he had landed back in the tunnel complex but at the same time, felt completely disoriented and confused by the transition that jolted his mind to its very core.

He heard a loud 'clunk' beside him and glanced round to see an old Enfield rifle settling on the dusty ground. The makeshift net was loosened and he started to free himself from the uncomfortable restraint. It fell around him on the floor as he scrambled unsteadily to his feet like a newly born deer.

"Oh, it's a relief to be paused again," breathed Ed as he turned round to be greeted by a British soldier from WW1.

"Who are you? Where are we? Is this Silicon Alley or Ancestors' Cove by any chance? Have you seen Thomas?" asked Ed as he dusted himself down, happy to be reunited with his familiar jeans, jacket and wrist watch.

"This is not Silicon Alley or Ancestors' Cove I'm afraid. The names ring a bell though. Maybe someone else has mentioned them at some point," replied the private.

"Really? Can you remember who?" enquired the life hopper as he reached out his right hand towards the young man, revealing the big shiny-faced watch that adorned his wrist.

"I can't remember. No one here called Thomas that I know of either," replied the individual as he reached out and gently shook Ed's hand before gathering up the strange net and tossing it to the side of the tunnel. Ed glanced over to see it land, and noticed a densely rich tapestry of leafless vines all over the tunnel walls. They stretched as far as the eye could see, illuminated from behind with the familiar recessed jets of light that he remembered from before.

"I don't remember any vines," commented Ed.

"This is the Koan Dome community, not Silicon Alley or Ancestors' Cove. We're one of the last ones before the white light sucks in the Transients. If I hadn't pulled you out then you'd have just got stuck at the end on the floor. Luckily I knocked you off that ledge with the butt end of my rifle and then caught you in the net and dragged you up. Christ, it took me over an hour to get you off that bloody ledge."

"Thanks. I appreciate it."

"Not a problem. We try and help out as much as possible when there are stragglers in the tunnel. Come, come and have a look. You can see the white light from here," replied the soldier, beckoning Ed over towards the entrance to peer back down the tunnel. There it was, the brilliant white light, perfectly still and sharply delineated, no shimmer or movement. With unstoppable omnipotence and power, it sucked everything in the tunnel towards it. The noise was horrendous and forced the duo back from the opening quickly.

"I don't really dig the noise too much, it reminds me of the war," stated Donald.

Ed looked at the young man, observing his head to toe khaki uniform, coarsely made hobnail boots, tight spats, unattractive canvas-looking matching trousers and ill-fitting green jacket. Over his right shoulder hanging down was a small cloth-covered water bottle attached by light green webbing straps whilst on the other side some sort of canvas pouch hung down over his fading grey cloth waist belt. The traditional domed metal helmet hung behind him and span around knocking him in the side of the head as he bent down to pick up his rifle. His young, innocent face and short wispy blond hair didn't fit at all with the harsh character of the uniform.

"Were you really in the First World War? You look so young; how could you ever have gone to war?" asked Ed, perplexed at the thought.

"I've heard some people down here call it the First World War, others the Great War. I can tell you, it was never known as the First World War to any of us at the time and it was certainly never fucking 'great'. If you want to know anything about hell then I know all the fucking answers, and I was only nineteen when I died."

Ed was momentarily lost for words. He walked over to the net, bent down and picked it up. It was tatty to say the least and appeared to be made out of old bits of cloth, probably clothes from Transients who had been and gone. He thought back to Thomas and his last departure from the tunnels and remembered how they were going to make nets to rescue stragglers in the tunnels. He lifted it to his nose, sniffed at the disgusting muskiness and then threw it back down where it had come from. He turned round and walked over to Donald.

"What now?" he asked.

"Let's get inside - we've a long walk ahead of us."

"A long walk? The last group lived near the entrance?"

"Not us. We have a six hour journey from here. It's a total killer in these fucking boots, let me tell you that. What sort of a crappy idea is that, train an army to march for miles and then give them crappy boots that produce agonising blisters after two hundred yards? It's better now after getting used to them for ninety years, but still not nice."

The duo started to proceed into the vine covered tunnel. It stretched into the distance as far as the eye could see. Behind the complexity of thick bare vines, there was a generous spattering of lights casting eerie shadows onto the deep red, dusty floor. He looked down at his round faced wrist watch and twisted the dials so the date was 01/01 with both hands pointing up at '12'. This would give him a good idea of how much time he had to play with later on. The sand was softer than before and was scuffed and disturbed with the footsteps, just like he imagined it should be naturally. He looked over at the vines enquiringly.

"Don't you have any Tumpleberries here?" he enquired.

"Timple what?"

"The last place had little flowers on the vines, although they only had one vine."

"No. We don't have any flowers on these vines, not to my knowledge anyway," replied the young soldier as they continued walking for a while. The temperature was cool in the tunnels with very little breeze to disturb the silence around them. It reminded Ed of the first few hours after a late night snowfall in the city. There would be a quiet and peacefulness that could rarely be found in such a place. The sand soaked up virtually all the sound of their footsteps whilst the vines further deadened the acoustic. Ed also noticed how dulled his sense of smell and spatial awareness were in comparison to his outings as a cat and dog. It all seemed very flat, even unexciting.

Soon his thoughts had turned to his objectives and what he was hoping to achieve on this second visit to the mysterious 'other world.'

"Have you heard of the Viking?" enquired Ed.

"A few murmurings. I'm not interested really. Do you want to meet him? I can set you up when we get back if you like? There are people that speak of him. I personally think it's a bit of a myth," replied Donald as they continued on their way.

"That's great. Please do introduce me to anyone who might know anything about him."

"For sure." replied Donald before they walked on for a few minutes in silence.

Ed glanced over again at the soldier's uniform, the coarse and itchy looking material, thick leather belts and various devices and pouches for carrying things. His beautiful short cropped blond hair, smartly combed, glistened in the darts of light that shot out from behind the vines and across the tunnels. His fine young choir boy features were astoundingly youthful. Ed found it hard to imagine this youngster fighting on a brutal battlefield.

"Anyway, what regiment were you in?" enquired Ed, curiosity getting the better of him.

"Berkshires, Royal Berkshires. More like Berks if you ask me, sent off to die like letters being dumped out of a postman's sack."

"You were in the Berkshires? My grandfather was in that regiment. That's quite some coincidence. Were you at the battle of Passchendaele?"

"I was in so many ass end battles. They didn't have names for us though. Just another fucking nasty situation to endure. Over the top, advance, kill, die or return back to do it all again. It all became a blur. All that 'bang' 'bang' 'bang' 'bang' 'bang' 'bang' 'bang' fucking 'bang'. My mind was blotting the whole thing out. I remember that name though, Passchendaele. I am sure I was in that area at some point. There weren't exactly lots of road signs, just burnt tree stubs, stripped of life and hope, stranded there erect in a quagmire of mud, blood, bones, metal shards, rats and a stench that soaked right through your clothes, even penetrating the thick leather of your boots into your socks and all over your mouldering, blistered feet."

"I've read about it. It really does sound like hell. My grandfather was there. He talked about it before he died. He fought in the battle of the Somme in 1916 and then at Passchendaele the following year - you might have known him," enquired Ed excitedly.

"I didn't really know anyone there. It suited you better to not know anyone. I watched people and noticed them but I never got to know them. The pain would be too much because they would always be taken away, usually right in front of your eyes and in the most barbaric way possible. Having a friend was your own worst enemy, it drove people mad. It wasn't for me. When I was first at the front, I was palled up with a kid who I went through training with. Eddie Stoner. On the first day we were ducking and diving with panic every time there was a bang, pop or squeak. Everyone was laughing at us. It was horrible. Strange to think that it was normal to ignore bombs dropping yards away . That was the crazy situation we were in. For fuck's sake, I went from being a kid terrified of the dark with a night light in my room, to an adult who was expected to stand up to machine guns and shrapnel with no fear. Totally mad stuff! Anyway, Eddie was there one morning, sitting down. It was all quiet and so he got up to pass me his ration tin and some bits of bully beef he didn't want. When he got halfway towards me there was a metallic ping noise and he stopped in his tracks. His eyes were focused on me, that little food tin in his hand. He just stared and stood motionless as if time stood still. Then I saw a little bit of blood drip out from under the rim of his helmet, first a trickle and then a steady flow, down over his eye brows, into his eyes, over his nose and mouth and down onto his chin and over his jacket. His eyes were focused hard on me as if he was trying to say his last will and testament right there. He collapsed, the ration tin fell onto the muddy wooden slats of the trench face up and he crumbled into a bent heap still partially upright against the trench wall. He was dead in a second. I leapt up and grabbed him and hugged him and hugged him. We both fell on the floor and I sobbed and sobbed. I had no idea how to deal with the situation. It was completely devastating. I was hollowed out right then and there. It felt like my innards and stomach had been scooped out onto a small shovel and tossed to the floor to be trodden into the mud. From that day on I would never have another friend, ever. It was too much."

"Man, that's terrible. Was it a sniper?" enquired Ed.

"No. What the Germans did for a while was drop heavy pointed bolts from planes over our lines. Basically there was no warning and if you were hit by one that was generally that. Normally people were not killed straight away. It might enter through your shoulder and exit from your stomach or whatever, causing an agonising death over days or weeks with infection. Eddie was lucky, it went through his helmet, down through his neck, right through his body. Unbelievable! I became a man that day. How I wish I never had. No more innocence or hope. Everything from then onwards was survival. Nothing more and nothing less," said Donald, his words tearing into the description of events like metal tore into innocent flesh and bone.

"Christ, I don't think I would even survive that," commented Ed, reflecting with surprise at how quickly he had adapted from being a violent killer hound to chatting with a nineteen year old WW1 veteran. By now they had proceeded out of sight of the original entrance and some way into the tunnel system.

"Mate, that was just the beginning. That was nothing. Believe me. With all that blood and guts I'm sure war did a lot more for vegetarianism than any vegan activist. There was something utterly terrifying about every moment and always a new grizzly bloodied sight to greet you around every corner. My first job was laying barbed wire fences in no-mans land in the depth of night. It was something else, crawling into a pitch black hornet's nest of potentially vicious machine gun fire. Three or four of us would slither out into the night, down into pot holes and craters, over decaying dead bodies, through mud and slime being as silent as possible. Then we would twist those metal cork screw posts into the ground and begin joining them all up with our bundles of barbed wire. It was crap in comparison to the Germans. Their barbed wire was so much thicker and nastier. I should know, I got caught on it a couple of times. If you were lucky you would get back to your trenches without being spotted by the enemy but if not, a long night of ducking into bomb holes to avoid the machine guns was on the cards. They used to call us the rabbits; always running helplessly from a gun. Anyway, I don't want to bore you with all this"

"No, please continue. It's fascinating," replied Ed as the couple got to an intersection in the maze. Both options looked identical but Donald knew exactly which way to go. He ushered Ed down one of the tunnels and was about to continue when someone came from the other direction. As he came closer, Ed could see it was a Roman centurion.

"Hi, Don," uttered the Roman as the three met in the tunnel.

"Hi, Frank. This is Ed."

"Hi, Ed, it's good to meet someone from more recent times."

"Well it's nice to meet a Roman centurion, Frank. Must have been quite a period to have lived through," replied Ed, curious as to the modern looking flat top haircut and small tattoo on his ear.

"Well I'm really from Aldershot and I died in 1990; a tragic accident in a fancy dress firework display. How I wish I had gone in normal clothes. I was a dreary tax inspector. Still interested?" replied Frank with honest irony.

"Well, maybe not, but Aldershot's okay," replied Ed before Donald added,

"I've left the net down there so keep your eyes peeled, Frank. Good that we saved this one."

"All right. I'll see you back there. There's going to be a knees-up later apparently."

"Oh good, see you there," replied Donald as they went their separate ways.

"I thought people kept themselves to themselves in here," queried Ed.

"Not really. I've heard some of the other portals are like that. We like a bit of a vibe in here. That's why I stayed. I had a few uninspiring transiences but when I landed here then it was enough for me. I never saw those Tumpleberries though."

"Anyway, do you remember my grandfather? His name was Albert Tindall," queried Ed.

"Albert Tindall, Christ! Yes, I do remember him. A very hard bastard with a real reputation; a real fighter by all accounts."

"Really, old grandpa? He was harmless later in life."

"I assume that he survived the war then?"

"Physically, but not mentally. He was always slightly absent up top. Spent his whole life waking up every night drenched in sweat, shouting. Other than that he had a hard life as well. He didn't get looked after by the government when he got back. He had been wounded in the lower back, really limiting his work options. However, they refused to be liable in any way whatsoever and their medical team never acknowledged the severity of the injury, even though he had more than ten independent assessments identifying him as partially disabled. He got very disillusioned and sorrowful. He had such strong beliefs at the start of the war about fighting the good fight and rule Britannia but it all really came to bite him in the face."

"That's terrible. I have heard other stories along those lines. If those politicians knew what we had gone through for king and country they would certainly have thought again. Truth is that they are spineless fuckers that would never be seen on a battlefield. It's all a con really. When I joined up as a seventeen-year old what could I possibly have known about politics, philosophy of life or anything meaningful regarding why wars should or shouldn't be fought or why it should involve me? In retrospect that war was down to a load of posturing wankers playing brinksmanship with other people's lives and destinies. It's a crime of inadequacy on every level."

"I know. That's why he wanted to come out at the end of his life and tell the real story for a TV documentary. The program was called '*What we gave and the price it cost and the lies that deceived us*'. It caused a lot of resentment amongst the modern armed forces who it transpired were being treated in a very similar way."

"Frankly, I'm glad I died, especially after I ended up here. I very much doubt if I could have lived a happy life out there after all I saw and experienced. What I would have given to be seriously injured and sent home. I thought I had bought that ticket when I got shot in no-man's land on a raid. We moved on from barbed wire duty to kidnapping. We used to sneak over at night and kidnap German soldiers from their trenches. It was terrifying. Stealthy crawling in the darkness and then jump in and grab one of them, knock them out and carry them back for interrogation. Anyway, one night we had got this little guy. My mate Danny smacked him over the head and we started to drag him back whilst the others tried to get some others. Unfortunately he hadn't hit him hard enough and he came round, grabbing his pistol and shooting me through my shoulder. It really fucking hurt. We dropped him down and Danny shot him at point blank range. Of course, this woke the whole fucking German army. The bright night flares went off and there we were, smack bang in the middle of no-mans land illuminated like a couple of ducks in the fairground. Immediately the machine guns started to spit their murderous vermin into the night. You could hear the bullets whizzing by like super speedy fireworks. Dan got hit straight away. I just saw his head explode, literally explode as I dived into a bomb crater about the size of a hot air balloon, rolling down into the mud and stench. The first flare faded and then another one went up, then another. The bullets darted off the top ridge of the crater, spraying dirt, stones and bits of metal into the hole. I put my head down, covered it over with my metal helmet and prayed like a goodun. They kept rattling away for over an hour. Then our boys whipped a few artillery shells over in that direction and hey presto, no more flares and no more gun fire. I just had to hold out there for a bit and then try and crawl back to the British lines. It was horrendous in there though. Bits of body, legs, arms, torsos, all severed and at various stages of decomposition. By comparison the corpses that had remained reasonably intact were pretty well outnumbered. I was so pleased the flares stopped illuminating the grizzly horror. I think the worst moment was a rat crawling out of the stomach of one of the dead. Disgusting little rodent covered in blood, all over its body, face and whiskers. I threw up right then and there, and shot that little fucker with my pistol. I knew I couldn't die in that spot. I had to get out of that hole."

"And did you?"

"Yes. I tell you though one thing drove me on besides my desire to escape the macabre nightmare. It was the idea of getting back and being in hospital with lots of young nurses mollycoddling me."

"I can see that would have been an incentive, especially in the circumstances."

"You're not wrong. I crawled back after a few hours, even though I was in agonising pain and bleeding a lot. Then after yelling the password, 'Pack of Marlborough', I was back with the boys and being whisked to hospital. It was overwhelming. A bed and sheets. No mud. A beautiful old chateau converted into a medical facility. Food on plates and women, lovely women. Those nurses did it for me. Man, once I was there I couldn't stop wanking. Even the old matron looked attractive after everything I had been through. If the bed had had a hole, then I would have fanaticised about that as well."

"Well at least you wouldn't have made it pregnant," replied Ed ironically.

"Yeah, it wasn't long till I was back at the front though, those fucking muddy trenches. Rats, worms and lice, that's all that lived there. Even the trees and foliage bailed on us. Sleeping was another problem. It was virtually impossible in full uniform and with all that noise, unless you collapsed from exhaustion of course. There were positive aspects though; you didn't have to wake up or get dressed in the morning."

"I can't imagine having to endure that. Even without the barbaric killing and murder it would have been hell. How did you finally get killed?"

"You know what, it's fucking ridiculous. I had been over the top five times, penetrated into the German lines three times and spent a massive amount of time in the thick of it right at the front. As time went on I became more fearless, dehumanised and bitterly vengeful. I stopped being a person. Morality and caring became completely suspended for me. Hardly surprising when you are in a situation where two groups treat each other without mercy or compassion. Every event hardened me more and made me even more of an emotionless warrior. It started to get out of hand. Once on an advance we overran the German lines and trenches in a small sector. I stormed along the trench alone, ahead of everyone, bayoneting the enemy one by one without even thinking twice. Then I turned around a corner into a small recess in the trench system where Germans would sit and rest.

"There was a solitary German sitting there, motionless, his hands down beside him, completely resigned. I held out my bayonet towards him, about six inches from his face and shouted at him with as much spitting, screaming, frothing, ugly anger that I could muster. 'Reach for your gun, you greasy cunt, fucking reach for it'. He looked unmoved and didn't react immediately. After a short while he reached his right hand into his pocket. I instantaneously sank the bayonet into his head, between his eyes without even flinching. As it went in they bulged and became bloodshot before blood started flowing from them like tears of blood. I stuck my muddy boot in his face and pulled out the bayonet, wiping both sides of it on his small cloth hat. It fell from his head forwards onto my leg and into his lap. Then I reached down and realised he was not clutching a gun but instead had a picture of his wife and beautiful little daughter that he wanted to show me. I was crushed. In that moment I remembered the world I had forgotten. Trees and lawns, dogs and cats, birds peacefully nesting, colour, women, beer and happiness, sport and food, recreation, simplicity and love."

"Christ, how did that make you feel?"

"Dead really. I knew there was nothing of me left. I had succumbed to the situation and had let the evil penetrate into my soul. My outer world had crumpled and it had led to a complete moral collapse. Everyone acted as vulgar and as cruel as one could imagine. From the various gas and fire weapons to bolts and bullets from the sky and bomb barrages that could last for weeks. It was an insane circus of horrors. I was completely confused. Soon we were pushed back by a fierce German counter attack and found ourselves back where we started. All that after a week's fighting and God knows how many deaths. It was appalling. The scary thing was that I got used to doing all this stuff as a matter of course but could never honestly say 'why?' It just was not an option. You either did it and stood a chance of survival or didn't do it and got shot by your own officers. Numerous times I saw that. I remember Johnny Briggs, a stocky little fella from Lewisham who had been a professional rugby player. He just sat in tears shivering in the trench when the whistle blew one morning, tears flooding from his eyes. The sergeant was adamant he must go over the top but he just sat there crying. I was thinking he would just leave him but he raised his pistol and shot him clean in the head, jolting his body violently backwards into the trench wall and down onto the muddy slatted wooden floor. I was already halfway up the ladder out of the trench and he looked over at me as if to say, 'so fucking what?' I was out of there and skipping over dead bodies like an energetic spring bunny before you could say 'criminal bastard'. It was horrendous. That bastard was killed some days later in a gas attack. I watched him struggle with his gas mask and didn't forward any help, even as he came towards me looking for mercy. The heavy yellow gas crept over the edge of the trench like a lumbering monster and engulfed him, causing him to cough and splutter with panic. I felt happy to know that he would die painfully over a few days, drowning from the fluid in his lungs. Fucker. How I had lost my humanity though on every level. I had decided I had had enough."

"That sounds horrendous."

"It was. It seemed that whatever happened or whatever I did, the only option was relentless pain and suffering. Some days later I decided to end it all. I had just eaten, which I'm sure contributed to my depression. It was a disgusting mess of fatty bacon boiled in water in my metal helmet. It was a common meal over there. After this, I made my excuses to exit the trench and go further back for a while into the support and logistics area. On my way, I deliberately slipped from one of the wooden walkways into the quagmire of mud. We were instructed not to help any soldier that fell in. It was like quicksand and often when one fell in, others would be killed trying to help. My kit was super heavy and I landed on my back a yard or so from the scattered planks. A big bloopy plopping noise and I was suddenly weightless and comfortable, more so than any time I could remember whilst out there. Everything went into slow motion. I could see a couple of the privates trying to help me before being hurried away by a commander. I looked upwards. It was a spectacular blue sky with little fluffy clouds scattered and bobbling. The contrasting shards of burnt tree branches and deafening gun rounds certainly gave it more edge than a normal autumn day though. I could feel the cool mud seeping into my shirt and pants. It was relaxing and quite marvellous, therapeutic and mesmerising.

I felt it go down inside my collar and come up over my neck. The shells continued to roar over my head from the gun position just behind until suddenly, total blissful silence. Nothing, not even a thud. The mud came up over my face and I felt totally at peace as it started to enter my mouth, its thick gritty texture enveloping my nostrils and filling the back of my throat. It tasted strangely aromatic and fragrant, not at all how I expected. I coughed and spluttered out of instinct but I never struggled, not one bit. I glanced to my left just before I went under, noticing the rows of men going to the front. Soldier after soldier marched past, covered in mud stains up to their waist. Only one looked in my direction. He caught my eye just as I went under completely, his face full of fear and trepidation. I, however, had freed myself and was on my way to another level. I was losing nothing and saw this as a great escape. Next thing I knew I was a fucking hedgehog. Can you believe it, reincarnated as a protuberantly pronged beast in what felt like an instant?"

"That's quite a story."

"I know. It took me many years to unburden myself of it psychologically. I just thought that I was the only villain in the whole scheme of things but in reality, I was as much a victim as those that I killed. Whether you survived that war physically or not, everyone that took part was a victim, dead inside. No doubt my bones are still there, deep in the soil beneath a tranquil and hopefully life giving crop of wheat."

"I'm sure it is a peaceful resting place. Certainly pictures I saw of those battle fields in the modern day show no evidence of the horrors that went on there. Whatever humanity can throw at it, the Earth can always repair itself," replied Ed reassuringly.

"Yeah, I think you are right there."

"I guess other soldiers from the war came through here, did they?"

"That one and many others. It was very interesting to meet soldiers from before my days: Roman centurions or guys from the Napoleonic wars. I'm not sure what would have been more terrifying, running into modern machine gun fire or facing psychotic ranks of sword wielding warriors. Truth is, they were all regretful and guilty about their actions when it came down to it. Time is a well trained healer though."

"Did it take you long to understand it all?"

"I'm not sure I understand it even now. I've come to terms with the whole thing though and stopped blaming myself. We might not have some of our physical attributes in here, but we certainly still have our feelings, emotions and memories. I often compare some of these emotions to waves. They often get choppy and rough but they eventually settle back into a calm sea at some point."

"That's a good way of putting it. You're right though. War's damaging even for the hardiest soul. All because of pig-headed, petulant politicians who can't resolve their differences like adults, especially when they know their mistakes will cost millions of lives. It makes me sick."

"Me too. We were blissfully unaware though back then. We didn't even know what we were fighting for really, other than an over-inflated idea of obligation to 'King and Country'. I was just glad to get out of it, Ed, to be honest," replied Donald.

"I can understand that." replied Ed as they continued trudging through the sand.

"After all that, I've ended up with the gun and uniform as a souvenir. Crazy that I can't get rid of them."

"Yeah, that is a little odd. I am curious though, after your death how long did it take to you to learn about being a Transient?"

"Well it wasn't until I got here. I was briefly a hedgehog that got run over by a tractor. Then I was a sparrow and got killed by an angry cat and then I ended up here. They told me about everything and I didn't want to go back into the fray, least of all go back into the physical world. It was bad enough the first time."

"I'm not sure I could commit to an eternity here though. Maybe it'll change if I get exhausted of going round in circles through different transient states. On the other hand I might just give in and stay as an animal after my time expires out there. I wonder what happens then, if I do go over the time limit and die at a later point?"

"I think that takes you out of the transient cycle and you just cease to exist. None of us have ever met a Transient who has done that and ended up down here. I guess the human soul dies when we cease to be aware of it, don't you think?"

"Possibly. But you cease to be a Transient by staying here permanently, isn't that much the same as opting to remain an animal?"

"Not really because we remain aware of ourselves. This might be the key."

"You might be right. Maybe there are also other options when we die in the first place. Maybe this transient cycle is not the only alternative. Maybe there is a selection process or something based on a judgement of the lives we lived. Did you ever wonder how you wound up as a Transient?"

"Yes, Ed, I did," replied the private as they turned another corner and continued walking along the maze of tunnels, all equally covered in the dense vines.

"I don't think there's a selection process or that it's to do with sin or punishment or anything like that. To be honest, there are so many people down here who've lived completely different lives that I can't see anything to suggest they might be here for similar reasons. I think it's random, just like life was. I never thought that my human life had any cause other than the lottery of who my parents were, or where and when I was born. I don't see why I should adopt a different frame of mind regarding any 'after life' or 'other lives', Ed."

"Good point. I'd also prefer to believe it's random like you suggest, although the first Transient I met seemed to think there was some sort of puzzle to solve."

"Well we all want to believe at some point that there is some god, head, or extra meaning for everything. What about it all being just as it is? That'll do me," said Donald as they turned into yet another tunnel.

"How do you know your way? All this looks identical," queried Ed.

"You get to know. Anyway, we've been chatting away a long time. We only have a little way to go and we'll be there."

"Good, I'm getting a bit knackered," replied Ed.

"Try these fucking boots, mate, then keep them on for ninety years. That'll teach you what tired is. Unfortunately we can still get tired down here, as you've probably noticed."

"Yes, I did. No hunger though, that's something, don't you think?"

"Certainly is. An eternity of hunger would really be hard to bear. As it is, a bit of tiredness and the occasional backache, isn't a problem for me."

The duo turned a final corner which opened out onto an impressively large dome-shaped hall, five times larger than St Paul's cathedral. All around there were balconies and tiers created in double spiral configuration, two spirals both starting at the same lower point going up towards the roof in opposite directions, crisscrossing at various points for easy access to all the levels. The outside of the walkways had small walls which seemed to be made from perfect, shiny, black granite. Behind them, the inner walls were covered with the tapestry of vines, back lit and casting an evocative illuminated texture across the whole dome. All along the walls were tiny doors with black curtains, similar to the rooms from the previous tunnel experience with Thomas.

"There are about three thousand rooms here, Ed. We're only about seventy percent full though at the moment," stated Donald as they walked over to the edge of the walkway. Ed could see they were about halfway up the height of the dome as he looked up at the marvellous back lit vine-covered dome and down into the large, red, sandy, open area below. There were dozens of people milling around and he couldn't help but feel he was in the biggest fancy dress party in the history of the world. Everything from sixteenth century policemen to cowboys, doctors, Chinese labourers, Baltic fishermen, pirates and Nazi guards, all happily intermingling.

"I can see why you learnt so many languages, Donald," murmured Ed, reflecting on the multicultural timeless mix.

"Well I have had a hundred years to sort it haven't I? You've got to fill the time with something. I'm on Mandarin at the moment. That's a really hard language," replied Donald.

"Come on, let's go down and say hi to a few people. Then we'll settle you down in a room for some rest and then decide what to do next."

"Okay, that sounds good. Let's do it," replied Ed, as they started to wind their way down the interlinking spiral walkways like mice in a maze. Ed kept stopping to marvel at the views over the balcony every few yards.

"It's an awesome place, Donald. I can see why you'd stay here. What did you say it was called again: Cohen dome?"

"No, Koan Dome, as in 'ko-an', like 'go-aan'."

"Oh! What does that mean then?"

"Well I never really understood it at first. Apparently it's to do with some sort of ridiculous question which can't be answered. After ages trying to figure it out logically, you go round in circles and get some sort of revelation, like a rubber glove slapped around your face."

"Sounds like some sort of 'Zen' thing?"

"Yeah, that's it. Zen. I spent years thinking it was 'Hen Buddhism' and that by figuring out how a hen became a monk I would get my rubber glove. I just misheard it."

"That's funny. Hen Buddhism."

"I know. Anyway, this 'Koan' idea has some things in common with being caught in the cycle of transience. We try to understand it with our old values, but in actual fact, a clearer understanding comes about by being less analytical."

"Yeah, I haven't got to that point yet. I can see why you'd stay here though."

"Yes, a lot of people like it. It was easy for me to make the decision. I miss very little of my previous life."

"If you could change things, what would you do?" enquired Ed.

"What, about this place?"

"No, I mean about your old life."

"Well I wouldn't have fucking volunteered for a start. I think a whole lot of innocent young people didn't need to be sacrificed so mercilessly with such meaningless actions. Walking into machine gun fire, succumbing to a gas attack, killed by a flying bolt; it was all pointless. I didn't even know the reason for the war until some years later after I was here.

When I found out, it made me downright angry. How could all those people die because some rich, posh, nobs don't know how to resolve their differences? It is farcical," replied Donald, as they got down to the floor level of the dome.

Ed looked up in amazement as they walked towards the centre where a large group of people was gathering.

"This'll be nice, it's the choral group. They sing some beautiful melodies and they sound amazing in here. Come on, let's sit on the floor and watch them. It sounds better at a distance. Then we can go and say hi and meet a few people."

"Sounds good. I really need to speak to someone who knows about the Viking. Can you arrange that for soon?"

"No problem. I know who to approach. We'll listen to this, then get you a room and then go and meet her. She is a bit of an oddball, but friendly."

"Fantastic," replied Ed just as the choral group started to sing a delicate whispering drone with a magical voicing. Slowly the sound swelled into the enormity of the dome, spiralling upwards all around, the sound echoing from the awe-inspiring walkways above. The combination of sweet female tones bolstered by the warmth and depth of the male voices created the perfect texture for the harmonies and interwoven lines, to be most effective. Long legato passages increased in intensity, punctuated by short staccato rhythmic chords sung in unison with the uppermost precision. Donald lent over towards Ed, his rifle resting in his lap and whispered in his ear,

"Majestic and glorious, but not religious at all. We don't do religion here."

"I can understand that. This music is just incredible though; I've never heard anything like it before."

"I doubt if anyone outside of this community ever has. This is what you get when Brahms and Bach have been living next door to one another for such a long period of time. They don't even use notation any more. They've just devised a way to conduct the whole group with nods, looks and head shakes. Look, can you see them there at either side? Bach is doing all the spiky staccato stuff and Brahms is doing the smooth legato. It's all totally improvised and will never

143

happen again. Every rendition is completely different. They both claim that it is the highest level of composition one can reach. Instantaneous composition, conducting and performance. Sadly I wasn't good enough to be part of the choir, but man, I love listening to it," commented Donald as he turned his attentions back to the music.

Ed looked over and saw the two plump gentlemen in similar black jackets with white silky neck handkerchiefs, one with a pronounced grey beard with white moustache, the other a little skinnier and clean shaven with a strange looking white wig. They both stood almost motionless apart from their heads which subtly jolted from side to side, occasionally looking at one another, nodding and smiling. He glanced up and around the dome as the music welled up like a stupendous and emotional tidal wave, sweeping around and around, toying with the innermost emotions and feelings.

"They've been here longer than me," whispered Donald into Ed's left ear.

"They are quite private chaps, but my goodness, that's talent on a whole different level," concluded the young man as the choir came down to a whisper and stopped all at once, perfectly synchronised. Ed had no idea how long they had been singing. He had been lost in time. A little bit of murmuring and chattering commenced as the majority of the group started to make their way up the spiral walkways like a bizarre mobile fancy dress party.

"Can we say hello to them? I mean Brahms and his mate?" queried Ed.

"Not now. They like it if you really have something meaningful to say. They don't waste their time with chitchat like us. Let's go and say hi to some of the others. You want to meet someone who knows about the Viking. I want to introduce you to Yedida. I saw her in there somewhere," replied Donald as the two men got up and walked over towards the dispersing group.

"Why do you carry that gun around with you, Donald?" queried Ed, looking down at the scary-looking item.

"Habit really, but I always take it down to the Transient tunnel. It can help me nudge people into the net. I'll drop it back in my room later. I don't have it with me always. Anyway, it's not loaded or dangerous. I don't think about it much anymore. If I loose it then it just reappears in my room the next day. Very strange"

"Okay. I just wondered, that's all," replied Ed, as they walked nearer the group.

"Yedida, Yedida," cried Donald, as he caught sight of a young lady in a white trouser suit looking the other way. She heard the cry and quickly turned around to see the two men approaching.

"Yedida, I want you to meet Ed, he's a new Transient, just arrived today."

"Hi, Ed, I'm Yedida, I am black, a female and Jewish, and I am fucking proud of it!" she exclaimed, slightly startling him and putting him on his back foot. An awkward silence followed, soon interrupted by Donald.

"She's pissing with you, Ed. It's all true, but she likes to confront people like that when she first meets them."

"Come, I won't bite. I'm Yedida," exclaimed the young lady in a much gentler tone with a smirk. As she reached her arm out, Ed caught sight of an ominous looking tattooed number on her inner forearm. He knew what that meant, but pretended to not notice it as he took her hand and warmly shook it, up, down, up and away.

"Hi, Yedida, I'm Ed. Ed Trew from England."

"Nice to meet you, Ed. Did you enjoy the music?"

"Absolutely. To be honest I'm still in a bit of a trance. It seemed to penetrate deep inside me. I've never experienced anything like that before."

"Yes, they've got it down. They know all about emotions and music. Did you close your eyes?"

"No, I didn't."

"Well next time, close your eyes. They have it so deeply developed that it generates a whole colour show internally, like a kaleidoscope of calming fireworks. It's an outstanding journey. Apparently they compose on the spot in colours. Not sure how they do that."

"Sorry, Ed, I forgot to tell you to close your eyes. Anyway, Yedida, Ed wants to know about the Viking."

145

"The Viking eh! He knows about the Viking? Well that's interesting," replied the young lady as they made their way through the emptying open space and up one of the spiral inclines.

"Yes, I was in another place like this before and got to hear about him. Before I commit to staying one place or another, I want to find out as much as possible about what options I have," replied Ed, as they reached the first landing.

"Indeed you do! Bring him over to my room later, Donny, and we can have a chat about things. You come as well and join in the conversation."

"Okay, will do. See you later then," replied Donald as she headed off in the opposite direction.

"Donny! That's sweet. Are you two an item?"

"Sadly, the term 'no sex please, we're British', really comes to roost here. 'No sex possible, we're Transients', is the actual reality of things".

"Yes, but I suppose you're settlers more than you are Transients, at least once you've decided to stay here permanently and not keep jumping back and forth?"

"That's true, although we still habitually call ourselves Transients. Anyway, back to the sex. I died a virgin, so I don't know what I'm missing. Was it any good?"

Ed thought back to the memorable night with Abella in the car before they were married and how he had an orgasm so massive he thought his whole head was going to be shot off his shoulders like a rocket. Then he simply decided to lie.

"Not much really, Donald. You don't need to worry about that. All hype really."

The duo arrived at the room where Ed would be staying. He turned round and looked back over the balcony into the large domed hall.

"It's such a wonderful atmosphere, the grand hall and the choral music. Don't you think it's quite spiritual?"

"To a point. I guess it depends on how you define spiritual though."

"Maybe. It reminds me though of a church I visited on a business trip to Bologna in the nineties. It was on a bustling square and when one escaped inside into the quietude and calm it gave a real Goosebumps feeling."

"That might have been down to the serenity of the building as much as you had been touched by the spirit of God. I would often feel a similar spirituality amidst the grandeur of nature, in a stunningly secluded but wondrous place with the birds singing and the wind gently caressing the leaves into an atmospheric symphony. In my short life I stopped associating that feeling from any 'presence' there might be in our conceptualised and pre defined spiritual locations and honestly put it more down to our ability to marvel at and be overwhelmed by the magnificence of nature."

"That's very true. The sheer scale and grandiosity of some temples and churches are quite capable of making us feel like that, even if we don't have an ounce of religious belief in us whatsoever. Maybe it is tapping into an archetypal spirituality deep within us, not defined by religious belief but more by an innate awareness of the sheer magnificence of the universe we're part of."

"Well said, Ed. It is certainly the conclusion a lot of people here have arrived at after much deliberation. Those places of worship did have an important function though, for people to experience that wonderment, and understand their place in the grander scheme of things, even if it only gave fleeting humility. Anyway, this is it. No mod cons, I'm afraid. Comfortable though," stated Donald, as he swept the curtain aside and they both entered the room.

"Same as the other place; simple but functional. Could be a Japanese hotel for all I know. I'll be fine," uttered Ed, as he slipped down onto the bed.

"By the way, she mentioned she was Jewish, but you said there was no religion here. Why would she say that?" queried Ed.

"She's not religious. She is just using that as a reference to her background when she was in the physical world. People tend to say where they are from and what their background is, but once you're here, it's impossible for anyone to continue believing in a god, whatever faith they are from."

147

"I can understand that," replied Ed, as he glanced at his watch and then slid flat onto the bed. It was now eight o'clock so he figured that after a six hour walk, the music must have gone on for at least ninety minutes, much longer than he thought.

"Have a good rest and I'll come back later, then we can go over to Yedida's. Are you okay with that?" queried Donald as he turned tail and started to leave the room.

"Cool. See you then," Ed replied, as the soldier slipped out of sight.

Ed slipped back into a relaxed position with his arms folded back under his head. He began to reflect on how fast things were moving and how extreme it all was, from the tortoise to the time tunnels, then the cat, the hound and then in a time warp with a WW1 soldier and famous classical composers hooking up to collaborate. Just then, Donald slid back into the room.

"Sorry, Ed, listen. Please don't judge me harshly on all those things I told you. If you'd been there, you would have understood. I was a timid child and youth, and never wanted to hurt anyone. The madness and cruelty of war turned me into a killer. That's the bitter sadness of it all. That's what I wanted to get across."

"I understand, Don," replied Ed using his abbreviated name for the first time.

"I cannot comprehend what you must have gone through but I can understand how it would have dismantled your reality and how that could desensitise you to all those horrors. I feel very strongly for you, honestly. There is not a single participant in any war that's not a pained and troubled victim at their core. I would never judge you on that," reflected Ed emotionally as he sat up on the bed and stared at Donald.

"Thanks. That's okay then. I'll see you later. Get some rest," stated Donald sheepishly as he left the room once more.

"Great. See you then. It's been good spending time with you and thanks for getting me out of the tunnel; I forgot to say that," replied Ed, as the curtain flowed down closed and he heard a distant "no probs" from the departing private. Ed lay down once again, drifting off into a calm sleep.

Chapter 12
Fritz the baker

"Come on, Ed, come on, we need to go over to Yedida, she's expecting us, come on," exclaimed Donald, as he gently shoved his shoulder back and forth, shaking him from his sleep like an apple from a tree.

"Arrghh, er, where am I? Er, oh, Thomas, NO, Donald. Sorry, yes, I'll be with you. Give me a second," spluttered Ed, emerging from his sleep like fog seeping under a door.

"I'll wait outside."

"Okay," replied Ed, as he span round upright on the bed, directing his feet onto the floor. He held his head in his hands and rubbed his eyes, quickly adjusting to the new environment. He jumped up and sprang across the tiny room, through the black silky curtain and out to the waiting Donald.

"Good. That was quick. Let's go, she's on the upper levels and it'll take a little while to get there. I've left my gun back in the room as well, just to keep you happy. Yedida doesn't like guns either. She's had quite a life – I'm sure she'll tell you about it at some point."

"Yes, I saw the tattoo on her arm. Does it mean what I think it means?"

"She'll tell you, I'm sure. If by 'what I think it means' you mean 'it's what I think it means' then yes, you are probably right, but it's not my story to tell. Put it this way, we both have a lot of common ground having lived through extreme cataclysmic events and it gives us a close bond," replied Donald, as they started to ascend the inclined walkways. The views into the large dome area grew more spectacular the higher they got, and Ed almost forgot about the mission to find the Viking, his transient predicament and all of the complexity that was now part of his existence. Soon they were up near the top and at Yedida's door.

"Yedida, we're here," exclaimed the British soldier.

"Great, come in, come in," replied the sexy and seductive voice from inside the curtained enclosure. Soon they had parted the silk covering and entered the room, politely kissed her on both cheeks and all three sat down, Ed and Donald on the bed and the striking black lady on a small stool opposite.

"You've just arrived then, Ed. What was your last transience?" enquired Yedida.

"A very brief one. I was caught up in a fox hunt as one of the hounds. Luckily though, I managed to sabotage it and the fox escaped. It was a horrible grizzly scene though," replied Ed.

"Horrible eh, the idea of fox hunting? Strange barbarism, although it's in keeping with the general demise of human character."

"Yes, quite," replied Ed.

"Anyway, you want to see the Viking do you? Donny doesn't altogether think he's for real, do you, Donny?"

"Until I've seen him with my own eyes, I'll remain a sceptic. Anyway, now you two are together, I'll love you and leave you," stated Donald, as he got up and put his hand out to shake Ed's.

"Maybe I'll see you later, Ed, if you stay on. Otherwise, thanks for the company."

"Thanks to you too and thanks for everything," replied Ed, as he stood up to shake Donald's hand.

"If you don't mind me asking, why carry the water bottle with you all day if you can't drink?"

Donald reached down to the canvas covered water bottle hanging from a canvas strap over his shoulder. He turned it round towards Ed to reveal a large dented hole.

"Of course, it's empty but it has sentimental value. It saved my life in my first few days at the front. It's a good luck charm," replied Donald with a smile on his face.

"Oh. Okay then," replied Ed, as Donald kissed Yedida on both cheeks before leaving the room and pulling the curtain closed behind him.

"Lovely guy," stated Ed.

"Yes, he went through a lot out there and really had to do a lot of soul searching when he came here. I guess he told you his story did he?"

"Yes, the whole thing. I think he felt really bad being

lured into that vengeance, hatred and loss of self. You can kind of understand it, given the circumstances, don't you think?" replied Ed.

"To a point. They were certainly extreme circumstances with a lot of psychological impact. That's sometimes worse than anything physical. You must, however, do everything you can to keep a sense of self in such extreme circumstances. That would be the only thing that could protect your soul and inner being. As long as you keep sight of yourself, there's hope you can make the right choices, whatever the situation," stated Yedida wisely, her smooth black complexion complemented even more by the pure white trouser suit. Her straight silky jet black hair cascaded down and framed her perfectly chiselled face whilst her proud straight posture gave her more than an air of grace. Ed guessed she was in her mid to late twenties.

"So tell me, Ed, what do you know about the Viking? I assume from the fact that you're here and aware of him, that you have been around the cycle a few times and that you know about the time deadlines?"

"Yes, I'm bang up to date with all that. I just want to make a few more trips before I commit to anything, although this place looks as though it could seduce an impromptu decision for many travellers to stay?"

"Yes, you're right. A lot of people do choose to stay, around fifteen percent I guess. However, I think you're right in wanting to find out a little more before deciding. I sometimes wish I'd gone round a few times. Mind you, I might not have ever ended up back here. We rarely see the same Transient twice. There must be a lot of portals along the way."

"Yes, I definitely won't stay this time. Anyway, how far is it to get to the Viking? It was a few days' journey from the last place?" enquired Ed.

"Not too bad, probably around a day or so. A little tricky though. There are a couple of obstacles to overcome on the way. It's not without danger."

"What sort of danger?" enquired Ed.

"Let's leave, I'll tell you about it on the way. It's nothing to be scared of. You're a big boy," replied Yedida reassuringly as she got up and moved over towards the door.

"Come on. We should get on our way now. Better to have too much time than too little. I hate rushing."

"Okay," replied Ed, as he got up and followed her out of the doorway, excited to finally be on his way to the Viking, cautiously optimistic for some positives, even if it was to give him a 'Koan' revelation.

They set off along the curving spiral pathway around the edge of the hall. Yedida proceeded over to the edge of the walkway and looked down at the open hallway below and the dome above. The hall was once again filling with people. She stood for a second with her hands on the top of the wall.

"They're going to sing again, Ed. Perfection isn't it?" stated Yedida.

"Yes, although it doesn't seem that long since the last performance, unless I slept longer than I thought," replied Ed, as the waves of melody began to drift around the extensive open space.

"This is a different group. There are a few. Sometimes they all sing at once, arranged around the walkways in the hall. It's really something. Anyway, are you scared of heights, Ed?"

"A bit, why?"

"We have to go up there," replied the young lady, pointing to what looked like a rope ladder which ran from the top walkway up and around the curved ceiling until about two thirds from the top. At this point, virtually horizontal, it disappeared into a small trap door.

"You're kidding right?" exclaimed Ed nervously.

"No, I'm not kidding. You'll be fine. Just hold on and don't panic. Let's go around there and start climbing."

"Okay then, it looks scary though."

"Another thing, Ed, this is a one-way trip. Once you get past a certain point on this journey, you can't come back. You have to go all the way and take your next transience from there. I'll let you know when we reach that point," said Yedida.

"But how will you get back?"

"I'm not going to go the whole way with you. I can only go so far or else I can't come back. There's a point of no return. Don't worry though I can go most of the way."

"Decisions, decisions, everywhere in this lifecycle eh," exclaimed Ed, as they reached the bottom of the cloth ladder.

"Is this safe?" enquired Ed, as he shook the tatty-looking item made from old clothes.

"Perfectly fine, come on, let's go."

"Okay, let's go," replied Ed, as he looked down at his watch to see that he'd been in this new location less than a day.

"You have enough time to get to the point of no return and change your mind to get back here. Don't worry. Watch me go up and when I disappear into the hole, then you follow me," stated Yedida.

"Okay then," replied Ed, as she leapt up the ladder with agility, hanging virtually upside down as she progressed towards the hole.

"Don't look down," she shouted, as she disappeared up and through the hole and out of sight.

Trepidations and fears gripped Ed as he grabbed the ladder with both hands and began to pull himself skywards. It felt surprisingly secure for a rope ladder, bearing in mind it was tied to little bits of the vine that covered the whole dome structure. The soothing waves of choral music washed over and around him, warming his soul and calming him from the increasing vertigo. He got more cautious and nervous with every grab and step as he felt his body getting worryingly horizontal. He continued to look up, clawing his way further towards the hole, the weight of his body feeling heavier by the second. Then he heard a voice from above.

"Don't look down, come on. You're nearly there."

"It was Yedida, her head poking from the hole, giving reassuring comfort to the novice climber.

Just as he thought the job was complete, his worst fears came and smacked him in the face. Against all instinct and advice he looked down and froze, directly above part of the choral group. He reached forward with his left hand to move closer to the trap door but in an instant his foot slipped on the rope. He fell dramatically away from the ladder, desperately hanging on with one hand. In a state of panic, he swung the free arm towards the ladder as he swung backwards and forwards, certain he would fall. Then he felt Yedida's arm grab his as she shouted firmly to hold on. Below, the choral group were oblivious to the goings-on overhead, as the melodies got more and more intense.

"Swing backwards and forwards and try to grab the ropes, Ed," she cried down to him. Soon he had done just that and was swinging his whole body so he could get his feet back on the rungs of the ladder. It took some while but finally he achieved his objective and was clambering up into the small hole and into a large tunnel. The young lady helped, securely taking both hands, pulling him up and into the opening and to safety. Ed collapsed on his back on the floor, astounded by the events.

"Thank goodness bodily functions are off the menu. I would most certainly have crapped myself there and then, Yedida. Sorry for the graphic."

"No problem. Honestly, very few people have the guts to do that climb. You're one of probably five percent. Congratulations."

"What would happen to me if I fell anyway, seeing as I'm already dead?"

"Good question. It would definitely hurt I know that much."

"There must have been a situation in the past where someone injured themselves badly, broke a leg or even something fatal?"

"Yes, there has. It is hard to explain but they kind of melt away and go missing for a few days. Then they reappear some while later unscathed and oblivious of whatever went on. Mysterious really. Anyway, look back through the hole at the choir," replied Yedida.

Ed moved closer back towards the hole and peered through. It was an impressive sight, the spiralled walkways spinning round and round the hall with the choir like tiny ants in a red sand garden. The brilliant wash of melody and harmony whispered up through the hole and around into the tunnel.

"Mind out, I need to close this," said Yedida, as she grabbed the trap door and flipped it shut.

"Look, check this out," she added, as she pulled the door open by an inch or so.

"Squint your eyes and look out through the opening, Ed."

"Why?"

"Just do it, you'll see," she replied. Ed did as she said and squinted at the partially open trap door.

"I can't believe it," he gasped, astonished by the myriad of rainbow colours that jetted through the small gap.

"What is it?"

"It's the music. I told you they were working with colours. You can see them if you close your eyes but it really gets exciting when the music squeezes through a small gap on the light. Far out eh?" replied Yedida, as she finally closed the door.

"Yes, indeed."

They both got up and began walking down the tunnel, which was slightly bigger than the previous tunnels but equally adorned with back lit vines and dazzling red sand. They walked for a few minutes in silence but then Ed couldn't help but ask about the tattoo on the young lady's forearm.

"I noticed the tattoo on your arm, Yedida. I hope you don't mind me asking about that?"

"Actually I was going to tell you about myself anyway. There are no secrets in here and it's really important to get to know what makes people who they are. I really need to explain my complex family history to you first though. It's quite a ride, trust me," exclaimed Yedida vulnerably.

"I'm a good listener," replied Ed, as they continued walking through the dramatically back lit vine-coated tunnels.

"Well, way back, my family comes from Africa. Not sure exactly where. My great grandfather had been slaved and ended up in Cuba. His son ended up in southern America and somehow after all that, after the abolition, my mother ended up in Germany, finally to be married to a white German tailor. It was not an easy place to be black at the time. The

First World War had ended and Germany was on its knees, crippled by the financial demands of the coalition of Europe and America. It helped give rise to the Nazi party who gradually went from strength to strength."

"Yes, I know all about that," replied Ed.

"Our family was okay though. My father worked hard and made a real success out of his business and my mother did absolutely everything to give me a stable and loving upbringing. She was my heroine. I went to college, studied and passed my law exams with flying colours and really got some good opportunities. However, the Nazis were going from strength to strength and starting to take a hold on the infrastructure of the country. They had lots of gangs of thugs that would beat up communists, gays, Jews, blacks and anyone else that took their fancy. After some years it started to become hell on the streets. We knew we would be targeted at some point but repressed the facts and thought that one day sense and logic would prevail and everything would be alright. How wrong we were.

"One day my mother came home with a torn dress, spattered in blood, limping and moaning. She slumped into the chair as my father and I rushed over to comfort her. We were in total shock. I hurried to the bathroom to get her plasters, towels, and antiseptic. She was distraught and pushed us away as we tried to help, sobbing with a pain I never knew could be possible. It transpired that she had been cornered by a small group of thugs who taunted and abused her, beat her and raped her over and over in a dirty alley, leaving her for dead, bleeding and crying.

"It was a tragedy from which she would never recover. She was completely ruined and finally killed herself less than a month later. Before she did though, she told me all about her time in America and how my grandfather and great grandfather had both been slaves and the suffering that entailed. She didn't want me to know about all that negativity previously. Were it not for the fact that this devastating attack had happened, I doubt I would have ever known. She hated persecution and bullying so much and after her stories I really got to understand why."

"That's terrible," replied Ed with concern as they continued along the long tunnels, a faint breeze brushing over their faces soothingly.

"I was mortified by the whole situation, the prejudice, the hatred. How could people be so incredibly violent and brutal to an innocent person just because they're different? It just didn't make sense to me at all. My father and I both responded in completely different ways. He became terrified, a shell of the man he previously was. Everything that happened was a cause for concern and scared him more until one day he went off and without ever really understanding what he was doing, joined the Nazi party. I remember so clearly that day he came home in the uniform, starched collars and perfectly shining boots as if clean boots cleaned a soul. His eyes were glazed over and he went straight upstairs without a word. By the next morning I had left, along with a small suitcase with a few clothes and basics in it. I had no idea which way to turn. The whole environment was getting more and more radical by the week and I knew I had to get off the street as quickly as I could."

"It must have been so painful? Why on earth would he have done that?" interjected Ed sympathetically.

"I don't know. I'll never understand that. Anyway, I had the idea of going down to the local Synagogue. I was shocked to find it covered in abusive graffiti and swastikas. The walls were charred with the signs of failed petrol bomb attacks and the broken windows were barely visible from the protective boards nailed in place haphazardly. I knocked and knocked at the door but there was no reply. I waited there for absolutely ages until by chance a young girl of about fifteen came past and ushered me along the side path, through some boxes and barriers and into a side door.

"Once inside I could see the main prayer room was barely a quarter full, maybe thirty or forty people. They called me over and gave me a hot drink, sat me down and continued their debate about escaping the city and leaving their possessions and properties to be ransacked. The debate went on and on, trying to unravel the impossible and unbelievable situation that was enveloping them. Round and round in circles they went, what will they do to us? How could that be humanly possible? Surely the human beings we have been living side by side with for generations could not even think of letting that happen? Sadly it was a grim reality and when bricks and bottles once again started to rain down on the building, logic took control and they agreed they needed to get out and find ways to hide people until it all died down."

"It must have been such a shocking realisation. Had you ever imagined that could have happened?"

"Never in a million years. My mother had preached understanding and love. Accept and tolerate, never react and aggress. She was a fine teacher and even in these extreme circumstances, I felt strong."

"You're such an inspiring person," replied Ed respectfully.

"Thanks. Necessity is the mother of pain management, eh! Anyway, I converted to Judaism right there and then. I begged them to let me in. They were reluctant and said it wasn't a simple ceremony but I pleaded that I wanted to share their plight religiously, not just because I was black but because I supported them with all my heart. After some while, the Rabbi conceded and did some sort of very quick ceremony whilst the bricks thudded on the building. Then they sewed a yellow star on my jacket, and I was united with them in their suffering. The missiles continued to fall until we heard a loud noise at the front door of the synagogue. All of a sudden it just caved in and a tatty open-top car burst through. Two middle aged men leapt from the car and opened fire with some sort of rapid firing rifle.

"We fled in every direction. The people directly to my left and right got hit and blood spattered out in front of them as they fell down face first into their own path. I just kept on running, out the side door and over a small wall with the fifteen year old girl I had met at the beginning of the evening. She had an idea where we could hide and took us through the dark myriad of small cobbled streets and alleys until we got to a small baker's. We darted through a tiny door at the side of the building and were greeted by a small, fat, balding German man in pyjamas who ushered us inside and locked the door behind. We heard the cobbled boots run past in the alleyway, stopping momentarily outside the shop before continuing on their way. It was terrifying."

"I don't think I would have trusted anyone at that point," commented Ed, noticing that the faint breeze had given way to a total stillness.

"I had to. I trusted Ellie, the young girl and I had to go with the flow. Anyway, it turned out well for a while. The baker, Fritz, looked after us, fed us, got us new clothes and made sure we were comfortable. We never went out at all though and stayed confined to his little back room. Then as the situation worsened he built a secret section behind a book case where we could hide safely, even if they came to search, which they did a few times. We were pin-drop silent, not even a flutter of hair to give the game away. Ellie was an amazingly strong girl, going through all that at such a young age."

"Both of you for that matter, Yedida," observed Ed.

"Yes, I suppose so. She was very philosophical and realistic though. When she was very young, she told me how she was attracted to the BDM just like all her German girl friends."

"What's the BDM?" replied Ed, as they came to a small junction of tunnels. He followed her lead as she took the second on the left, equally enchanting with the back lit vines casting delicate shadows across the smooth sandy floor.

"The League of German Girls, another one of Hitler's ideas to go along with the Hitler youth boys organisation, which dated back as far as the mid-twenties. Every little girl wanted to join it and go on their weekend excursions and camps with their plaited hair, singing songs and learning all the requirements of being a good German woman."

"Must have been like the girl guides for psychopaths?" replied Ed.

"Yes, that's one way of putting it."

"But you said she was Jewish? How can she have wanted to join those un-travelled, uneducated and uncouth racist bigots?"

"I guess she was just caught up in the hype and fashion of the whole thing. Virtually everyone joined and those that didn't were sometimes kicked out of their school. Ellie didn't realise she was classed as 'different' until she tried to join and was rejected. Then the school bullying started and that was the beginning of a very nasty few years for her. I remember her saying that it was as though everyone in her school had been hypnotised. Girls that had previously been her friends turned on her. Everyone apparently got possessed with idolising the Fuhrer and demonising Jews, Gypsies, Blacks and anyone else that didn't fit into their strange illusion of a perfect world."

"It's strange that people didn't feel guilty enough en masse to just stand up and say 'Look! This isn't right, we have had enough,' don't you think?"

"Listen, Ed, in a room of mad people the sane one is the odd one out. People wanted to believe the hype just like they believe over-inflated religious doctrines. They wanted to join, belong and obey, to not stand out or be the black sheep. Of course, as time moved on, their decisions were more based on fear than anything else," replied Yedida.

"It must have been a hellish thing to live through and see developing in front of your very eyes."

"It was indeed, corroding everything civilised, like water slowly eroding rock. It was so subtle that people didn't even realise it was happening. I guess their need for security and belonging was greater than their need for freedom."

"Someone else said that to me recently. Can't remember who."

"Age old wisdom."

"What's enlightening about speaking to you is how I get to see it all from a personal perspective rather than a chronologically watermarked historical analysis."

"It's just my personal experience."

"Yes, I know but it's very powerful. Terrifying to see how normality can drift into chaos and hatred in no time at all."

"Yes, a slow painful process leading to me hiding in that cramped space with Ellie," replied Yedida, as the duo came to an intersection in the tunnels. Ed followed Yedida's lead as she steered them onto the right fork and they continued without a pause.

"How long were you there for?" queried Ed.

"I lost track of time. It was definitely years. It was strange because it got more intense as time went on. Fritz, the baker, got more and more uptight about the whole situation and in the end it started to get really difficult. We thought he was going to throw us out but then figured he wouldn't risk it in case we told the Germans who had hidden us. It carried on incessantly until one day we heard the allied bombers overhead. The bombs got closer and closer and Ellie and I huddled together in the corner, terrified. Then there was a deafening explosion right next to the house and it blew the wall clean off, exposing us and our secret little lair. As we got up and dusted ourselves down we were exposed for all to see.

"I could see the smoking bomb crater with bits of wood, brick, plaster and pottery mixed up in a confused and nasty mess all around. I could see the bloodied severed arm of a German soldier lying neatly on top of a small pile of random rubble, balanced delicately as if by design. Then as the smoke cleared further, to our amazement we were suddenly face to face with two young German soldiers, also dusting themselves down and staring in disbelief at what had been uncovered. Ellie was still half-asleep. She panicked and freed herself from my clasp and then started to run around the crater. One soldier clumsily tried to pull his rifle from over his shoulder as if he had never had to do it before and started vomiting the word HALT over and over again with guttural disgust, waving his gun angrily in the direction of the tiny girl.

"She continued to run and stumble in panic and then BANG! She was gone with a single shot in the middle of the back, ripping right through to the front and dropping her on the spot in a pool of blood. It was total horror for me. This sweet little girl who had been such a close friend for that period suddenly vaporised in a moment of mindless impurity. I was devastated and resigned. The tears ripped out my lungs and heart as I stood up, put my hands behind my head and walked out towards the soldiers. They grabbed me, shook me back and forth and shouted abuse in my face."

"We've got a black one here, my first black Jew. Might get a promotion for this one."

"It was just a joke to them. They tied my hands behind my back and marched me through the rubble of the streets like a wild animal on display. I could see though from the tatty look of the soldiers and the rubble everywhere, this was a war they definitely were not winning. It filled me with joy, even though I knew I likely had only a very short time to live."

"Do you know when this was?"

"Not exactly, but I do know that the fighting ended a few weeks after my capture, at least in the area that I was finally taken to."

"What happened next?"

"They were very disorganised. I thought I would be interrogated or taken to a nasty police station but there was none of that. They kept me locked up for one night and then bundled me on a train, a wooden cattle train absolutely jam-packed with people, all with their little yellow stars. I wore mine proudly. I would have chosen being one of the persecuted every day of the week over and above becoming a mindless animal destroying human souls like disposable crockery."

"That's so incredibly brave."

"It's just standing up for what you believe in. If you honestly believe it then you have no choice anyway because you couldn't suddenly start believing the opposite."

"Well your father did," replied Ed, wondering if he had pushed the boat out a bit too far, nervously aware of the sound of their feet squelching along in the sand. There was a brief silence before she replied.

"You're right. In fact that became incredibly clear to me when, after two days of agonising discomfort in the train, we arrived at our destination and started to be unpacked like a delivery of coal bags. We jumped down from the train in little clumps of people, some falling and getting crushed by the next group that jumped down. Then we were funnelled like sheep into lines, all facing the train. Inside the carriages you could see the corpses lying motionless, the faeces and urine running between their pained bodies, dripping across the slats and out from the open doors onto those lucky enough to be trampled to death. That was our dignity and pride draining from those carriages right there.

"All around the vicious dogs barked on their strained leads and the guards shouted with terrifying violence. Then I saw my father in his Nazi uniform, rifle in hand. I cried out to him,

"VATER! VATER! It's me, Yedida, Yedida."

"He looked away instantly, focussing on another part of the line, whilst another guard came over and started laughing.

"Father? He's your father is he, you fucking piece of shit. I've heard it all now. SHUT THE FUCK UP," he yelled as he smacked me in the kidney as hard as he could with the butt of his rifle. It crippled me, doubling me up in two but luckily the people either side caught my arms and held me upright. One whispered in my ear in German mixed with Hungarian. 'Don't fall over, you'll be dead. I managed to keep hold of myself with their help and by the time they had marched us over for selection, I was able to stand on my own. I had to walk past my father in the array of guards. I just looked ahead and ignored him."

"I really have no idea how you survived this, Yedida."

"It wasn't easy. Anyway, soon I was in a big wooden hut and dressed in a revolting itchy, stripy uniform. It was disgusting. Every day we got up at the crack of dawn, marched for two hours, worked until dusk and then marched back. People were dying everywhere, all around at every point during the day. It was simply terrifying. These people had been stripped of every ounce of dignity. Everything eroded away at them, from the cold and cramped discomfort of the hut, the agonisingly humiliating open-plan toilets, the slave labour and the cruelty. It chipped away at one's deepest psyche leaving only a shell, a zombie of death."

"I cannot imagine all that, on such a grand scale as well," replied Ed, looking down at his feet as they indented the fine grained red sand, one after the other. He glanced behind him to see them disappear into a perfectly smooth surface, just like he remembered from one of his previous communities. Yedida continued,

"It might have been on a grand scale but we all experienced it as individuals. People who I've met since tend to refer to the macro rather than the micro view. They refer to it like it was a school of fish or something. It's much more horrific if you start to think about every single individual story. Everybody had their own very personal tale and they were all as heartbreaking as the next," said Yedida emotionally.

"There was one middle-aged woman I met early on. She was quieter than the rest, very solitary and defensive. I never knew her name but she told me her story one day in the strictest confidence. She used to sit alone outside the hut on the uncomfortable ground for hours, staring into space like someone in a trance. Winter was coming in and it was starting to get much colder. One day I went over and sat beside her.

"It's cold out here, you're not helping yourself. Come inside, at least there's a tiny bit of warmth from the stove and the other people."

"She sat motionless, not even turning her head. I put my arm on her shoulder and reassuringly tried to lure her inside. She turned to look at me, her piercing eyes looking even more pronounced with her prominent malnourished cheek bones and shaved head.

"I don't even deserve that. The hut is more than I am worth. You people are at least noble victims. Maybe you'll get gassed finally, but at least you would be able to do that with innocence and pride."

"What do you mean?" I asked, "We're all equal now - we stand together in the face of this adversity. Come inside."

"I can't, really. I should be alone. If I told you my story you would agree," she replied.

"What story?"

"I'll tell you but you must promise that you'll tell no one else. Please?" begged the frail individual.

"Okay, but only if you feel it'll help you. I don't want to know for knowing's sake. I just want to help you."

"Up until a few months ago I was a regular German woman. My husband was a war hero, killed at Stalingrad and my son, my beloved son, Jürgen was living his dream."

"Your husband was a soldier, a German soldier?"

"Yes. Worse though, was my son. He was doing very well in the Hitler-Jugend and I was supporting his dream. I believed in the whole thing, his training and development as someone who could be a servant of the Fuhrer. I was as fanatical as him and Hitler was my hero, even though I was covering up the basic fact that I had a Jewish grandparent. We had framed photos of Hitler in every room and went to all the rallies and events. We were devout to the religion, seduced by the powerful illusion. Then Jürgen came home one day and told me he had been funnelled off into the Wafen SS. He told me how the authorities had identified him as a 'big, tall, strong Aryan boy' and complimented him on how ruthless he had been in his training. He was to report for duty at the end of the month. In the meantime he'd been given some time off to be with his family.

"I was so happy and yet so extraordinarily sad. I didn't want him to join such a brutal section of the German army. I knew about the camps and what went on there from my husband's gossip and really didn't want to see Jürgen involved in all that. I burst into tears and didn't know what to say to him. I hugged him with all my being, grabbed him by the shoulders, looked into his eyes and told him how much I loved him. He didn't respond at all, totally cold and unemotional, not at all like he had been as a little boy years earlier. That training had changed him into a monster. It was ruthless and dehumanising. The stuff they had to do was unbelievable, from barbaric bare fist fights to competitions to see who could kill the most animals. They would put chickens and rabbits into an enclosure and send the boys in one by one. They each got a minute and the one who killed the most was the winner. Jürgen won every time, sometimes proudly bringing his blood stained shirt home to show me. That's why we don't stand a chance in here. That is how they are trained and we're the chickens. They have had every vestige of emotion, compassion and fairness pounded out of them in their Fuhrer training. They are nothing more than heartless killers now."

"But this doesn't make sense. How did you end up in here?"

"I just got to a point where I couldn't live the lie anymore. Not only was I suffering but my son had been converted into a machine whilst tens of thousands of people were being deported every week. I knew where they were going and I just cracked. I went down to the police station and handed myself in. I knew that would at least stop one SS officer from being recruited. Maybe it could have also saved his life, I don't know. I do know he was arrested as well though. I saw him being taken into the cells as I was being led out to the train station. He spat at me and tried to 'SIEG HEIL' as much as he could in handcuffs. I just told him he was as Jewish as me and that now he could see the lie we had been living for the last ten years. Reality would overcome illusion finally."

"I didn't know what to say to her. It was such an extraordinary story. I just comforted her as best I could, told her a little of my life and advised her to go inside. She didn't come in until much later."

"Did she tell anyone else?"

"No, not to my knowledge. I certainly didn't pass it around either. She wasn't around for much longer anyway. A few days later I saw her running away from the hut towards the fence. 'HALT' 'HALT' 'HALT' rang out before a single shot burst into her head as she approached the fence. At least that was an end for her. I'm sure she felt better for having purged and offloaded her story. I had no idea how she lived with that at all."

"To be honest, Yedida, I have no idea how you lived with all that either. What a view of humanity in a very short period of time," replied Ed.

"Yes, it wasn't easy. When I was a young girl I read a lot of novels and really looked forward to discovering the moral of the story or finding out how the characters were rescued, enlightened or gained salvation. In the camps, however, it was completely different, tragedy following tragedy, day after day, month after month, and year after year. No happy ending. It was truly devastating, a real book of horrors. I tried to be strong and tried to keep going and be positive. I put everything into it, losing count of time, day after day after day. Then one morning, they were all gone, every one those SS pigs. We were left roaming around the camp stepping over meatless shrivelled bodies, all with our yellow stars and stripy uniforms. It was like a surreal scene from another planet. We had got so used to the tormentors and then to suddenly not have them there was like walking without a floor. It was a complete shock. Then the Russians came and started to feed us and assess the situation. They raided the local town for clothes and we all got much more comfortable outfits to wear. Hence, this white trouser suit I am wearing now, and for the rest of eternity."

"But weren't you safe then? What happened?"

"A few days later I got terribly ill, like a tidal wave of pain and sickness to my innermost core. I remember being up and about one day and then flat on my back on a stretcher the next. I don't even remember dying. I must have just blacked out and been in a coma."

Ed was lost for words, shocked at what some people had to endure in their lifetimes. How could there possibly be a god in any world where there was such suffering? There and then his journey with religion ended with abrupt disillusionment.

"Don't you think people like this should never be forgiven though, I mean, those that have committed absolutely unthinkable crimes against other people?"

"That's certainly a thought that one starts with but then where would it all end? We cannot choose to hate forever. Then there really would be no hope."

"I'm not sure I could stop myself hating them with a vengeance forever, Yedida."

"Hatred and vengeance are feelings that eat away at one's own inner being as much as it is projected outwards. There is a reason people use the term, 'consumed by hatred'. It has no positive function whatsoever for the 'hater' and just drags remnants of the past negativity into the present. I don't hate them, blame them, resent them or forgive them. Most of all I do not want the repugnantly unfavourable elements of their psyche in my inner consciousness. It's more about trying to understand them. Up to a point, I can see how a generation of civilised Germans could have been hijacked by a crackpot leadership with oppressive means of persuasion. Make them believe in a superiority based on the demonisation of others, pushing the belief that the economic suffering is because these 'aliens' were taking more than their fair share. Then build such an oppressive wall of fear around them that they are terrified to disagree to the point of convincing themselves of the validity of the message. Then they will either join the ranks or sit on the sidelines and condone the consequences. As long as they felt secure and comfortable why shouldn't they have turned a blind eye to the odd group of Jews being marched off or the odd barbed wire camp in their very back yard? Denial is a powerful tool in the hands of evil."

"It sounds like you are saying it was all okay," stated Ed strongly, noticing the tunnel was veering on a curve slightly to the left.

"I'm not looking to justify it at all. The most we can ever hope for now is to understand it. How could such negative brainwashing be possible in an educated society? What strands of weakness can be common to so many individuals? I put it down to power and greed at the top and subservience, fear and denial at the bottom. These elements went hand in hand not only with the Nazi regime but also with the kidnapping and victimisation of my distant relatives. They were taken without mercy or conscience, ripped from their homeland and separated from their bloodline and soil. Inspired by greed and condoned en masse with subservience, fear and denial, we had plumbers, postmen, lawyers and janitors becoming death camp perpetrators. They killed me, murdered my mother and destroyed my country, along with god knows how many other innocent people. Nothing can change that. It is history and in the past. What we have to do now is put ourselves in a position where we can prevent that happening again, for a whole society to become completely brainwashed into a belief that can create a pseudo justification for mass murder and slaughter," replied Yedida emotionally, slightly raising her voice.

"Well isn't religion the same in that it brainwashes whole swathes of the community?"

"Exactly. Power, fear, guilt, manipulation, obedience, self-negation and servitude. They all play their part. However, we can't confuse all religions with mass negativity such as the Nazi ideology. Of course the human pattern of subservience is similar but the outward message can be very different, even sometimes positive," replied Yedida.

"I hear you there. You've really got a well-rounded and wise attitude to it all. One question though. I noticed there was an SS guard in the crowd yesterday. How can you possibly interact with him?"

"Like I say, you can't hang onto things too long or else you'd never be free. It was never easy to speak with him or share any space with him to begin with but that's no different to what a lot of the Jewish survivors had to go through when they returned to their homes in Germany, Hungary and Poland. I'm sure they walked down the street concerned that every postman and policeman had previously been a Nazi. Truth is that Niklas, the SS guard, was as much a victim of the whole thing as everyone else. He was so damaged by everything he saw that he killed himself. He had been studying medicine when he got drafted into the army and suddenly found himself in a position to obey orders or die. When the orders got beyond the realm of his personal morality he felt suicide was the only choice."

"You're probably right. Jews returning to Germany and Poland would have found it tough but there were a lot relocated by the British in Palestine. That all got a bit confrontational. What did you think of all that when you heard it?"

"Well the first I heard of that was from an English soldier who had been killed in a Jewish terrorist attack on the British at the King David hotel in Jerusalem. He told me about a Jewish group called the Irgun who had carried out that attack, and many more, trying to force the British out and assure an armed Israel state in Palestine. Apparently it is still one of the largest terrorist attacks in Israel ever. I was shocked and disappointed. After all the violence and oppression we had endured, we were doing the exact same thing to others. I felt we had lost our innocence and had been perverted away from the righteous peaceful path and onto one that demeaned our wisdom and depth as a people. It's only my personal standpoint, but I was frankly disappointed."

"Do you think it's wrong then?"

"It's not about right or wrong. Being oppressed and persecuted gives a deeper understanding of how painful it is to be in that situation. We should rise above it with wisdom and an understanding of how it should never be inflicted upon others. Anger is an emotion of unwise stupidity whilst oppression and persecution is the language of the fascist. There's no place for any of that in a civilised world."

"I agree. It would certainly be an improvement if people took an ethical lead rather than a physical one based on brute force," replied Ed, noticing the breeze in the tunnels getting stronger as they proceeded.

"It's certainly a complex issue. Anyway, what about yourself, Ed? What sort of life did you have?" enquired Yedida with a gentle, but authoritative tone, changing the subject.

"Well I have to say, my life has nowhere near as much shocking content. In fact, you'll probably nod off if I even begin telling you about it," reflected Ed ironically. Yedida, however, was having none of it and soon Ed was into the whole saga of solar-powered lamps and tortoises. Before they knew it, they were approaching their first major obstacle on their route.

Chapter 13
Marks in the sand

"How in hell are we going to get across that?" he exclaimed with disbelief, staring at the powerful gushing hurricane of wind enveloping the transience tunnel in front of them.

"It'll be fine. Come over and I'll show you what we're dealing with," she said as she led him to the entrance and pointed up at the matrix of solid vines that clung firmly to the walls and ceiling. They stretched from the doorway upwards in every direction around the inner surface of the tunnel.

"We need to squeeze between the vines and the walls and make our way over to the entrance on the other side which is about two hundred metres down the way."

"You're kidding, right? How is that going to be possible? There's no way those vines will be strong enough," pleaded Ed, a little shocked by the proposition and startled at the prospect of crawling through the small space between the vines and the walls.

"Of course they're strong enough. It's a bit of a squeeze but it's definitely okay. I've done it a few times before, both directions."

"That's terrifying. I don't like the look of it, but what choice do I have? I guess if we go back, I'll have to use that ladder again, is that right?"

"Yep, that's kind of about the shape of things. Well are you up for it?" queried Yedida.

"I guess so. Another bizarre step along the way. Let's go. I assume you'll go first?"

"Yes, I'll go first. Follow me. When we get over the top of the tunnel we have to turn around so we are going feet first. Otherwise by the time we get down to the doorway we'll be upside down, and it's then too difficult to turn round and jump out into the side tunnel."

"Okay, I'll just copy what you do."

"Cool. Be careful though. The first bit before you get

properly under the vines is the most dangerous. Same at the other end, you need to be really careful jumping into the side tunnel. There are a lot of gusts that side."

Yedida went to the opening and edged along the ledge slightly into the tunnel with her back to the wall.

"Follow me, Ed," she exclaimed, as she started to clamber and climb up between the vines and wall, the wind rushing past and pushing her loose clothes tight against her body. Ed followed suit and nervously stepped out onto the ledge and pulled himself up, higher and higher around the curvature of the tunnel. He looked down on the violent gushing river of wind and noticed in the distance the all too familiar bright white light. It was smaller than he remembered.

"Is this a different tunnel than the one Donald got me from, Yedida?" shouted Ed.

"Pardon? I can't hear you! Shout louder," yelled the young lady, now almost at the top of the curved roof, and a few feet ahead of Ed.

"Is this a different tunnel from the one Donald got me from?" he shouted again.

"Yes, it is. When you get up here, look down into the stream - it's quite a sight," shouted Yedida in a penetrating voice before adding, "We need to crawl along the top in line with the tunnel. Then we'll turn around and go backwards down towards the door. Can you hear me?"

"Yes, I can. No problem," bawled Ed, as he too got to the top part of the tunnel and began to crawl along the vines against the flow of the gushing current. He looked down into the violent wind stream, shocked to see bodies being whisked along in the current, helplessly tossed every way up. He continued to keep an eye on Yedida who was beginning to twist around sideways and descend down the other side, feet first. He followed suit, and before he could even have time to get nervous, he was jumping down backwards and was pulled back into the side tunnel by the assured lady.

Soon they had dusted themselves down in the sheltered area.

"Right, I'll make some marks in the sand, so if you come back this way on your own, you know it's the right tunnel," stated Yedida as she bent down and started to dig a small hole beside the wall. As she dug away so the hole filled in, forging itself back into a smooth surface.

"Oh, I forgot about that. The sand won't allow us to do that," she exclaimed despairingly.

"Anyway, it might get disturbed by someone else in time anyway," replied Ed, before peering in between the vines at the remarkable black wall.

"Look, Yedida, there's a small crevice in the wall here. We could fill that with sand and that would be another landmark. I could even put my watch in it."

Ed pointed to a small opening in the rock hidden behind the vines. Yedida got up and looked at the hole.

"Yes, that's a much better idea. You should check the time on your watch now though, to see how long you have left."

"I agree," replied Ed looking down at the big clock face to realise he had well over a day left, almost two. He took off the watch and put it in the hole on top of some of the sand that Yedida had just placed there.

"Another thing to look out for is the white vines in the tunnel that mark this entrance. As I understand it, this is one of the only places that has them, so it's a good way to ensure you're in the right place if you need to get back to see the Viking."

"Why would I need to visit him twice anyway?" asked Ed.

"I'm not sure, it's just that people often end up visiting him more than once, but maybe you won't need to."

"I assume you mean after another transience?"

"Exactly. Apparently he can have some influence over where in the tunnels you come back to. I don't know how he does it though."

The duo proceeded forward along the vine-clad tunnel and into the distance with an eager intent.

"Did you see the bodies whizzing by back there? It is one very powerful stream, Ed."

"I can't believe it. I guess that was us at one point or another?"

"Yes and soon it will be you again. Luckily there is never much of a memory of all that, apart from a strange dream-like recollection."

"That's good at least. I didn't notice any animals though. Are there any?"

"Not in these tunnels. I'm not sure how it works. Maybe this whole process is only for human souls. Some say that the soul stays with the body for a few days which would explain why we see the bodies in the tunnel and also why we have this cycle of transience and rebirth."

Ed thought about what Yedida was saying and how all this had suddenly become logical and believable to him since his death. Trying to believe any of it in his previous life would have been a lot harder indeed. His mind wandered to the vines and tunnels and how they were all so similar.

"Crazy how all these tunnels are so alike don't you think?" enquired Ed.

"Yes, I suppose so. It means you really have to memorise the route we are about to take in case you need to travel this way again," replied Yedida.

"Yes, good point."

"Indeed. Do you know the 'mummy daddy' roll?"

"Is that a dance?" replied Ed.

"No silly, it's a drum roll: Mum-my – Dad-dy, right, right, left, left. That's our route, that's what you need to remember. There are four turns in that sequence which correspond to the tunnel intersections. Have you got it?"

"Yes, I'll remember that."

"Mum-my – Dad-dy, right, right, left, left," reiterated Yedida.

"Yes, yes, I've got it," grumbled Ed and they continued on their way, trudging through the perfect sand. They remained silent for some while as they squelched onwards.

"How do people know how long they've been here? Do you count your sleep cycles? What do you do?"

"That's the best way, although I gave up interest after forty or so years. You would always get an approximate guideline from new arrivals telling you what year they died. To be honest, I am not overly interested what year it is. Why do I need to know? I haven't even asked you what year you died, have I?"

"That's true. For your reference though, just in case you do need to know, I died in 2009."

"Thanks."

"Not a problem. Anyway, I was meaning to ask. Bearing in mind how long you've been here and how much opportunity for reflection you've had, do you think there is some great omnipotent force manipulating us into this transient cycle, judging us for what we did or didn't do, punishing or rewarding us accordingly?"

"Honestly, Ed I don't think so. The people here are so varied, from serial killers to charity workers, murderers and criminals to nurses and Samaritans. It is just too much of a cross-section to be anything like that. I honestly think it's just random and that transient souls cannot live in a new body for more than a few days without losing their energy, fading or else becoming permanent. I really think that's all there is to it and there are a lot of us down here that agree. People on the outside were always talking about enlightenment, nirvana or something mystical to veneer over their true selves.

Maybe realising that 'this is your lot' is all there is to it and that we are nothing more or less than the reality we are in at any time."

"What about having to solve the mystery of why this is happening?"

"Maybe there is no mystery. It just is as it is."

"Then I would be chasing a folly."

"Possibly. It might also be that searching for the answer helps you understand the situation as it is, rather than seeking to influence change. The more you travel between transient embodiments, then the more you learn and develop naturally. Perhaps instead of realising there's an external mystery or question you need to penetrate, it might be that you need to discover something about yourself. Maybe the answer to a question – if there is a question in the first place – is within you all the time," replied Yedida with introspective wisdom.

"Is that what you felt personally?"

"Yes, for sure. I spent some time feeling that there must have been something up with me and my people for us to have been treated like that. Why else would people act en masse and make us slaves or send us to concentration camps and murder or exploit us? I couldn't unravel how that could be possible without blaming myself and demeaning my own self worth. Even in the camp whilst I was still alive, I felt that if I acted well and tried to please them then I would stand a better chance. How wrong that was. It was no more than pleading for mercy by compliance. It took a long time once I was here, to balance my thoughts, feelings, sensations and intuitions on the whole thing and stop blaming myself."

"That can't have been easy. How on earth did you come to terms with what your father did?" queried Ed, his memory jogged unconsciously by the 'mummy daddy' roll that Yedida had used to illustrate the route.

"That was a very difficult one to unravel without self blame. He had been a hard-working man but was always a bit remote from us. He would work every day of the week, only surfacing a bit in the evenings. It meant that we were not that close which I suppose made it easier for him to switch sides like he did. I know he was getting abused for having a black wife and daughter, and his shop had been attacked a couple of times. Maybe he just got sick of being scared and decided to do what he did. Truth is, he was as powerless as a doormat with all the ambition of a napkin."

"Ha, nice one. Of everything I've heard so far though, all the horror stories from various people and all the bad and negative things, this is the thing that disturbs me the most. How could he have abandoned you like that? What a scumbag and coward – if you don't mind me saying?" replied Ed emotionally.

"No, I don't mind. It still hurts. I really hope he never arrives here. It is resolved in my mind on the rational side but it would be a hard cross to bear."

"What happens in situations like that, when people come face to face after an extreme conflict in their human lives?"

"Well one thing's for sure, if they stay here then they have time on their side to be honest and understand the issues. If they're reluctant, they usually decide to move on. If they do stay, they have to sit together in a debating group. It can take decades to understand all the complex feelings but as time moves on, things nearly always get resolved."

"I find it hard to imagine how some situations and relationships could ever be reconciled."

"Absolutely. It's sometimes very problematic. There's hope though, if someone comes to terms with their wrongs and acknowledges them and is at the same time forgiven, or at least understood by their victims. In here, people somehow seem to have more empathy and respect for each other. They're less selfish and tend to have their perspectives on life more in balance. There are a lot of things that cause conflict in the physical world such as sex, ambition, greed, lust, gluttony, ownership and so on. We simply don't have that here. Without it, people seem to adjust to one another in a more humane and natural way. Once they've been here for a while, they get used to that way of life, making it easier to apologise and forgive or understand, regardless of the misdemeanour."

"Isn't it a bit of an over-simplistic or idealistically naive approach?"

"What's the alternative? Eternal conflict? Civilisation seemed to specialise in never-ending bitter resentments that would fester from generation to generation, destroying people's hopes and prospects. Surely it's better to bury the hatchet and move on with a clean slate, don't you think?"

"Yes, I do. It would obviously be preferable, some sort of redemption at the gates of heaven - not that this is heaven of course."

"Yes, redemption - but one you have to work for, not just a clean slate for being a disciple of something."

"Pity that mankind can't learn from the work you do in here. Such potential as a species but certainly not destined to realise it. Makes me feel almost relieved to be dead. Talking of heaven, don't some people think they have arrived in heaven when they first arrive?"

"Sometimes. They soon realise it isn't though when they

see who is here. Then we have to convince them it isn't hell either."

"Ha, yes. I guess so." replied Ed as they carried on along the way through the dimly lit vine tunnels.

Chapter 14
ONE, TWO, PUSH

The duo had come to a halt and rested against the vines at a complex intersection. It had been a tiring uphill walk since the tunnel crossing and Ed felt it in his legs. They sat for some while in a calm meditative state, comforted by a reassuring silence. Ed felt the soft thumping of his heart and noticed the delicate exhalations from his mouth passing his dry lips.

"Listen," whispered Ed, piercing the silence.

"What? Listen to what?"

"Exactly. It's perfectly silent. You don't notice it so much when you're squelching along in the sand but there's a pin drop hush, not even the faintest rumbling," replied Ed, as they both fell paused to listen to the emptiness.

"It's beautiful, eh, something to behold," said Yedida, her voice softly rippling into the quiet.

"I don't remember that too many times when I was alive. A few times we went camping when I was a kid but there was always some sort of animal bleating or a couple of foxes having noisy liaisons. This is quite special though."

Once again the couple fell silent and Ed began to reflect a little on the environment. The temperature had been consistent, approximately around twenty degrees, not too hot and not too cold. However, as they proceeded on their current journey it started to chill by a degree or so. Ed was very sensitive to temperatures and thought back fondly on the friendly battles he had with his wife to gain control of hotel room air conditioning thermostats when they visited warm countries.

He put his hands through the vines and onto the shiny granite stone walls, first his left, then his right. It felt cool to the touch but not as cold as he imagined stone should be. He rubbed his hands up and down over the uneven but smooth, almost polished surface. It felt glorious, making his hands tingle as they moved back and forth, to and fro.

"It's awe inspiring isn't it," he exclaimed, pulling his hands away and between the vines to turn and look at Yedida.

"Yes, really nice to touch, eh. Have you noticed it's getting a little chillier as well?"

"I did notice that. Is it much colder where the Viking lives?"

"Not much, maybe a degree or so. You won't notice it once you've been there a while."

Ed started to feel a little trepidation about his visit. Everything seemed to be masked in uncertainty and it was starting to make him feel disoriented once more.

"It's weird being in here, caught in this whole cycle of things, Yedida."

"In what way? I thought you'd been dealing with it really well up to now."

"Yes, but that's because I keep getting caught up in the mystery of the whole thing and blot out what's really happening. It's a real quandary and everyone I've met so far seems to have a different view about it. It makes me very ambivalent and very depressed about everything, all this guesswork, inconclusiveness and uncertainty. It's psychologically exhausting," replied Ed despairingly, his posture slightly slumped.

"Whatever you do, Ed, you have to believe that one day you will become enlightened. You have an awareness and consciousness that helps you make definite decisions. Even if you don't really know what the decisions are about, they are decisions all the same and they put you in a position of power. However minimal that power might be is irrelevant. You still have something and you have to cling onto that for all it's worth."

"You're right. I am getting down on myself. I really need to snap out of it."

"Look how far you've come already. The tortoise and then the other tunnels; the cat, the hound and the determination to climb the ladder and come all the way here. The glass is half full, not half empty. Come on, let's go. We should be on our way."

181

Yedida started to head off into the tunnel.

"Thanks, Yedida. You are a real support."

"I've had to do it before. Don't worry. The worst that can happen is that you get used to all this. Anyway, from here the journey gets a little trickier. The tunnel gets smaller and smaller and by the end we have to crawl through it. It becomes rather tight and we'll have to push ourselves through the last section. I hope you're not claustrophobic," announced Yedida.

"Not particularly but I don't altogether like the idea. How tight does it get?"

"Pretty tight. First timers feel they'll never be able to push themselves through. It feels kind of elasticated and pushes in against you but that's only for the last few yards."

"Okay. Another step along the way. Is there anything after that?" enquired Ed.

"That's where I'll leave you, the other side of the tunnel."

"Oh," replied Ed with more than a degree of sadness in his voice. He looked down the length of the tunnel and saw how it narrowed into the distance. The vines and lights also diminished in size proportionally making it look like a strange experiment with the 'free transform' tool in Photoshop. Soon they were off into the tunnel, bending their heads and stooping over as it got smaller and smaller. Soon they were on all fours crawling, arms stretched out in front of them in the soft sand, Ed first followed by Yedida. The sturdy vines got tighter and tighter across Ed's back as he crawled deeper into the tunnel. He started to feel more like a champagne cork than a reincarnated hunting hound or suicidal Tortoise.

"Are you sure we can get through this, Yedida? I might be too big," enquired Ed anxiously.

"Yes, I've taken bigger people through than you, don't worry. If you feel you're stuck I'll help to push you," she replied reassuringly.

"Thanks. I think that moment might be coming."

"There's not far to go, push, just push," shouted Yedida.

"I am, but I feel like I'm going nowhere," groaned Ed

despairingly, feeling he was getting stuck in the restraint of the tunnel.

"Okay. I'll push. You just have to believe. We're nearly there. When I count to three, you push and I'll give a shove on your feet from behind."

"On three or four?"

"On three, exactly on three."

"Right then, let's do this," anguished Ed, as he desperately tried to muster more strength.

ONE, TWO, PUSH.....

  ONE, TWO, PUSH.....

    ONE, TWO, PUSH.....

      ONE, TWO, PUSH.

With this push, Ed's hands and head popped out into an open chamber. He felt dazed, like a new born puppy.

ONE, TWO, PUSH.....

  ONE, TWO, PUSH.

All of a sudden he was rocketed from the tunnel like a giant pea from an oversized elasticated pea shooter. The chamber floor was about two feet below the opening, and he landed hard, flat on his face in the sand. Tiny grains clogged his mouth, nostrils and ears. He picked himself up, spluttered, coughed and then saw Yedida's arms poking from the hole. He gave them a tug and she too shot from the tunnel towards him, pushing them both to the floor, culminating, with her landing on top. Quickly they got up, dusted themselves down and looked around the small space.

"Beautiful isn't it?" remarked Yedida, shaking sand from her silky hair.

"Yeah," replied Ed, as he looked round at the intriguing shiny black granite walls with seams of equally opposite white stone. The sand was a piquant two-tone red and white, almost in a leopard skin pattern. The chamber was circular and small with seven cave openings opposite from their point of arrival. Ed looked back to where they had come from and was shocked to see a full sized tunnel entrance diminishing off into the distance.

"Did you see that? Look, it's expanded! Did you notice it?"

"Once you're through and there's no one else in the tunnel, it switches to the opposite way around. It is bigger at this end and smaller at the other end for now, until I've gone back through it and then it reverts again."

"Is that why I can't go back?" enquired Ed.

"No. It's when you've done the next leg of your journey, that's when you can't come back, at least not without another transience. We need to go into the fourth cave from the left, Ed," stated Yedida, gesticulating with her arms.

"Why can't I come back after the next leg?"

"Apparently it's a one-way ticket. Anything we've discovered about the other side has been from people like you who have been there, then gone through another transience and landed back on our side."

"Okay," he replied as they counted off the caves and proceeded to the fourth one of the seven, all with uncut white granite archways around their side.

"Do the other caves lead anywhere?" queried Ed as they neared the entrance.

"Not to my knowledge. It just seems to be this one," replied Yedida knowingly.

Once inside, they were greeted by a small and strange man dressed in light brown robes and an odd pair of homemade blue canvas sandals. He stared down at the ground almost motionless his bald head brilliantly shiny like a polished gobstopper.

"This is the fortune teller. You need to meet him," stated Yedida slightly nervously. Ed looked around, wondering what this strange fortune teller was all about, sitting inside a small cave with no entrances or exits other than the one they'd entered through. The odd man started to shuffle towards them, his arms jutting out from the torn sleeves of his robes. Ed noticed he had no hands, just round stubs where the wrist would have been. They were battered and worn and looked like they'd been amputated in a very messy and haphazard manner.

"I need to leave now, Ed. Give me a hug. It's been fantastic meeting you. Thanks for being a sympathetic listener," said Yedida, as she grabbed Ed by the shoulder, span him around, hugged him and left the small enclosure in a hurry.

"He is deaf, dumb and blind. You need to grab both his arms with your hands and you will find out what to do next. Good luck my friend, enjoy Denmark," she shouted as she sped along the tunnel and back towards her home.

She disappeared from sight before Ed could respond with much more than 'goodbye, thanks for everything'. He was shocked at the sudden turn of events, and felt sad to have lost her companionship. What's more, who was this man, why would he need him to observe his future and what did she mean by 'Denmark'? Besides, how the hell would he do it if he was deaf and dumb? Reluctantly he reached out towards the man, grabbing the two sticky, sweaty stubs, noticing the empty eye sockets covered in scarred skin. Instantly he was pulled with violence into a fast moving vacuum, like a human canon ball.

He couldn't see or hear anything apart from the super-loud rushing noise that virtually penetrated his ear drums. Next he was in a cavernous blue ceramic bowl, enveloped by total silence. A blinding sun shone warmly on his face. He drifted in and out of consciousness, things getting fuzzier and fuzzier until he finally awoke between two strange red brick walls. He looked down and saw an urban street scene; a deprived area with young men brandishing automatic weapons. They were firing randomly into the scruffy apartment block on the other side of the street. He felt like he was in an un-liberated East Berlin.

It had all the hallmarks of a war zone but not a war between countries, more a local riot or civil chaos gripped by lawlessness and anarchy. He was sinking down upon a small open-top lift, but when he looked down there was just a cobbled street, and no lift. He descended in relation to the building opposite but could still see over the wall next to him. He saw the young thugs fire their guns into the building once more. Shots were exchanged with the occupants, before the fighters inside changed sides and started killing the other residents.

He feared for his own life as he got lower and lower, and

then out of the blue, commuters started passing between the two walls either side of him, brushing shoulders and pushing him rudely. He followed them, away from the young armed men and found himself crossing Brooklyn bridge with hundreds of commuters, packed in neat uniform lines. He chatted freely to his comrades and noticed that he too wore a dark blue pinstripe suit and duffle coat. The comrades commented on how hard it was living in such a deprived area of town and that they must really get out and escape.

Once over the bridge he found himself in an old Georgian style house. It was dark and he struggled with a huge bag of bongo drums. Dazed, confused and with no money he reached for the light switch, illuminating a bare and violently bright bulb. An angry voice shouted loudly and he was punched in the back of his head knocking him down. He came around to realise someone had nailed his duffle coat to the table, imprisoning him in a small kitchen. He was tormented and abused by his captors for waking their leader, Shirali. They ripped his coat from the table and kicked him out into the street, leaving him panic stricken, separated from his bag of bongos. He felt he must get back inside at any cost.

Nervously he sat in the street wondering how to get his drums back. Shirali emerged from the house to tell him he would never see them again, showing off his revolting oversized teeth in the process. The desperation grew stronger and stronger as he ran up and down the street like a crazed dog. Then a loud bang, a kaleidoscope of darkness and finally silence.

"Sorry about that."
　　"Sorry about that."
　　　　"Sorry about that."
Soon the voice started to penetrate into Ed's consciousness.

"Jumping over is never easy. I imagine you had a horrible dream. Was it the Brooklyn bridge one or the pyramids? I prefer the pyramid one myself."

"Urgghh." Ed stumbled up to his feet, catching sight of a

fine white sand floor and a brilliant white granite tunnel wall.

"Umpgh, that was a dream then? Thank goodness for that," he breathed, as he got to his feet to see himself standing in front of a small Indian man dressed in black silk Kota pyjamas.

"Yes, everyone who comes through the fortune teller has a nasty dream and thumping headache for an hour afterwards. Not ideal, but one must survive. That's a 'psyche jump' for you, eh? Welcome to Denmark."

"Denmark! I thought she was joking. Do you need to see my visa then?" replied Ed jokingly.

"No need for that down here. It's not 'that' Denmark anyway. It's just what we call this sector. How's your head anyway?"

"Arghh, yes, you're right, I've got a thumping headache," said Ed in reply, realising he had a throbbing gelatinous medicine ball on his shoulders.

"You would be here to meet the Viking, I assume?"

"Yes, I am. Can you take me to him?" queried Ed.

"Yes, for sure. It won't take long to get there, maybe twenty minutes or so if we keep a sprightly pace. Are you okay to walk?" enquired the mild mannered Indian gentleman.

"Yes, I'm fine. Let's go. I'm Ed."

"Hi, Ed. I am Pritvijaj," replied the man as they set off into the white granite tunnel.

"Does he speak English, Pritvijaj?" enquired Ed eagerly.

"Yep, that and dozens of other languages fluently. Mind you, he has had nine hundred years or more to fine-tune it," replied the gentle Indian man.

"Yes, I guess so. Time certainly helps, eh."

"He was on the other side for four hundred of those, in the Basheri community."

"Basheri? I don't know that one. I just came from Koan Dome."

"I know. You came through the Koan portal."

"You mean there's more than one entrance like that?"

"Yes, there are a few. We don't get many visitors though, mainly because they can't go back. Anyway, Koan, that's where I was. Lovely place, eh. I stayed there for twenty years or more, at a guess. Did you meet Yedida? Did you hear the choir?"

"Yes, the choir was incredible, as was Yedida. She showed me the way here."

"What a lovely person, so sweet."

"She's pure, what a soul," replied Ed as they continued into the white tunnel.

"Proof that you can survive anything with your dignity and pride intact. Anyway, Ed, what are you hoping to get from the Viking, what do you think he can do for you?"

"I'm wondering if I can go back and find out what happened, maybe change things? I don't know why, but I feel a strong impulse to pursue these ideas with the Viking," replied Ed thoughtfully.

"I'm sure he can help you. He is very instinctually insightful. Don't be surprised if he tells you what you are thinking before you even know it yourself."

"Sounds intriguing. I can't wait," replied Ed, as they turned a corner and into a similarly white tunnel, this one covered in deep black vines from top to bottom. Familiar lights in the walls cast an enchanting matrix of shadows across the fine white sand.

Chapter 15
Welcome to Denmark

Soon Ed was being whisked into a large white-walled circular room, equally decorated with dramatic back lit black vines. Arranged in a circle on the floor were dozens of white furry sheepskins, all vacant apart from one on Ed's left as he walked in.

"Ed, this is Jahani. Jahani, this is Ed. He's just arrived and was sent over by Yedida," announced Pritvijaj as he ushered Ed in further, before turning tail and leaving the room.

"Good. Welcome to Denmark. How much time do you have?" enquired the Viking directly, as he calmly stood up.

"I think I'm good for a couple of days, Jahani," replied Ed, as he went over towards the ancient man. As he got closer the first thing he noticed was his ancient looking, gnarled and wrinkled face, like he had been head-on in a blizzard for the whole nine hundred years since his death.

Greyish, gingery, brown hair shot out with profusion from all over his bulky head, long and slightly knotted locks flowing down past his chin and a fine beard that looked more like a waterfall flowing from his bottom lip. A fat and chunky moustache resided on his upper lip like a tatty Cuban cigar underneath a vast, round, bloodshot nose. A hard stare came from his intense deep set blue eyes focused all the more by the bedraggled and thicketed bushy eye brows. This was crowned with a pronounced and tall forehead making it look as though the top of his skull had been hydraulically raised up from inside. He was indeed a daunting sight of a man with a domineering presence. As he stood upright his powerful physique made Ed feel quite demure.

He looked down at the clothes on his muscular frame, a light brown fur skin over his broad shoulders, cut into a zig-zag finish at the bottom, covering a long sleeveless under jacket made from a canvas looking material, also cut in a zig-zag line just below his waist at the bottom. This covered fairly plain-looking cream leggings and knee-high, black, furry boots. Underneath the sleeveless jacket on top was an equally plain long sleeved, off-white shirt with two leather forearm protectors on each arm. In the corner, Ed could see a long-handled axe and the customary long-horned Viking helmet.

"I can see you are a lot more modern than me, Mr Trew," boomed the powerful-looking Viking.

"That's right - Mr Trew! How do you know my name?" exclaimed Ed with surprise.

"You'll get used to that. Come, sit down over here," replied the Viking as he shook Ed's hand and pointed him towards one of the animal fur seats. The thick hedge eyebrows danced on his face excitedly with every word as if they were actually speaking themselves.

"How did they get in here, Jahani? I thought there were no possessions?" enquired the solar power expert with regards the animal skin.

"They were my clothes. I died with them all on. It was a bloody cold night, you have no idea," exclaimed the Viking animatedly, as they both sat down a metre or so from one another on adjacent furry seats.

"I assume you're curious about your death and want to find out a little more about the circumstances? I'll tell you in advance though, I don't help anyone that killed themselves and left their children behind. It cannot be condoned at all."

"No. Don't worry, I didn't do that and yes, that's exactly it. I'd definitely like to know exactly what happened," replied Ed, noticing his oversized and magnificent hands, each finger looking like a baby's arm.

"I understand. It's most common in murder cases though, people wanting to know the exact details of who finished them off and why. Some people don't even know how they were killed. Do you know how and where you met your demise?" replied the Viking with a perfect 'middle England' voice, nurtured among many languages over the centuries.

"Yes, a car accident near Dummer in south England."

"Well, that'll make things a lot easier. Saves me doing any detective work," replied Jahani.

"What, like a Viking Sherlock Holmes?" retorted Ed.

"Yes, indeed. Anyway, we need to start with some words. Huayna, Huayna. Can you come in?" bellowed the Viking at the top of his voice towards the door. Soon a small Native American man entered the room and went over to Jahani.

"Huayna, Ed. Ed, Huayna, please meet one another," stated the Viking as the young man, dressed in a Mexican-looking Clint Eastwood shawl, curled up in a ball on the floor in front of him. Huayna looked at Ed blankly with as much emotion as a roast potato.

"He's Peruvian and doesn't speak a word of English. He was a coal miner but his real ability was as an acrobat. I bet you couldn't get into that position could you?" stated Jahani looking at the small man in front who had suddenly formed himself into a perfect ball.

"I couldn't. You're right. Why is he doing it though?" replied Ed.

"Come, get up and sit on him, he won't feel a thing."

"Sit on him. Why would I do that?"

"Trust me, just do it. It's how he got the nickname 'the chairman', after all."

"Whatever," replied Ed as he got up and sat upon the small man who didn't even flinch.

"Right, now hold my forearms and start reciting words to me, any words you like."

"Erm. Well, I won't even bother asking why. Last time this happened though I had a horrible dream. Is that going to happen again? I need some warning -the headache's only just going," replied Ed.

"No, nothing like that. Nothing at all. I just need to make a connection with you on another level. Huayna acts as a conductor for all the psychic energy. It won't take a minute," replied the elderly man as Ed reached forward, grabbed his arms and began reciting random words, immediately sensing an electric energy moving between the three of them.

"Ambidextrous, ambient, feeling, supervision, cold, terrified, medium, trough, bacon, meaningful, tenuous, promotion, slouch, hay, farm, journey, Saturday, phobia, trepidation, horn, Monday, watch, wind, fuelled, jelly, trench, ante, antenna, sagged, agent, moon, night, monk, priest, pressing, custard, aubergine, text, skid, perpendicular, science." Ed was bought to an abrupt halt.

"That's enough, that's enough. You can sit on the floor again now. Thanks, Huayna. You were on top form yet again," stated the Viking ironically, as the small man unravelled himself, stood up, and disappeared from the enclosure.

"If he doesn't speak English, then how did he know what you were saying?"

"Intuition possibly, more likely though was the fact that I was pointing at the door for him to leave," replied the Viking, as a big grin broke out into a face expanding smile causing his beard to ripple with the movement.

"Fair enough," replied Ed, also grinning as Jahani swept his hand over his moustache and down over his long beard as if he was pulling on a rope. Ed was glad to have finally met up with the Viking. He was starting to feel a lot more relaxed in his company and had stopped feeling quite so intimidated. He was certainly a gigantic man with a colossal presence but underneath he seemed to be a gentle heart in the body of a lion.

"Anyway, what did you discover about me with the words?" he asked.

"Nothing. It's just about opening the channels between us. Seemingly pointless but equally important in the grander scheme."

"Well that's good to know. What happens now? What can you do for me and what can I learn about this whole situation from you? I've come to understand you are the 'go to' guy for information in here, is that correct?"

"I've got to be honest with you, Ed. There's not a lot I can do for you this time round. You'll need to come back after another transience and then we can start to control things a little bit more. There are a few things you need to know. These are all very important points if we are to move on. You will need to kill yourself within two miles of where you originally died. It's important that you kill yourself and are not accidentally killed by an external influence. At the moment of death you need to be focussing on an object in your possession which you need to bring back with you. It can be anything, a dog collar, bow, anything. It's really important you focus on that object and try to stay consciously aware after death and during the first moments of the transience. Then when you come back to me, I can work on getting you back to approximately that same spot each time for you to find out a little more about your death. Unfortunately, all I can do this time is help out with trying to make you more agile on the other side. There is something we can do for that to ensure you are not a tortoise again or a snail or some such thing.'

"That's a relief. The tortoise was the worst. Beginner's luck I suppose."

"Maybe. Anyway, we should get a move on and get you on your way. No point in hanging around here for chit-chat. Let's go over to the tunnels and send you off," exclaimed the Viking as he got to his feet and ushered Ed up and over to the entrance of the room and into the tunnel past the vacant white furry rugs. Soon they were ascending some black rock stairs and entering a smaller tunnel, bright white granite perfectly polished like a marble bath. All along the long tunnel there were small holes in the floor, just about large enough to fit one person in. They walked calmly alongside the holes until the Viking drew them to a halt.

"Right, I think this one will do. I'm not going to tell you the significance of these holes for now but I most certainly will when you come back. Suffice to say, this one is a vertical drop and it will propel you into the transient stream below. It will be very quick and you will be whisked into your next embodiment."

"How difficult will it be to get back to see you again? I might end up in tunnels days away?" asked Ed curiously.

"Give me your jacket. As long as I keep that, when you depart there will be a high likelihood you will land within a day's travel or so of this location. Most people know of me within that radius, so you should be fine to find a way back," replied the Viking.

"Okay, here's my jacket. This is all going so quickly though. I'm not in a rush. There's so much I wanted to talk to you about, not least of all about being a Viking. Can't we just back up for a while?" enquired Ed.

"You'll be back. I've heard your words, you will be back. Trust me. Then we can spend some time together next time. If all goes to plan, that should be in a few days," replied the Viking.

"Okay then. I trust you. What do I do next?" replied Ed.

"Just sit on the edge of this hole facing away from where we walked and just jump in," replied the elder man as he folded the jacket in two and put it under his arm.

"Okay. Well here we go. Hope to see you again soooooooooooooooonnnn," replied Ed as he sat on the edge of the opening, accidently slipping in and disappearing from sight quicker than a meerkat down a pot hole.

Chapter 16
Biltong and smoked salmon

Ed came round to a barrage of noises that covered the complete spectrum, from Tarzan's monkey to an aviary of birds chirping in eighth notes. He felt restrained and struggled to move his arms or legs. Underneath and all around he could feel feathered, fidgety warmth that panicked and squirmed with desperation. He tried to turn over to get a better view but remained completely constrained. As he came round more, he could see a muted light leaking through beige material that completely surrounded them.

Then in a flash the material above opened, letting in floods of light that momentarily dazzled and blinded him. Instinctually he turned his head away, offended by its perverse intensity. Then he saw an overpoweringly large hand reaching through the hole and down over his whole body. Without thinking, he nipped at the invader, forcing it to retreat slightly before reaching down again, this time with more confidence and authority. All around the fervent impassioned noises rang out in a chorus of panic. He felt four massive fingers wrap around and underneath his body whilst a fat thumb completed the lock on top. He was then raised up gently out through the opening. As he fought and squirmed he began to realise he was being removed from a sort of cloth bag filled with other animals. From the noises, he assumed these were some sort of flying creatures, feathered animals, fowl or game.

Hopefully not a sparrow, he thought as he was pulled from the bag into an all-consuming bath of vivid light.

As his body span with the movement of the hand, he found it hard to focus on his surroundings until he finally came to rest facing a middle aged and plump man full in the face.

"Don't worry, little fella," said the man, as he moved him down from in front of his face onto his knee, "we're not going to hurt you; you'll soon be back in your nest," he said, as he turned him up, facing towards the top of the trees, bringing a second man into view. He was slightly younger, but wore a ridiculous red bobble hat which fought hard to restrain a full head of blond hair flowing out in every direction. The wind tossed it this way and that, as Ed started to feel the chill of the breeze.

"With this, we can have a good record of where they live and breed over their lifetime. With a rare bird like this it is really important. They're just starting to reach sustainable numbers after so many were wiped out with pesticides," proclaimed the man to his companion as he withdrew a medium pair of pliers with bright red handles from a small bag.

"Really? That's great news. What do you know about this family?" replied the first man.

"Well this one's quite old now, forty or fifty days or more I think. The mother was tagged living in Chichester cathedral a few years back."

"Really, that far away."

Ed listened intently, reassured by the fact that they were only tagging him and not ripping off his limbs with the pliers. It was still a mystery what bird he was exactly, but it was useful to know he was rare.

"Yes, not surprising though," replied the man in the red hat as he took Ed's right leg and held it still in front of him before adding,

"They are fast little mothers. Highest recorded speed of these is over two hundred miles an hour."

"You have got to be kidding," responded the man, as Ed mused at the possibilities.

Wow, I can fly at two hundred miles an hour. That's bananas. How brilliant. This is going to be something else, he reflected as the man took out a piece of flexible bendy metal and forced it around his leg with the pliers, forming a loose and lightweight engraved anklet.

"These can't be too heavy or else they can confuse the bird in flight. It weighs practically nothing," declared the man as he let go of the bird's leg. Ed looked down and saw a fearsome looking bird foot, long yellow fingers with sharp and offensive black claws, almost as long as the fingers. It looked to him like he had the equivalent to a thumb and three of these fingers but before he could properly inspect them, he was hurled into another bag which was immediately tied.

From inside Ed could hear the muffled tones of the two gents discussing what needed to be done next.

"Now we just have to weigh him and measure him and we can pop him back where he came from. We can weigh this one in the bag."

"Great, then we can go to the pub. This is the last one isn't it?"

"Yep, then we are free like the birds, although I don't think we'll see them in a pub. Imagine a peregrine falcon turning up at the bar."

"Yeah, can I see your ID, sir, please?"

With this, the two men went about weighing Ed. A mysterious journey followed, bumping, tossing and turning as they made their way to wherever they were going to set him free.

"I bet I've lost quite a bit of weight since the last time I was weighed," joked Ed to himself as they came to a halt and he felt the bag land gently on the floor. With all the kicking and jostling he could feel around him, he realised he'd been dumped on top of the other bag of birds.

"Right then, let's get the rope and everything ready. We'll be down this cliff in no time at all and get them all back in the nest."

At least I'm in my own bag, not with the others, reflected Ed before considering what life would be like as a peregrine falcon. He had seen a few documentaries on TV but hadn't really taken it in.

If I had known I'd become one, then I'd most certainly have taken more notice, he thought ironically.

At this moment, he felt the bag being swooped up, and from the speedy movement, imagined they were abseiling down a rock face. Soon they came to an abrupt halt and the bag was opened as they swayed from side to side in the wind.

"This one won't be in the nest for much longer by the

looks of it, John. He's much bigger than the others," shouted the man to his companion on the top of the cliff. He reached into the bag, grabbed Ed and plonked him out on a cliff edge barely as wide as his body. An uncomfortable, twiggy mattress was all that kept his bum from the white chalky surface as the wind battered him from every side. Instinctually he turned away from the gusts to protect himself, not particularly bothered to miss the cliff top sea view.

One by one he heard the other birds placed back on the cliff before the man abseiled back up to the top.

"Are any of you Transients? Are any of you Transients?" he shouted at the top of his voice amidst the deafening noise of the wind and the endless penetrating bleats coming from the other birds.

"Fuck it, this is not going to be much fun," he reflected as he tried to protect himself from the elements. Just at this moment, a larger bird arrived and perched itself next to him. It was stunningly exquisite, a beautiful, light brown front with tiny black spots and grey back. The feathers fluffed up slightly as the frightening looking yellow and black claws clung on to the side of the tiny rock ledge, steadfast in the gale force conditions. The bird's head was a dramatic grey with light brown under the beak and tasteful yellow trim around the eyes and face. The piercing shiny black eyes peered out at Ed as it moved closer with some sort of edible treat hanging from its mouth. Instinctually he found himself opening his mouth as wide as he could as the big bird stuffed the food into him.

Great! A bite to eat, and then I'll fly inland and get away from this abusive wind, thought the bird, as he consumed the offering and watched his new friend fly down from the rock and out to sea.

Oh my god, it tastes like biltong crossed with smoked salmon. I've no idea what I've just eaten but it was certainly tasty, thought Ed, turning back away from the brutal wind, wondering how difficult it would be to fly.

Mmmm, that's a point. I've never flown before. That will be a real test of nerve. I guess I just fall off and see what happens. Ed settled down into a ball, curled up his body and tried to protect himself from the elements as best he could.

I'll try and sleep here for now, build up my energy and maybe there'll be less wind when I wake up. I have a few days after all – unless I end up killing myself immediately cos it turns out I can't fly – that would be really stupid. Anyway, if I can sleep here then I can sleep anywhere. With this, Ed resigned from the day and settled for a symphony of wind to send him to sleep.

When the morning came, it was indeed less windy. He turned around away from the cliff to assess the situation. The sky was a brilliant blue and the sun had just meandered into the sky. The temperature was cold but his feathers seemed to divert the worst of it around him. He stretched out his wings for the very first time and shook his body with a stretching yawn. They were massive and felt like they stretched the whole width of the white chalky cliffs. He flexed and flapped them gently and felt their power ripple through his whole being. He looked down at the hundred or so feet drop to the rocky shore below. He might well have become a bird but his human consciousness had retained its fear of heights. He thought back on the terrifying rope ladder climb with Yedida just a day or so earlier. How useful the wings would have been then.

I just have to jump off and trust in nature. I've got wings like a 747. What could possibly go wrong? Even if I did die, I'd just come around again anyway.

With this reassuring thought, Ed moved a little closer to the edge of the tiny ledge, looking down at the terrifying sheer drop.

Well here goes, bungee without the cord. Arrrrggghhhhhhhhh.

Off he went, plummeting straight down towards the rocks, coming dangerously close to crashing back into the cliff face. He flapped his wings frantically, but nothing.

Oh my god, this is crazy. Get hold of yourself. You must be doing something wrong.

Ed stopped flapping and decided to glide, wings stiff and

erect like a small aircraft. In no time he was in the flow and becoming one with the air. It was like diving into a swimming pool without the resistance of water. He glided freely, swooping down to the left and speeding just a few feet over the tide drenched rocks before soaring to a dizzying height, looking down on the cliffs like it was toy town. Instinct guided him to glide on the various air currents, using virtually no energy whatsoever but travelling at a phenomenally blinding speed.

Up and down he went, descending, plummeting and falling before climbing and surfacing back into the heights, only to once more repeat the process.

I could live with this. This is brilliant. It makes my tortoise incarnation feel even more miserable. Weeyyheeyyyy, he thought, as he cut into and out of the wind streams like a fighter jet.

"I'm the racing car of the sky, the bullet train of the clouds, here we go again," he gasped as he swooped down low over the top of the breaking waves before reaching back up to the top of the cliff and coming to rest on a protuberant, grass-topped, chalky rock.

I guess I must be somewhere on the south coast, probably Eastbourne or Dover. That's some way from where I died. I should pay a visit to the area though, just like Jahani suggested. This is the ideal opportunity to get an overview of the whole scene, for better or for worse.

Ed considered his options and decided to fly inland, get his bearings and try to gather some more information on the circumstances surrounding his death.

Two hundred miles an hour, that would take me a very short time to get to the M3. I would just need to follow the A27 towards Portsmouth and then pick up the M27 and then on to where it meets with the M3. It won't take long at all.

The falcon swooped down off the cliff before ascending high into the sky and heading inland. It was a bright autumnal day. The trees had half shed their browning, crumpled leaves, and the colours of autumn adorned the landscape below. Ed surveyed the splendid palette, reds, browns, yellows and greens randomly arranged as if targeted by a wacky paintball gang. He wove into and out of breezes and winds, left and right, up and down. In no time he had picked up what he assumed was the A27 and followed its path along the coast towards Portsmouth.

I guess this really is 'as the crow flies', even though I'm a falcon, considered the feathery beast, as he continued on his way, gliding for seemingly vast distances without even flapping his wings.

I want to get up to the area where I died, trace back my steps and see what I can remember, thought Ed and he made surprisingly quick time powering himself along the south coast. It was an astonishing feeling, toying with the currents, surfing on air. As he proceeded, he swooped down every few road junctions to check he was on the right path. A27, Portsmouth / M3, then M27, Southampton / Bournemouth and finally M3 London / the North.

The M3 was one of Ed's favourite motorways, especially in Hampshire where it meandered its way through, over and around the South Downs, carving a path through massive white chalk hills and off into the distance. He glided down to get into the flow of the traffic, to feel once again the exhilaration of travelling at ninety MPH in the fast lane. He got in the slip stream of a speeding truck, riding against the unpredictable air flows that came from its surfaces and angles. His powerful muscular wings easily matched the task as he ducked behind and above the vehicle, much to the amazement of a coach of Japanese tourists alongside. Soon he climbed skywards again, speeding past and leaving the coach in the distance.

"Where're your speed cameras now?" he murmured to himself as he swooped down and past a hurrying police car. Just to confuse them further, he held his speed and flew in front of them before shooting upwards again, twisting and turning like a spitfire in an air display.

Ed Trew, caught on camera at last. That will surely get on a 'cops with cameras' TV show, he thought, as the two middle aged men stared with shock through the windscreen, instinctively reducing their speed.

Ed knew the road fairly well and decided to head north at

Winchester along the A34. He knew that this intercepted the A303 and then he could fly along the route he took on that fateful day driving back to London. The more he could remember, the better he would be in trying to piece together a plan in helping him decide on his future. He knew from his research that he had died somewhere west of Basingstoke near Dummer.

Can't get much dumber than texting whilst driving, reflected the Falcon, momentarily getting angry with himself for being such an idiot. He was at least relieved that no one else had come to harm in the incident.

What's done is done. I have to think ahead. If I fly north up along that route and then across on the A303 onto the northbound M3, then it might help jog my memory, thought Ed, inquisitive for any little scraps of information that could help.

Below him, the patchwork of fields created an enchanting landscape, yellows and greens, browns and greys all shapes and sizes, completely randomly carved into every sort of asymmetrical shape imaginable. Through it, the road carved its ugly, unending path, segueing off into junctions and smaller roads, like a life-giving organisation of concrete and tarmac veins. Through them a myriad of vehicles squirmed and flowed like millions of little red corpuscles speeding to fulfil their duties in the service of the all-encompassing master society. It made his death seem almost irrelevant as he looked down in awe at everything.

He sped on to the easily recognisable junction of the A34 and A303, swooping down to check the road signs before ascending once again and resuming his path along the A303, dipping into and out of the various avenues of wind.

I'd better get down lower and slow down a bit to get a better idea of things, thought Ed before plummeting down and flying just above the fast moving traffic for a while before suddenly swerving left and taking a moment's rest on a small wooden fence adjacent to the road. He looked on curiously at the traffic speeding by, each car battering him with a stomach blow of pressure and a deafening 'zwooshhh'.

I can't believe it - was I really going faster than that? he thought, surprised by the speed of the traffic.

He was soon up and off again and in no time was flying at the same speed as the London-bound vehicles, swimming in the wind. It was a depressingly barren environment, the road cut through empty countryside with little else other than fields, a railway line and a few isolated farm houses. Further on there was a small airfield, loaded with dozens of tiny planes and two healthy looking airstrips. '26' he could see clearly painted on one of them as he glided overhead.

Opposite was a small service station and restaurant. He could clearly see the big red sign 'Little Chef' adorned with a picture of a small fat cook obviously happy to serve up some tasty English breakfast.

Might I have gone in there on that fateful day? thought Ed, as he swooped over the road to look a little closer, soon realising there would have been no way of getting over from the London-bound carriageway. He continued on, and a little further he came across another service station, much smaller and next to some sort of industrial unit or scrap yard. Behind this, there was a large scale off-road dirt track for bikes, cut into the landscape like a never ending squiggly line carved by some sort of large lunatic monster.

He flew down to get a closer look, perching on the roof of the fuel stop. Soon he was overwhelmed by the fumes coming up from the pumps and was forced to swoop over to the roof of a small provision store and pay centre adjacent to the pumps. In no time people started to gather below him, outside the shop.

"Look at that little beauty," exclaimed one young man, dressed smartly in a silky, shiny, grey suit. Impatiently he dug around in his pocket before extracting some sort of smart phone device, holding it aloft in Ed's direction, and snapping away merrily. Soon the crowd started to swell, staring and snapping away at the falcon.

Might as well give them some good photos, thought Ed, as he stretched his wings to their full powerful span.

"Wow, Wow," he heard from below as they clicked with their cameras, conversing with eager enthusiasm.

"That's not something you see everyday," uttered one gent as the queue of cars started to build up, unaware of the situation and impatient to get to the pumps. Not wanting to draw too much attention to himself, Ed decided to fly over into the cover of some adjacent trees, but only after swooping down over their heads, giving them all the fright of their lives.

Once in the trees Ed reflected on the location. He was sure he had stopped off there to get petrol before the accident. It was sketchy but he could clearly remember the external décor of the place and the layout of the pumps. However, he also remembered stopping off at a café but he could see no café there. Did this mean he was in the wrong place? He decided to get a better view and flew higher into the trees.

From this new vantage point he could see another building, part of the same complex but hidden around the back. It was some sort of café and so he decided to fly over and check it out, this time from a less conspicuous position than the roof of the mini mart.

Having swooped down, he perched himself on a cluster of bushes beside a small car park and started to check out the area. The car park was virtually empty but he estimated there was space for approximately thirty or forty cars. Steam poured from the kitchen vents on the roof of the adjacent café and bright lights inside suggested that it was open for business. The building itself was a cheaply built, strange, square bungalow construct with bright yellow placards around the top displaying the name;

'303 DINER, THE PLACE TO EAT'

It looked anything but the place to eat, but on the road, if it's edible then it's a friend. The diner sat slightly on the top of a mini-incline and behind it, away from the road there was a stunning panorama of rolling hills and fields, stretching off far into the distance. The horizon was dotted with trees, clinging longingly to their last remaining browning leaves, hoping for just one more day of sunshine.

A dark grey Ford station wagon pulled into the car park and reversed into a space just along from Ed, partially obscuring his view. As the engine died into its last revolution, the final vestiges of carcinogenic smoke trickled out from the exhaust in a puff. He ducked down onto a lower section of bush, as the man got out and made his way into the café, twisting his body around half sideways, and flicking a switch that electronically locked the car, omitting a loud, single-toned staccato 'beep' in the process.

Ed jumped up to see the man heading through the front door and into the building, most certainly inspired by the big yellow sign that read; 'FULL ENGLISH BREAKFAST - £2.99' He instantly remembered that sign and how he had almost missed it and had to reverse back. This was definitely it; this was where he ate just before he died.

Eagerly he glided up onto the roof of the car before using his wing power to fly over a little closer to the café. The building was generously endowed with large windows that stretched across each side of the building, giving a clear and unhindered view of the inside. He perched on a small coin operated parking ticket machine covered in a yellow plastic cover that read: 'FREE PARKING.'

Not often you see that, thought Ed, as he stared into the café. It was a large, open plan interior, American diner-style with tasteless grooved yellow leather upholstery. Fixed six-seater booths with plastic-looking tables juxtaposed with laminated menus and paper napkins. Waitresses wearing virulent yellow costumes, and halogen lighting with yellow and red stripy walls rounded off the décor of the establishment. Ed stared and stared, wishing he had sunglasses rather than top spec falcon eyes.

Why in God's name would they think that anyone would want to eat in an environment like that? pondered Ed, as he tried to remember more about his last visit there. He could remember that he was dealing with numerous urgent matters and he was making a lot of calls on his mobile.

It was something to do with solar cubes for the Olympics, he remembered. A change in spec to meet EU requirements and a lot of hassle over some pointless technicality. Whatever it was, it didn't really matter now. He just wanted to get a clearer idea of the moments leading up to his death.

Just then he noticed a tear in one of the leather seats at the back of the restaurant. He recognised it. This must have been where he sat. With this, the door flung open, and a middle aged, fat man emerged with a large plate of sausages, bacon and eggs. In his other hand he had a small plate piled high with crispy toast. Ed ducked down and hopped behind the parking machine, as the man took up a position on one of the wooden tables outside, lifting his legs one after the other over the long stool which was joined to the table at either end.

He was soon followed by one of the bright yellow waitresses.

"You forgot your coffee, sir," she exclaimed, as she approached the table and carelessly placed the large mug down, spilling it over its edges and down through the slats of the table and onto his legs.

"Oh, Christ, can't you be careful?" barked the man.

"Sorry, sir, you forgot your coffee. Isn't it a little cold out here for you? We don't have any heaters I'm afraid."

"I'll be fine. I'm fat and I get hot. I love the cold. Would you be able to bring me some tomato sauce please?"

"Sorry, sir, you'll have to pop inside for that yourself, it's self-serve. I only came out with the coffee because you forgot it."

"Well I forgot the sauce as well," exclaimed the man as he dried his leg with the paper napkins, getting grumpier by the second.

"Sorry, sir," replied the young woman, pretty and in her thirties, and notable for her proud cleavage.

"Alright. No worries, where is it?"

"I'll show you, sir."

The man jumped up from the stool, slightly stumbling but catching his balance before the woman noticed. They disappeared into the building. Ed took his chance and flapped up onto the table, and within a very short time had consumed two sausages and made off with three slices of bacon. He headed behind the bush, dumped the bacon on the floor and started devouring it as the man returned outside.

"What the fuck! Where's my food? What the fuck is going on?"

That saves me killing some innocent bird or rodent,"

206

thought Ed, as he snapped away at the bacon, tossing it from side to side as he severed it into pieces with his beak. Soon he was up in the air again on a recce of the local area. He streamed up into the sky, and north away from the road. On his right was an intricate patchwork of tall trees arranged in square fields and straight lines. He swooped down over them, across the adjacent fields and over the small grass runways of the private airstrip, carrying on along the line of a small road and past a tiny farm with deserted outbuildings. He descended down lower and flew amongst the buildings and over the grand farm house with its luxurious garden and swimming pool, covered for the approaching winter. Up and away, he soared high into the sky once more and over numerous misshapen fields and then lower over a small village. He went down lower still and settled on top of a lamppost, looking down at the unusual combination of sweet, white-walled, thatched buildings alongside cheaper red brick bungalows, probably built in the late fifties without an eye for décor or style. He zipped off from the resting position and down along the evocative small country lanes: Yew Tree Close, Cuckoo Lane, Frog Walk. The names seemed so quaint amidst this array of accommodation they made identifying its affluence very difficult.

He soared out and away from the village, past the Fox pub and over towards the M3 motorway, proceeding to fly with the flow of the traffic back towards the service station, darting in and out of the cars like a speeding motorbike. Soon he was back over the fields soaring high, marvelling at the illogical textures and colours of the higgledy-piggledy fields below, before nearing the café and service station once more. He flew down lower and sped over a large pond, enchanted by his reflection in the glistening water. The underside of his wings looked incredibly impressive as he slowed down and swung back and forth over the water, empowered by the reflection.

Night was soon drawing in and Ed started to feel impatient about doing the nasty deed and prompting his next transience. He wanted to get back to see the Viking as soon as possible. He was enjoying the manifestation as a bird but wasn't going to be hanging around for longer than he needed to. He headed back to the diner area and took up residence in the tallest tree on the edge of the café car park, reflecting on his pending suicide.

Well I have a few options. I could just sit under the wheels of a truck and when it pulls away, that would be that. Alternatively I could simply dive bomb myself into the ground at full speed. That might be quicker. Decisions, decisions, but not ones I ever thought I would have to make.

He didn't feel comfortable with either choice but knew he had to decide one way or the other. He had learnt that the fear of the suicide was much more daunting than the actual deed itself and that once he had made the decision, he should put that out of his mind and carry out the act with total conviction.

Soon he dived down from the tree and calmly outstretched his impressively powerful wings to their full span and with a swift jerk of his body angled to his left and began to ascent skywards. He calmly manoeuvred the wings up and down with very little effort and swept over the site once more, across the busy road and back again, circling the petrol station and café. Then he flew out across the dirt bike track, swooping down to see the young boys on trial bikes as they zoomed over the bumps and humps and around the twists and turns of the course.

Darkness was falling fast and he knew he had to make a decision quickly if he was to choose the dive bomb suicide method. The last thing he wanted was to land on a patch of grass and be injured, not killed. He went higher and higher and then in an instant, snapped around and started hurling himself towards the ground, special nostril baffles enabling him to breath during the descent. Faster and faster, sleeker and sleeker he zoned in on the wide concrete floor in the middle of the industrial yard. The earth came towards him like a freight train at full speed. He remembered what the Viking had told him, bring something back, whatever you do, bring something back. Focus on it and not your death, concentrate as hard on that object as you have ever concentrated on anything before in your life.

The only thing Ed had to focus on was the anklet around his leg. He focused hard on it, directing all the power of his mind onto that little metal ring as he powered to earth at a colossal speed. Around him the ferocious sound of the wind and the friction against his body compressed his whole being, making him feel like a space craft re-entering the atmosphere. He could feel the heat around his body as he dived faster and faster, completely focussed on the ring.

The sound became unbearable and the forces around him dazzled his senses until suddenly a release, like diving into blancmange or fluid jelly bathed in a warm glowing darkness. He remained focussed on the ring, still moving at breathtaking speed but aware he couldn't see the ground anymore. Nothing was in front of him, beside him or around him. He drew to a close like a racing car slowed by a parachute. Then came the white light, a blinding pinprick slowly expanding its aperture and aspiring to engulf him.

He continued focusing on the metal ring, keeping partially conscious and trying to force his mind towards thoughts of pause. It was like trying to wake from a dream, completely powerless and yet aware to a degree where one knows action is required.

"Anklet, pause, metal ring, anklet, pause, pause me, pause," he murmured and murmured to himself over and over before drifting away, slowly falling down into a deep, deep soft black mattress of invisibility. He could neither see nor be seen, down deeper and deeper, further and further into an abyss of nothingness.

Chapter 17
The dreaded Peabody estate

He awoke abruptly to the sound of the deafening wind. He could see the portal entrances as he zoomed past but felt helpless in the strong current. Painstakingly, he tried to wriggle his body out towards the edge of the flow, putting all his energy into contorting and manoeuvring his body like an acrobat submerged in a blancmange white-water rafting circuit. Slowly but surely he got closer to the edge, the violent current calming slightly, giving him a little more power over the situation. He wriggled and wriggled further towards the edge, bringing the smooth granite walls into a clearer focus. He continued speeding in the flow, keeping in the forward stream but at a slower pace than in the centre. Beside him he could see people zapping past in the core of the ferocious wind stream.

The smooth granite tunnel walls changed appearance as he passed by, with the odd spattering of vines beginning to appear. These were similar to the ones he had witnessed with Yedida. He manoeuvred further over, reducing his speed a little as he neared the edge. The vines got thicker and denser just like he remembered. Suddenly he caught sight of a patch of white vines around a portal entrance. He realised that was his stop and jerked his body violently towards the edge of the tunnel and started to grab out towards the vines.

He grabbed and grabbed, squirmed and twisted until finally he got hold of a branch and came to an abrupt halt. The wind pressure at the edge was still powerful, and it took all his strength to keep a firm grip and get himself into a position where he could get down to the bottom opening and crawl between the vines and the tunnel wall. The whole episode had taken a lot out of him, and it was a real struggle to pull himself up onto the top part of the vine structure and crawl back along the tunnel against the flow.

The wind and gusts hit him full in the face as he struggled back towards the white vines and doorway. It took him some fifty minutes to reach his objective and the portal entrance. He climbed down, twisting his body around backwards towards the entrance. Soon he had jumped off and had landed in the side tunnel, aided by a gust of wind. Anxiously he got his bearings and went over to the area where he remembered they had hidden the watch.

Maybe I'm in the wrong tunnel, he thought, as he nervously reached behind the vines, reaching with his arms at full stretch to explore the walls and hunt for the small opening. He fumbled as he peered through the vines, running his hands along the smooth black rock, searching for the hole. Soon his eager hand discovered a small opening and delved deep excitedly to search out the sturdy watch.

"Yes, yes, yes. This is the place," he yelled as he pulled out the watch, startled to realise there was a second one on his wrist.

"How can there be two of them? I wonder if they say the same time."

He looked down and compared both timepieces, surprised that they differed in time by more than six hours, even though both had actively ticking second hands evenly dancing around the circle of numbers on their infinite endeavour. He wondered momentarily as to how the discrepancy transpired, but in the scheme of things, it was one of the least important.

He put the older watch in his jacket pocket and then remembered the anklet and how he needed to bring something back with him from his transience. Nervously he bent down and lifted his trouser leg to realise it wasn't there. He checked the other leg also but nothing, no anklet or even any mark where it had been.

Of course, how stupid can I have been, that would never have fitted around my human ankle, what a jerk! Maybe I've completely wasted my time with this transition," thought Ed, as he began to scramble frantically through his pockets to see if it could have ended up there.

"Bingo, absolutely brilliant, here it is. This is absolutely incredible!" exclaimed the intrepid traveller, as he pulled the tiny object out from his trouser pocket.

That's unreal. It's just too much. I never thought in a million years that I could have brought something back. This is brilliant, thought Ed, as he proceeded into the tunnel system remembering Yedida's advice out loud.

"Mum-my, dad-dy, right, right, left, left. That's my route. Easy."

As Ed set off into the tunnel, he could see the silhouetted figure of a man just in the distance sitting down against the wall with his head in his hands.

"Hi, I'm Ed. What's your name? Are you okay?"

Ed's greeting startled the man who jumped to his feet and stood with panic some twenty-five feet away.

"Don't come any closer. Who are you, what do you want? Why am I here? I'm going to call the police, do you hear me?" exclaimed the panicky individual in a northern English accent.

"Have you been in the tunnels before or is this your first time? Are you alright?" asked Ed, as he moved closer to the man who started to back away. Ed could see he had a fire-fighter's costume on, regular UK issue as far as he could tell.

"Have you been here before?" enquired Ed once more.

"No. Who the fuck are you and where the fuck am I? What's going on? I've just had the nastiest and most realistic dream that I was a fucking snake and now I am in this god awful tunnel. I don't even know how I got here," replied the man with confusion.

"Were you in the other tunnel with the wind?"

"Yes. Terrifying."

"Did anyone help you out of it?" enquired Ed, continuing to edge forward.

"No, no one helped me. I woke up clinging to the branches just by that entrance over there and crawled in here. That must have been six hours ago at least. Where are we?" said the man pointing back past Ed towards where he had just come from.

"Listen, I'm a friend. My name is Ed Trew. I can help you but you need to trust me. What's your name for a start?"

"Johnny, Johnny Rathbone. Am I glad you have come

along," he replied, as he cautiously moved forward and the two men shook hands.

"Listen, Johnny, I know you must be disoriented right now. I've been there and I know it's not easy. What I'm going to tell you won't really help how you feel a whole lot," explained Ed.

"Well I'm prepared to listen to anything right now, mate," replied the fireman.

"Have you ever been in a bar and someone has told you a story that you could never believe, even in a million years?"

"Many times."

"Well I'm about to tell you something which will make you think I am a mad, deluded, liar, probably escaped from the local nut house."

"I just want to get out of here and back to my life. If you can help me do that then I'll believe anything. Can you do that?" replied Johnny.

"Well yes and no. Your dream was very vivid and real wasn't it?"

"Yes, it was and it lasted for what seemed like days. I kept waking up and then realising I was back in the dream, it was terrible."

"And I guess you died at the end, didn't you?"

"How do you know that? Yes, I did. I thought if I killed myself in the dream then I would have to wake up at home. I was sick of feeling like a slimy, fucking snake, wriggling my body and slithering around in the grass. It was disgusting. I ended up crawling into the middle of the road to get run over. I can still see the headlamps bearing down upon me with the terrifying noise of the engines and then -" Johnny was interrupted mid flow.

"And then you saw a blinding white light and you were travelling at the speed of light towards it and then you blacked out and somehow found yourself clinging to the vines."

"Yes, that's it. What is this, SAW 6 or something? How the fuck do you know that?" shouted Johnny aggressively.

"Lets sit down, there are some things you need to know," replied Ed, sitting on the floor against the wall. Johnny did likewise and the two sat facing each other across the tunnel. Ed thought for a moment about how he could break the news to the young man, probably no older than his mid-twenties. He sat silently for a while before taking a deep breath and launching into his whole story, the tortoise right through to the Viking and the falcon. Johnny sat in disbelief with a smirk on his face as Ed brought the story into the present.

"And that's when I heard you shouting along the tunnel."

Johnny sat for a moment in silence looking down at the ground with his head in his hands.

"And you expect me to believe that do you? You expect me to believe that I'm dead and was reincarnated as a snake? It's preposterous," replied Johnny, obviously annoyed and upset by the whole thing.

"Honestly, mate, I don't really care whether you believe it or not. In a few days you'll know it as fact. I'm not here to convince you of anything. It's by chance that we've met and to be honest, that's fucking lucky for you because after too much time in this tunnel, you'd be here for the rest of eternity, whether you like it or not. Now you have choice, something that thirty minutes ago you didn't. This predicament is all about the choices you make and believe me when I tell you that you have to make them pretty god damn quick."

"Alright. Don't be angry, Ed. You can understand my reluctance to believe this bullshit, can't you? Less than a few days ago I was fighting a fire on a council estate in Middlesbrough being pelted with stones by the local youths, then the next thing I know I am a suicidal snake followed by this bizarre scenario. It's a massive nightmare."

"I understand. Man, it was easier for me to believe it all when I looked at my reflection and saw I was a tortoise. I totally feel for you. It's so beyond belief, I know that. I have no idea what else I can say to you apart from the advice Sam gave to me. Try to remember as much as you can. It might help somehow in the future. You say you were on a fire job - is that the last thing you recall?" enquired Ed reassuringly.

"Yes, the dreaded Peabody estate. They would set fires in

car parks and on waste land and then we'd come to sort it out and get pelted with stones, rocks, lumps of metal and anything they could lay their hands on. It was like a sport to them."

"Why? Why on earth would they do that?"

"Christ, ask me one on science? I have no idea. I would like to have seen how they reacted if it was their house on fire with their possessions in it. I'm sure they'd be more friendly then, mother fuckers," replied the fireman angrily.

"I've never heard of anything like it. It's such a strange thing to do, battering firemen with rocks. It's beyond comprehension."

"I know. We had to endure that at least twice a week, often taking resources away from other emergencies that needed attending."

"Do you think you might have got hit with a stone?"

"I don't remember that, maybe I did though. It was known to happen. Sandy West got hit once and was in hospital for a week. Nasty fractured skull, even with his helmet on. Really nasty."

"Well my advice to you, Johnny, is to think back as much as you can, try to delve deep and gather as much info as possible. I, however, need to be on my way, mate. Sorry. You're welcome to come with me, but it's not an easy journey and honestly, not one I think you should take at this moment. There are some strange intersections to say the least."

"What shall I do then, stay here?" replied Johnny with desperation in his voice.

"I would suggest two possibilities. One is that you go back to the big tunnel where you arrived, climb up onto the top of the vines and jump into the flow to zap you into your next transience. The other is to climb over the vines and up stream by a short distance and then down into the tunnels on the other side. You'll find people there who can help you. Bear in mind though, you would still only have a couple of days before you needed to jump or else you'd get stuck here permanently. I think that's something you should only commit to if you are really sure."

"It's all so confusing. I really don't know what to do. Do you think I should see the Viking guy you mentioned?"

"Yes, but not now. That's a one-way ticket and I have no idea what would happen if you've only been through once. Apparently he prefers more experienced Transients anyway. My feeling is that you should get a few reincarnations under your belt and get a better understanding of what is happening here."

"Maybe you're right. Listen, you go off and I'll sit here for a while to decide. I'm totally strewn. Maybe I should go and meet more people first. I can't believe I'm in this situation."

"Up to you. Remember though, you only have four days to do it on each transience. After that you will lose your human awareness and consciousness and melt away into the animal. Maybe that's an easier choice anyway."

"Do you then get reincarnated after that animal dies?"

"I don't think so. I think it's only the human consciousness and soul that survives. Once that's gone I think that's it, you'd just disappear from existence," replied Ed as he got up.

"Okay, whatever. Listen, you go, I'll be fine," sighed the fireman gloomily, still sitting down whilst Ed stooped, shook his hand and turned off into the tunnel and into the distance.

"Thanks, Ed. Good luck and hope to see you again," he yelled, as Ed quickly walked around a slight bend and out of sight.

"Yes, hope so. See you, Johnny," he shouted back as he continued on his way, wondering what would happen to the novice. In no time he was squeezing himself through the elasticated, shrunken tunnel and was again confronted by the strange fortune teller in the cave. Cautiously he reached out and grabbed his arms, which were still sticky and sweaty just like last time.

Chapter 18
Sambar for breakfast

Ed rushed from the front of the hotel and had not got more than a few yards up the street when he remembered his precious bag, a bag he could not be without, a bag he'd carelessly left in his room on the third floor. He shot back into the lobby and over towards the stairs, only to find a flowery wallpapered wall where the stairs once were. Anxiously, he rushed along the corridor to the lifts and other stairway but nothing, just walls and doors. Sheepishly, a room service maid brushed past him with her laden trolley, looking up into his face with her green, lizard-like eyes. He clambered out of the window and began climbing up the outside of the building, clinging onto half dead vines, the roots springing from the soft sand and cement mixture between the crumbling bricks.

He tried to pull himself up further but continuously fell back, each time damaging the surface and the vines a little more, making further progress impossible. Hurriedly, he rushed back inside, panicking to get to his room. This time the lift was there and he jumped in, pressing the illuminated third floor button with angst, prompting its speedy ascent. It screeched to a halt. Urgently, he swung open the metal cross braced door and ran out, only to realise it was the fifth floor, not the third. He turned around to see the lift had disappeared, and in its place was just a solid wallpapered wall. Terrified, he ran along the corridor and found another lift, once more pressing the third floor button with desperation. It couldn't travel fast enough as he willed it downwards, desperate for his bag. Finally, it reached its destination after what seemed like an eternity and he ran out, only to find he was running out of the front of the hotel, full circle but this time with his bag in hand. Ferociously, he ran down the street and into a dark tunnel and blackness, silence and calm. He slowed like a fish in jelly and came around to find Pritvijaj looking over him.

"Where's my bag?" he shouted angrily as he looked all around for the leather satchel, still caught in uncompromising 'fire drill' mode.

"Ah, the bag one, that's always entertaining. Not my type of hotel, I can tell you that. Good to see you again, Ed. You weren't gone long. Come on, up you get," said the Indian fellow as he reached out his hand and helped Ed up to his feet.

"Headache again?"

"Umpgh, yes. Horrible. I feel like shit!" exclaimed Ed.

"Don't worry, come and lie down for a bit. Jahani is out walking and will be back in a few hours. You can rest in his room and have a nap. I will sit with you, come on," urged the small man, as he ushered Ed along and into the familiar circular room he remembered from last time.

Pritvijaj arranged some of the sheepskins in a line on the sand, folding one of them up into a pillow and guided Ed down onto them.

"Sleep here for a while, Ed. I'll sit over there. If there's anything you need, give me a shout."

"Thanks, Pritvijaj. You're very thoughtful. Actually, one thing puzzles me. How come these sheep skins aren't worn out after hundreds of years?" enquired Ed.

"No idea whatsoever. It's just another mysterious element in an altogether mysterious setting. Positively mysterious, I would say," replied Pritvijaj with a wry smile, as Ed nodded straight off into a deep sleep.

Luckily for Ed, his sleepy dream state was a lot calmer than the psyche jump with the fortune teller. Soon he was stirring back into the present and the company of Pritvijaj.

"A little more relaxing this time, I hope, Ed?" enquired the small man.

"Yes, quite so. Thank God, eh!" replied Ed.

"Well, maybe not God, but thank goodness if you like. What were you on this last embodiment?"

"Some sort of falcon, incredibly fast and powerful. I even had a full English breakfast on this trip."

"Really, I preferred idli and sambar for breakfast. I do miss food you know. That was a passion of mine. Even if I could feel hungry again, I would be grateful but alas, that's not possible anymore," exclaimed Pritvijaj sadly.

"I can't imagine an eternity of not feeling hungry. It must be hard to come to terms with?"

"It was at the beginning. Like many things, you do get used to them after a while. It's such a distant memory but one that surfaces every now and then really strongly, like a distant echo floating in on the breeze."

"I must say, I really look forward to that moment when I jump back over into another transience and get the chance to gorge myself. Anyway, how long have you been, er, dead?" asked Ed, still surprised to be addressing such a question.

"Nineteen forty-seven, just before India was officially partitioned by the British. I was a Hindu living in Karachi and had to get over the partition line before the deadline. Things got very nasty between the Muslims and the Hindus. I had never seen such barbarism of man upon man. The British were pretty heartless and cruel but when Indian was unleashed upon Indian, the violence was equally merciless. I sadly never got to my destination. I so wanted to see the free and independent country that we had wished for over so many years. That's what hurt me the most."

"Everyone must have resented the British so much for pulling out of the country like that?" replied Ed, sitting up and crossing his legs Indian-style on the floor.

"I don't think people were all that aware of how it was going to pan out. By the time the violence took hold, people were too busy ripping each other's throats out to be blaming the old masters."

"Well I've read a little about that point in history and frankly, Pritvijaj, it makes me ashamed to be British, as does the manner in which they abandoned the Palestinians and divided the peoples of Sri Lanka. So much of that could have been avoided with some sort of responsible governance and considered withdrawal. It really was the bedrock of the brutal conflicts in those countries and really came to influence the new millennium in a negative way. It's so sad, most particularly for people like you who never got to see their dream fulfilled," replied Ed passionately.

"I don't know too much about the more recent events, but certainly the religious divisions created during the British Raj were very harmful to the Indian people. However, I was always a fatalist. Things are so for a reason, even if we never know what that reason is."

"That's very philosophical. It's certainly an attitude that helps to prevent burning resentment. I'm learning so much from all the people I meet on this journey. I really respect you all," reflected Ed thoughtfully. Just then, there was a stirring at the entrance to the room and soon the huge-framed Jahani was entering.

Ed noticed the Viking had donned his characteristic horned helmet, forced over his thick hair at the top which splayed out uncontrollably from the bottom like he'd been spontaneously ejected from an electric chair. His large eyebrows inhabited his inquisitive frown like two rolled-up sleeping bags. His fixed stare locked onto the Englishman like a laser guided weapon.

"Oh, greetings, Ed, that was quick. How was it? What were you this time? Did you get any further information? Tell me," enquired the old man as he removed his helmet, flung it in the corner and sat down by the Englishman. The exposed hair burst out instantly with spring-loaded urgency.

"Yes to everything, I even got something to bring back," exclaimed Ed, as he reached into his pocket to retrieve the small metal anklet, while wondering how all that hair fitted into the helmet.

"That's extraordinary, Ed, it usually takes people years and multiple incarnations to do this. You must have a very powerful psyche," replied the Viking as he took the article from him and inspected it.

"Excellent. What is it though?"

"I was a rare falcon and this was the identifying ring that was attached to my leg soon after I transitioned," replied Ed.

"Marvellous, this is great stuff. Tell me what happened. Did you get back anywhere near where you died and find out anything new?" enquired Jahani actively excited.

"Yes, I'm pretty sure I have traced my last steps before I

was killed. I'm certain I know exactly what happened and where I was moments before the accident."

"And is that where you killed yourself, on the transition I mean?"

"Yes, very close," replied Ed.

"Excellent. We have a lot to go on here. Leave this with me and give me your watch as well. It's an article that's been close to your body and will help."

"I have two, well, two of the same article I mean. I have the one that always appears on my wrist when I arrive here and also one that I had left in the tunnel when I was with Yedida as a landmark to find this place again. I hid it behind the vines just near the transience tunnel."

"That's very good. Have you changed the time of either of them?"

"No. They were both different times though. I don't understand that," replied Ed.

"Marvellous. Give me them both. I'll keep them with your anklet and jacket. This is all most helpful." With this, Ed realised there were two identical jackets, the one he was wearing and the one he had left with the Viking on the previous visit.

"I'll need some time to think things through, Ed. I don't make decisions on the spur of the moment with things like this. Let's relax a little. There are plenty of places to stay here. Why don't you let Pritvijaj show you to a private room where you can rest. Then we can meet later and spend some time together. I'll tell you some Viking stories."

"Sounds good, Jahani. All positive. I just had a sleep but will rest anyway," replied Ed, as he and Pritvijaj got up and he was shown out and along the outer tunnel to a quiet room, equally white with characteristic jet black vines. The layout was similar to all the rooms he had slept in before, a soft spongy bed and small bedside chair. It also had similar silky curtains but this time they were pure white and not black.

"Don't you feel insecure not having a room with a door and lock?" enquired Ed, as he sat down on the bed.

"Not really. You get used to it anyway."

"I think I was a bit more insecure in my day. I can't think

221

of a time when I stayed in a hotel room and didn't block the entrance with a chair or double check the door was locked at least five times when I left the room."

"You might want to look at that."

"What do you mean look at it; I'm dead?"

"That's very true. Anyway, I'll leave you to rest and build your energy up. I'll come and get you later on."

"Sounds good," replied Ed, as Pritvijaj swept out of the room leaving the curtain swaying to and fro behind him. Ed lay back and watched it swinging, getting calmer and calmer until it was perfectly still and unruffled. Pristine silence filled the air, pure and simple. Ed stared down at his thick gold wedding band with sudden and unexpected deep sadness. He missed Abella immensely.

Chapter 19
Arctic Bear Haggis

"Wake up, Ed, you've been sleeping for over a day, come on, wake up."

Pritvijaj rocked Ed's shoulder gently, bringing him into the present, albeit in a drowsy and bleary eyed state.

"Oh, really? A whole day? That's mad. I guess I really needed a rest eh," replied Ed as he span round and sat on the edge of the bed.

"Look, come on through when you're ready. Jahani is waiting for you in his room."

"I'll be through in a minute when I've pulled myself together," replied Ed, watching Pritvijaj depart around the edge of the silk curtain.

He sat still for a moment, wondering what decisive insight the Viking could be serving up. He was still not sure what this quest for information was doing for him in the long term. At one point or another he would have to make a decision on staying somewhere permanently. He knew he didn't want to continue forever in the uncertain world of transient hopping.

Well at least I'm better off than I was at the beginning. I'm a lot better informed and at least I have an opportunity to consider options in detail rather than being whisked into immortality against my will. I must continue to approach this positively, thought Ed, as he got up, slid past the curtain and ambled the short distance to Jahani's.

"Oh, Ed, good to see you, come in, come in and sit down," said the Viking, gesticulating for Ed to sit near him.

"Take a look at this," he said, handing Ed his Viking helmet.

"That's not too practical is it?" stated Ed, as he came and sat opposite the old man.

"Not very comfortable either - try it on," replied Jahani.

"Okay then," said Ed, as he popped the large helmet onto his small head only to see it fall off and straight to the floor.

"I guess I haven't got the right head to become a Viking. Were they all big built like you?"

"No, not really. It was a mix like everywhere else. I was born in Sicily, not Scandinavia like most people think."

"Sicily? Were the Vikings in Sicily?" enquired Ed.

"Yes, not many of us though, maybe a few thousand at most."

"I never knew that, although Viking history was never my strong point," replied Ed.

"It was a good place to be brought up. It was very liberal in comparison to the rest of the bigoted medieval world. It was tolerant and respectful towards all the diverse religions and cultures. My mother was a native Sicilian woman. She was called Agata, which means good and she really was that," replied Jahani.

"Respectful of religions; you know that Vikings kind of got a bit of bad press, raiding, raping, pillaging and all that? It wasn't like that then?" enquired Ed nervously.

"Not in my circles. We were just migrating from the frozen ice lands where we came from, looking for warmer climates. Often we would mix with the local populations and try to live side by side. Sicily was the prime example of that. Many aspects of daily life got intertwined: religions, food, marriage, you name it."

"Really? Intertwined religions? I thought the Vikings were pagans?"

"We just had a multitude of gods that were worshipped for different purposes and at different times. That's why the integration of Christianity was so easy for us, it was just another one to put on the mantelpiece and add to the set. Mind you, it did start to take over a bit."

"Tell him about the giants, Jahani," piped in Pritvijaj.

"He probably knows that already."

"Erm, giants? No, I don't know about them."

"Well, like good and evil in Christianity, we had giants that were the counter force that challenged our gods," replied Jahani.

"How do you think Christianity started to take over? Vikings seem so strong-willed from everything I've read."

"Business. All because of business and money. Christians were not allowed to trade with us for religious reasons. To get around that, they instigated a scheme whereby Scandinavian traders could partially convert to Christianity to make deals possible. It was called 'primsigning', and although falling short of baptism itself, served the purpose. It led to a lot of full conversions though," replied the Viking informatively.

"I never knew that. Was that happening in Sicily?"

"Yes, everywhere in the trading Christian world as far as I know."

"Did you spend your whole life there?"

"Apart from some overseas excursions, I was based there throughout."

"Somehow I was expecting swashbuckling stories of sea-borne invasions and ferocious battles with swords and axes, maybe even some Walrus ice cream and Arctic Bear Haggis?" replied Ed.

"There was a bit of that - swashbuckling adventure that is, not the frosted mammal cuisine. We used to go over to Sardinia, North Africa and other random islands in the Mediterranean. They were scared of us and there was normally a bit of friction, but that was how things were back then. There wasn't much severe fighting that I was involved in. Just as well, because I was really a man of peace and enjoyed the calm serenity of Sicily."

"If you don't mind me asking, how did you die?"

"Again, an anticlimax for you here as well. No tales of bravery and craziness. No death in battle or falling on the sword. Just a quiet and natural death in my sleep. I remember clearly nodding off after a night of fine wine and steak and then suddenly being in the tunnel with the bright light. That was that, nice and easy. I had a good life with no regrets."

"Any children?"

"Yes, eleven children and three wives," replied Jahani with a wry smile.

"Goodness, that's definitely not an empty pistol," replied Ed.

"That's right. I've met three of my children again in here.

Very strange. They all moved on to other pastures though, just like you want to."

"Yes, indeed. Maybe we should touch base on that. What have you been thinking?" enquired Ed.

"The only bit of information I'm missing at the moment is your approximate date and time of death. It was in the UK wasn't it?"

"Yes. I can do better than approximate. I looked it up on the internet when I was a cat. It was September 22nd 2009 at approx 17.00 near Dummer in southern England," replied Ed.

"Ah, that's excellent. More detail than I normally get. Give me a little while to work out some figures in my head," requested Jahani, going into himself.

"Okay then, no probs," replied Ed, as the two sat in silence whilst Pritvijaj left the room.

"See you later," said Ed, as he disappeared, only to be put in his place with a big 'schhhhhh' from the Viking's road-mapped face. They sat quietly for a while, Ed reflecting back on Johnny in the tunnel.

"Right, I'm set. Let's go up to the departure tunnels and we can talk further," announced Jahani as he got up and headed towards the door, followed swiftly by Ed.

"Jahani, I forgot to mention. I met a first-time Transient in the tunnels on the way here earlier."

"Well I'm glad you didn't bring him here. I hate babysitting first-timers. Did you leave him there? What did you tell him?"

"Yes, I left him there and advised him to jump again or else head back through the tunnels and meet up with others. He had plenty of time, it was his first day," replied Ed, as they proceeded along and up the same black stairs they'd used previously.

"Good advice. You can't get involved emotionally with Transients until they are permanent. It's important to remember they're temporary. He'll find his way for sure. Maybe I'll see him one day. Did you tell him about me?"

"Yes, I certainly did, although he found it really hard to believe any of it. You can see his point."

"That's true," replied the Viking, as they got to the top of the stairs and into the smaller long tunnel with the various portals in the floor. They walked through and past where Ed had jumped before, standing still at a point where the white granite floor turned to black, making it look like a tube of oil and milk. Jahani got Ed's possessions and put them on the floor on the dividing line between white and black, first one of the jackets, then the two watches the anklet from the bird and finally the second jacket.

"Now then, Ed, you need to make a decision. I need to let you know that this could all go terribly wrong. I can control some things but I cannot guarantee one hundred percent success. What are you expecting out of this?"

"I don't know yet. What are the options on the table?"

"Well, basically, right here, where we are standing, marks the middle of a varied selection of portals and departure points. Each one is angled differently, getting less steep and longer as we move away from the central point."

"Well what does that mean?" queried Ed.

"It means that if you travel down the longer ones then you are travelling at a faster speed when you enter the flow of the tunnel. This gives the opportunity to be propelled slightly further forward in time depending on the speed you enter the tunnel. If you go down the one in the middle, between the white and black granite then that is a sheer drop and you will enter the time continuum closely linked to the exact time of departure. However, the further down the tunnel you go away from this point then the longer the descent and the greater the speed at time of entry into the flow. In this instance you will speed ahead of time slightly, departing into the future. Quite simple really," exclaimed Jahani.

"Yes, quite simple, although if I hadn't been through all I have been through recently I wouldn't believe you. As it is, I do, although I can't see what use it would be for me to jump into the future," replied Ed.

"That's just it. It works both ways. If you look back along the tunnel the opposite direction, you also have hundreds of portals pointing into the stream in the opposite direction, against the flow."

"And?"

"And of course, you can speed into the flow in the opposite direction at various speeds to delay your position in time. The further you go along the tunnel then the further back in time you can go. Some people like to go back and witness their own death, to see what really happened. I have enough information and objects from you to be able to accurately place you a day or two before your death. Because you also finished your last transience in that area, you'll definitely end up somewhere nearby. The choice is yours."

"That's some choice. First I'll need some time to think about whether I want to witness my own death," exclaimed Ed, pensively.

"It certainly is. In your own time, young man," replied Jahani, leaving a moment for some quiet reflection. Ed sat down by the side of the tunnel, head in hands doing an accurate impersonation of Socrates. Jahani stood motionless and quiet, looking the other way, with Ed in his peripheral vision.

"You mentioned that something can go wrong. What could that be?" enquired Ed, looking up at the gent.

"In this case, with all your information, I think we're pretty safe. Normally I can't be sure of an exact time because I don't have enough information. Worst case scenario you can land months or years out and it's then really hard to come back round and do this all again because the whole personal time continuum gets really messed up. Also, I've no idea how you will manifest. You could become a snail. It all gets much harder to predict and therefore harder to be accurate," replied Jahani.

"You have to hope you don't become a fish."

"Yeah, I might very well get eaten though."

"That's true. I just wanted you to be clear of the risks anyway."

Ed sat thoughtfully.

"I can see the risks. I'm prepared to take them though. I've come this far, so why shouldn't I push the boat out further?" stated Ed confidently, as he got to his feet.

"Right, in that case let's go then. We need to walk along to the fifty-seventh tunnel going against the time flow. I'm pretty sure this will set you up a day or so before your first death."

The two of them began walking along the tunnel.

"Don't we need my things?" enquired Ed, stopping in his tracks looking back at the articles.

"No. They stay on the dividing line until you've gone, then they just disappear into thin air. I have no idea why," replied Jahani.

"How come you know about all this stuff anyway, like a wise sage, or wizard or something?" enquired Ed.

"It's just that I've been here for a long time and have been interested enough to experiment. Maybe there are other places like this in other tunnels. I don't know. Anyway, I would send people off who were interested and when and if they came back, I would remember the data and in that way I built up a library of information in my head."

"How could you remember all that? It must be an astounding number of equations?"

"I don't know. I must have an elephant's memory or something. That's what one girl called it. Anyway, I started to get more and more accurate with it all."

Soon they had arrived at tunnel fifty-seven and stood staring into the sloping chute.

"I can't believe it, it looks so long."

"Yes, indeed. It won't be any different for you from before though. There'll be a similar white light and deafening wind noise. I think you're used to it by now."

"Thanks, Jahani. I know the drill. I've become quite fond of tornadoes," replied Ed ironically, still gazing into the daunting-looking opening, a terrifying and infinite well of darkness. He could feel his heart pounding faster and faster, throbbing at his chest as if there was an angry boxer inside. His stomach churned as his legs felt drained of strength, although still able to shake nervously at both knees. He was aware of what a big moment this was for him. All his endeavours and pursuits as a Transient had led him to this point. It wasn't long before he came to his senses and slapped the fear around its face with a determined fist of rational awareness.

The two men stood in silence for a while, Ed staring down chute fifty-seven and Jahani staring at Ed, giving him time to come to terms with the task at hand.

The silence didn't last long.

"The time has come. You should go now. I wish you all the luck possible. Maybe I'll see you again."

"Maybe. We'll see," replied Ed, as he sat down on the edge of the selected portal before slipping himself in and disappearing like a rocket-propelled skier down a steep slope. He remained fully conscious when he sped out of the entrance and slammed into the powerful contrary flow, thumping to what felt like a 100mph emergency stop against a brick wall. Everything froze; time and space stood completely still.

Soon he became aware of people floating slowly past him, looking like they'd been filmed with super slow motion cameras as they drifted eerily along. He started to spin, arms and legs outstretched like a big star. Faster and faster he span as the noise of the wind became overwhelming. Soon it engaged all its might and the familiar rapid flow of movement started to overcome his senses.

As his body was tossed, turned and spun, he intermittently caught sight of the brilliant white light, burning into his skin like a powerful laser. Then suddenly he was inside the light, completely restrained and motionless, surrounded and baked in the violent, blinding, brightness. He could feel it penetrating into his body and through his organs as if he was a pudding in a microwave, before a high-pitched deafening tone of ten thousand kettle whistles ripped into his brain and rendered him unconscious.

Chapter 20
Strictly come cooking

Ed awoke with a painful sensation around his neck. It dug into his wind tunnel, dangerously restricting his breathing, causing a slight panic.

"Come on, Beamer, get over here, please. Come on, dog," he heard as he felt his whole body yanked backwards, dragged by the restraint around his neck.

"What's up with you, for Chrissake? Come on," cried the voice of a young female, impatiently.

The whole commotion woke him fully and he soon realised he was once again transitioned into a dog. He looked down at his light brown, furry paws as his legs straightened, succumbing to the pulling on the lead whilst being yanked from a small basket. He was soon trotting along politely in the direction of the taut lead, feeling much daintier than he had as a killer hound. He looked around to see a neat and tidy house, smart white leather sofas, large flat screen TV and tasteful sand colour carpet. The walls were newly decorated and painted in a soothing light blue colour with yellow trim. He looked ahead and saw two fine legs in silk stockings with evocative open high-heeled shoes, crowned with a black pleated skirt just above the knee.

I could be up for a good view here, he thought, as he trotted behind the lady, catching up to loosen the tension on the lead. Soon they were heading through the front door and along the garden path and into a small one-track road with hedges either side. He looked around at the house as they exited through the gate, recognising the bungalow style from his excursion when he was a falcon. If it was the same village, then he was indeed very close to the filling station and diner. He hoped deep in his heart that Jahani had got the calculations right and that he had arrived a day or two before his death in the car.

They proceeded along the lane and into a slightly bigger

road, still barely enough for two cars to pass. The weather was clear with a perfect blue sky peppered with small fluffy clouds. There was a chill in the air and a slight breeze that ruffled through his fur, but nothing that caused him discomfort or misery. As they proceeded further down the lane, he recognised one of the white thatched buildings from his flight, and then the road name on a small long sign fixed to two small posts about a metre high.

'Yew Tree Close', and then a little further on, 'Cuckoo Lane'. He now knew exactly where he was. All he needed to do was whip down the road past the Fox pub and that would take him towards the M3 from the north. Then he would just need to turn right and the diner was less than half a mile away.

They turned the corner into a small park and the young lady undid his collar and let him run free. He galloped off away from her, wondering what his next move should be.

What to do? Should I run away now and try to find out the date and go to the petrol station? If I have a couple of days to kill, I might get caught by pest control or dog services or something. Maybe it would make sense to find out the date first. That might involve going back with her though and possibly getting locked in and trapped in the house.

Ed mused and debated internally, working on the best course of action. As he ran to the other side of the park he noticed a little old man sitting on a bench reading a paper. He wandered over quietly and peered at the front and back of the broadsheet as the man held it aloft, habitually consuming its stories of doom and gloom. Ed peered up inquisitively at the paper trying to focus on the date at its top.

'FURTHER CRISIS FOR LIB DEMS AS KEY MP'S SWITCH ALLEGIANCE TO TORIES,' read the bold headline negatively, underneath which there was a graph of steep social decline.

Ed remembered the headline clearly from the few days before his death. He had joked about it with Abella and had defaced the graph with an alternative and opposite one of bankers' profits. He squinted to get a closer look at the date, but was disturbed by the young lady coming from behind.

"Beamer, what are you doing? Reading the headlines, you silly dog? Stop being so daft," she exclaimed, startling the reading man and causing him to fold his paper in on itself temporarily.

"Sorry, I didn't mean to disturb you."

"Not a problem at all, always glad to be disturbed by a young lady," replied the older man, greasily, believing he was still able to woo and charm the younger of the opposite sex.

"Oh, well, Okay then. You carry on, I must be off," replied the lady, nervously aware of his scruffy stubble and dirty ears. She backed up and reached down for the dog. Beamer was having nothing of it and squirmed out of her grip and up onto the bench, trying to grab a view of the paper.

"Beamer, come here," she shouted.

"Beamer? That's a cute doggie name. What's yours?" interjected the man, slime dripping from every word with over-inflated and irritating self love.

"I'm Georgie," he added, ignoring the dog, putting the paper down between him and the hound.

"Mia, I'm Mia," replied Mia, feeling anxious and repulsed by the individual as she reached down to manhandle Ed from the bench.

"That's a nice name. It means 'golden flower' in my native Polish," replied the man, lying outright.

"Oh," replied Mia, her eyes staring emptily over his right shoulder as she grabbed Ed, just as the dog caught clear sight of the date at the top of the folded page: September 21st 2009. Excitedly, he accepted Mia's embrace and looked into her perfect face, big blue eyes and glowing dark-red, shoulder-length hair. His muddied paws dirtied her white blouse as she turned away from the man, flustered and confused.

"Bye, darling," he exclaimed, as she retreated, clutching Ed whilst trying to fix the lead back onto his collar.

"Yeah, bye," she replied with dismissive contempt as she clipped the clasp and gently put the dog down onto the short grass, extending the lead to its maximum to let him roam a little more freely. The man returned to his paper, whilst Mia dusted her blouse off as they proceeded back across the small park towards the gate. Ed now knew he had a whole day before the death of Ed Trew and decided to go along with her back to the house.

"Beamer, why did you do that?" she whispered angrily at the dog as they passed through the gate and along the road, restricting his lead back to the shorter length. Ed looked up at her adoringly and continued on his way. He was hungry and hoped for some food once they got back. All those days in the tunnels without food, hunger or taste. It really built up a big appetite when reincarnated as an animal again.

Soon they were back at the house and he was off his lead and in the kitchen being presented with a big dish of doggie meat lumps. He tore into them like an animal possessed, and then followed it down with the whole bowl of water.

"Naughty little fella, you're hungry today, Beamer," exclaimed Mia, as she came back into the room having changed from her muddy shirt. She refilled his water bowl and then gathered together her laptop and handbag and disappeared from the front door. "See you tonight, baby," she exclaimed upon departure.

Ed was relieved. He had the whole day to himself to chill out and make a plan. He could really spend time thinking about what to do the next day and what plan of action was available to him. Should he just sit by and observe the tragic events or should he try and influence the outcome? He got more and more confused as he thought through the various options, making the whole thing much more complicated in his head than it actually was. This was exaggerated further when he came to consider the choices he would have to make on his future transitions.

He also started to analyse the logistics of the plan. How would he get out of the house and over to the diner undetected? If he did escape when she took him walking, then he would have the collar on. The collar would surely result in him being returned back to Mia. How would he get around that? The best option would be to somehow get the collar off and escape from the house. How would that be possible? Then how could he get to cross paths with Ed and what would he do if he did? He had so much to think on and organise, he didn't know where to start.

Well I guess the first thing is to go and check what sort of dog I am, thought the hound, as he leapt out of the kitchen, through the living room, into the corridor and on into the bathroom of the bungalow. Soon he jumped up onto the toilet, up again onto the sink and stared at what he saw.

Oh that's ridiculous, thought Ed, as he looked in the mirror to see a scraggly light brown, long haired, terrier puppy. He inspected the collar, a firm looking black leather strap about an inch wide with a regular looking belt buckle and restraining strap. From it hung a very clear 'Beamer' pendant with an address and telephone number. It looked difficult to undo and he was certain he would not be able do it. Disgruntled, he jumped down from the sink, danced across the bathroom and back through the living room into the kitchen. He jumped up onto a chair and then up onto the work surface and decided to check the windows for a possible escape route.

At the back, they all looked prohibitively secure, big sturdy security locks on the top and bottom of the windows, too high to reach and too awkward to tamper with. Disillusioned, he jumped down and ran over and up onto the sofa and then onto the front window ledge. These looked a little more likely with the windows having brass Victorian casement bars on the bottom and handle fasteners on the side. He was sure he could reach up and dislodge one of these handles and then lift the brass casement bar off the protuberant nodules screwed to the window ledge. He tried squeezing his paw under this brass fitting and hey presto, after a couple of attempts it sprang off. Then he batted it backwards and forwards from side to side until it settled back in place. He then reached up to the window handle which was very loose and lifted easily. He stopped just before it came open and jumped back down to the sofa and further onto the sandy carpet. It felt so warm under his paws, just like the climate of the house with its central heating on a reasonable thermostat setting.

He headed back through the house into the kitchen and his

basket, still confused about how to get out of his leather collar. He knew that was going to be a tricky one.

When in doubt, sleep, thought the dog, as he settled down on his blanket to nod off.

Before he knew it, night had drawn in around and Mia was back at home, feeding him more doggie lumps and lavishing more attention upon him. She had changed into her jeggings and a loose white tee-shirt that was kind enough to let her pert nipples arouse and dent the surface. He was a happy dog sitting on her lap watching inane TV.

"You're being a good boy tonight, Beamer. What's gotten into you? You're usually tearing all over the place," she said, as the 'strictly come cooking' theme tune blurted through the speakers offensively. Soon Ed jumped down and returned back into the kitchen. As he took refuge in his basket, he drowsily wondered what exactly causes animals to be so sleepy for vast portions of the day.

Chapter 21
17.49, 17.52, 17.56, 17.59

The following morning, things were a carbon copy of the previous day: the strained lead tugging at his neck, then the walk in the park followed by the meat lumps and Mia's departure for work. Ed was then left alone. It was September 22nd 2009, the day he once died. He wandered around the house still a little bemused how to get out of the collar. He strayed from room to room looking for something that might assist with the task, finally ending up in the kitchen and on the work surface by the window. He looked around at the cutlery and general utensils in the small plastic drainer beside the sink. Then he ventured over to the other side of the work surface where the plates and saucepans were stored, along with a wooden knife block with three of the five slots filled.

Cautiously, he nudged it with his black button nose, knocking it over and causing two of the knives to shoot out and onto the floor. The other one remained half in and half out of the wooden retainer. He looked at the knife on the surface and the two on the floor knowing that whatever he'd attempt with them would be dangerous. He remembered what the Viking had told him about the time continuum getting messed up if he went around again. This might be his only shot at being there for the fateful day. He looked around the kitchen for other articles that could help, but all to no avail. Distraught, he sat thoughtfully back on his haunches, staring down at his basket, blanket and bowl of water.

He sat on the work surface for over an hour, stuck for an idea. The collar was far too securely fastened for his paws to be effective in opening it, and so he soon came to the conclusion that one way or another, he had to cut it off. Again he looked round at the knife on the work surface and then – bingo! It all clicked into place. Excitedly, he went over to the wooden block and nudged it out of the way, forcing the knife to come loose and lie in the open. It was a bread knife with a ten inch serrated blade and a five inch handle. He batted it with his paws into the tiled corner. Patiently he manoeuvred its length so it was face down and upright on the surface with the handle directed into the corner at forty five degrees. He stooped down over the knife with his chin resting on the unsharpened back edge which was erect towards the ceiling. He put his paws either side of the blade and manoeuvred his neck so the tip of the knife was slipping between his neck and the collar. He was soon juggling with the elements to get them perfectly aligned but time after time the knife slipped loose and fell over.

He persisted again and again until finally he got it wedged in the gap, the blunt edge rubbing on his neck and the sharp serrated edge digging into the leather like a saw. He manoeuvred back and forth, keeping the knife lodged into the corner with the pressure and weight of his pushes. He was well aware that one wrong push at the wrong angle and the knife would slip right into his body and most likely kill him. Undeterred, he continued, determinedly cutting through the collar until finally, after what seemed like an eternity, it cut right through. Quickly, he stepped back from the knife and dug with his paws at the severed collar, prying it from his neck and down onto the work surface. His throat ached agonisingly from the friction of the blunt side of the blade.

Excitedly, he jumped down, thirstily drank his way through his bowl of water and leapt across the room and up onto the window ledge via the sofa. He levered up the window casement bar with ease from its receptacle and turned his attention to the brass side handle, just within his reach. Soon he had loosened the latch and the window swung open, assisted by a gentle nudge with his head. He crept out onto the wide ledge outside and pulled the window shut with his furry front paws, giving it a firm push with his bum to make sure it stayed closed. It was a fairly tight fit so it was quite secure once shut. He didn't want Mia to be burgled because he'd left the window open.

He jumped down into the garden and over to the gate, peering around the corner before diving out and speeding along the lanes towards the Fox pub. He rushed along 'Yew Tree Close', and then onto 'Cuckoo Lane', not a soul in sight. A little further on and he was in the village centre with its post office, police station and corner shop all collected around a small central war memorial and flower bed.

Stealthily, he ducked and dived behind bushes, between parked cars and onto the main road which led to the Fox pub and M3. He sped down into a small ditch which ran parallel to the road, and continued at full pace, reaching the Fox pub some fifteen minutes later. Outside, two elderly, plump men came out dressed in tatty farmer's attire, getting into a rusting Ford transit van before speeding off. Ed continued on his way, unconcerned whether they saw him or not. He was feeling nimble and fast enough to get away from anyone and anything.

The grass-covered ditch carried on for another half mile or so before petering out and up into flat land beside the road. Ed ducked in behind the hedgerow and sped further towards his destination, undeterred by the odd cars that zapped by on the quiet route. Soon he reached the M3 and followed it along, weaving through the matrix pattern of fields he'd marvelled at from the skies not so long ago. In no time at all, he was darting across the small airfield and towards the off-road trials bike course he recalled was next to the diner. It was deserted, its muddy, ragged, trail criss-crossing its way back and forth across the small piece of land, no bigger than a football pitch. He ran impatiently along its straights and around its bends with excitement as he came to realise he'd nearly reached his destination. Continuing with determination he proceeded and forced his way through a bush at the edge of the course and into the grounds of the diner.

He snuck across the car park, up a small grass embankment and took refuge behind a small concrete post. He wasn't sure what the exact time was but by the look of the sun's position in the sky, it was nearing late afternoon. Nervously, he peered around from the hiding place hoping to see Ed's silver Volvo estate appear on the slip road. Each new vehicle noise marked another chord of disappointment in the dog as they passed by the diner and drove out onto the dual carriageway. He waited anxiously, his ears shooting bolt upright every time anything moved or made the slightest noise. He could see the lights in the diner and the steam coming from the kitchen vent. The bright yellow waitress fizzled past the window every now and then, carrying oversized cups of tea and bacon rolls to lonely customers.

Ed looked on nervously until the sound of an engine drew closer and closer. It was a silver Volvo estate, just like Ed's. It stopped along from the diner on the slip road just past the petrol station. The engine revved as the driver looked at the big sign:

'FULL ENGLISH BREAKFAST - £2.99'

Next, the silver car reversed backwards, causing a minivan coming past to swerve, resulting in a meaningless exchange of horn abuse. Then the car steered over to the left and into the diner car park, pulling up just along from where the small furry dog was hiding. Excitedly, he leapt out from his position under the adjacent van and over towards the door of the diner where he peered out from behind another of the big breakfast signs. He watched in complete disbelief as he saw the car door fling open, revealing Ed's feet, then legs, body and head. He was shocked to be staring at himself. Of everything that had happened so far, this was by far the most extraordinary to come to terms with. Two Ed Trews.

He pulled a jacket from the car, put his iPhone into his shirt pocket, slammed the door shut and headed over to the restaurant. Ed could smell him even from that distance, the familiar aftershave, the slight underarm development from a day in the car. It was all so instantly recognisable and comfortable. He got closer and closer, brushed past the sign and pulled open the heavily sprung glass door, walking in to let it slowly close behind him. Sneakily, the dog popped in through the diminishing gap and dived behind the paper stand. Ed turned around as if he had seen him, went over to the stand and grabbed one of the free papers before turning around and heading over to the table with the ripped seat.

"Can I sit you here, sir?" he heard from one of the ultra yellow waitresses, pointing to a completely different table.

"No thanks, I want to sit here by the window."

"That's for six, sir, can I sit you here?" replied the waitress unhelpfully pointing towards a two-seater.

"Look around, can you see any groups fighting over who gets the last six-seater booth, darling?" replied Ed angrily, gesticulating around at a virtually empty diner, apart from one elderly, bald man in a seedy-looking stained raincoat and a couple of old bikers recounting their youth.

"Whatever. I'm getting off in half an hour so why should I care?"

"Now you've said that, why should you have cared in the first place?" retorted Ed angrily, causing the woman to disappear behind the counter along with a massive sigh that could have taken at least fifty percent of the oxygen from the room. Ed remained unmoved, picked up the menu from the table, gave it a quick glance and headed over to the self-serve counter to order his £2.99 'all day' breakfast, even though it was late afternoon.

"I'll need to bring it over to you; the sausages aren't ready," said the same girl, relocated behind the till.

"That's fine," replied Ed, as he handed over a five-pound note, took his change and returned to the table with a generous mug of coffee. Meanwhile, the dog had slinked under the tables and was hiding next to Ed's booth. Ed plonked his coffee down on the table, took out his vibrating iPhone from his pocket and stared at it in dismay.

"Oh, for fuck's sake!" he uttered with annoyance, as he slid the screen lock and began tapping away at the device. Meanwhile his small furry alter ego had jumped up on the seat next to Ed, startling him and causing him to drop his phone next to the coffee, just as the two bikers took their leave.

"Crikey, where did you come from?" said Ed, as he stared at the dog. He put his two front paws up onto Ed's upper legs, trying to look as sweet and fluffy as possible, finally resorting to stretching upwards on his hind legs and licking under Ed's chin. With this, Ed pushed him down onto the seat, grabbed his arms around him and holding him aloft, exclaimed,

"Is this anyone's dog? Hey, is this anyone's dog?"

The grumpy girl came over with his bargain cuisine.

"You can't have pets in here. Didn't you read the sign on the door? NO PETS," she shouted nastily.

"Christ, it's not mine. It just came over and started licking me. What can I do?"

"George, is this your dog? George?" she shouted at the only other person in the diner, getting a muted negative grunt in response. The seedy man continued to stare down at his empty plate, unmoved.

"Well it's not mine either. Sorry, but I'll have to serve you outside. Come on and bring the bloody dog with you," she exclaimed, as she marched off out the door with his food and coffee.

"You're polite. Where were you trained, Michelin school?" replied Ed angrily.

"I'm just doing my job if you'll let me. Come on. You'll have to go outside," replied the girl.

"Chrissake. It's freezing out there. Bloody hell!" exclaimed Ed, as he followed her out, dog under one arm, jacket under the other, the free newspaper left with disregard. Once outside, he put the dog down and tried to get rid of him.

"Go on, go over there," he exclaimed, pointing towards the bushes. However, the hound followed in the footsteps of the girl with the food as she plonked it disrespectfully on one of the tables outside the window. He jumped up onto one of the wooden slatted benches fixed to the table and waited for Ed. He remembered it was the very same table he had stolen food from when he was a falcon.

Ed joined him as the girl rudely brushed past and back into the diner without a word. Ed put his jacket on and sat clasping his coffee with both hands. The dog sat obediently looking up at him with endearing seduction.

"You mutt, look what you've done. I'm freezing out here," moaned Ed, as he put the coffee down and began munching through the breakfast, accompanied by a pining, whimpering sound from the dog, outstandingly happy to be back with himself.

"Christ, if I give you this, will you shut up?" exclaimed Ed, as he passed him down a piece of bacon, wondering what he was going to do with the refugee puppy. He devoured the tasty meat as Ed switched his attentions to yet another text, after which he put his phone down and drank more coffee. Soon the coldness bit a little deeper and Ed headed back into the diner for another plea to find the dog's rightful owner, just missing a new text arriving on his phone. The vibrations shot through the whole table and into the wooden planks, shaking the dog's internal organs like a mini-blender. Meanwhile, inside the diner, Ed headed across to the counter to speak to the girl once more.

"Is the manager here?" he enquired.

"No, I'm in charge. It all goes through me," replied the girl.

"I bet it does," replied Ed ironically, under his breath.

"What did you say? I'll have you for racism," shouted the girl in immediate response.

"I said I've got cold toes. What did you think I said?" retorted Ed.

"Whatever," replied the girl, tossing a dishcloth behind her without care, missing the work surface completely and accidently directing it into a large pot of beans.

"Anyway, I'll have to leave the dog here. It's not mine. I can't take it," pleaded Ed.

"Try the petrol station. You can't leave it here. It's a restaurant not a zoo," replied the girl with no concern.

"Your cloth is in the beans, look. Call it a restaurant? Another thing, it's sexism not racism, get it right," replied Ed angrily, as he turned round and marched out, leaving the girl to retrieve the bean-soaked cloth. Meanwhile, outside, the dog had seized his opportunity and grabbed the mobile phone from the table, dragged it over to the bushes and hidden it. Soon his new master had returned, scooped him up and began walking the short distance up the small slip road and into the petrol station.

"Has anyone lost a dog?" he shouted, as he wandered around the five or so people pumping fuel into their cars.

"Has anyone lost their dog?" he shouted again to no response before marching into the mini-mart payment booth.

"I could hear you from in here, mate. No. It's not anyone

in here, all the customers are outside," shouted a small British Chinese man behind the till.

"Can I leave it here? It's not mine."

"Sorry, mate. You'll have to take it. I suggest taking it to the RSPCA or dog home or something like that," replied the little man as one of the customers came in and impatiently started wafting a credit card in his face.

"Oh for fuck's sake. This is ridiculous. I can't take a fucking dog home. Why did you pick me, you fucking little mutt," exclaimed Ed angrily, as he headed out of the petrol station and back over to his car.

Oh, my phone. I must have left it on the table. Stupid git, thought Ed, as he fumbled through his pockets before returning to the empty table. Once again he headed into the diner, dog in arms.

"Have you found a phone outside?" he shouted across to the girl.

"You can't bring a dog in here, I told you that already. Please leave the premises," she retorted nastily.

"Oh fuck, fuck, FUCK, **FUCK!**" replied Ed in a less than articulate manner before heading out and over to his car, perplexed with the dilemma of the dog.

Lose my phone when I need it the most and get kidnapped by a fucking dog. What a day. I wish I'd never stopped here, thought Ed, as he popped the hound onto the passenger seat, buckled himself up and sped out into the night.

The dog looked up at the digital clock in the dashboard of the car; 17.40.

Maybe I've delayed Ed enough to avoid the accident, he thought, as they sped onto the M3, zapping past cars, lorries and bikes. The speed crept up to 70, 75, 80, 85 and then settled around 92MPH. The dog kept very still and quiet, nervous to his core about what would most likely happen next.

He mused on the idea that it might have been him that caused the accident in the first place, his intervention and interference. He tried to unravel the complex chronology of that and then finally gave it up as a farfetched idea. The clock ticked on, 17.49, 17.52, 17.56, 17.59, 18.03, 18.16, 18.24. On and on as the journey continued, further and further towards London and their home. He sat quiet and still, keen to not make a noise or disturb the environment and cause an accident. He stood up with his hind legs on the edge of the seat and his front paws on the glove compartment staring at the road signs as they counted down towards London. He double-checked the date on the small calendar above the car clock, Sept - 22 - 2009. It was definitely the right day and by now the time had moved on to 18.55. He hoped to his inner core that he had guided Ed away from the fatal accident and towards a fulfilling future and the realisation of his dreams. What would this intervention do to his next transience though.

In no time they were well into London, turning onto the M25 and along the M40. Soon they would arrive at Ed's West London home and he could get his first glimpse of Abella. He had missed her so much, even though he'd shagged a white furry pussy in a bush.

Chapter 22
Little telepathic monster

Ed threw his leather satchel over his shoulder, grabbed the dog under his arm and marched over towards the front door. As he fumbled in his pocket for the key, the hound squirmed free and barked at the closed door, jumping up and down in excitement. As soon as Ed slid the key into the lock, twisted and opened the door, the dog shot in like a bullet, up the stairs, round the corner into the bedroom and through to Abella's secret relaxing spot. Ed rushed in behind him, slammed the door, threw down his bag and ran after the hound. Abella was lying on a XXL beanbag in a hidden alcove in the corner of the room. The furry beast ran in and leapt on top of her, licking her face excitedly and forcing one of her iPod earpieces to fly out as he showed his uncontrolled emotion.

"Who are you, how did you get in, you naughty little fella?" exclaimed Abella, as she embraced the animal with both arms, gently stroking his silky fur. Ed entered the room and went over to see her being mauled with affection.

"This dog is something else; I have no idea how he knew you were here. It's like he's a little telepathic monster."

"Where did you get him from, he's gorgeous, a gorgeous Border terrier pup?" replied Abella, as she stroked and hugged the hound who was still lavishing affection on her face.

"He kind of hijacked me at the diner and became very insistent to come back. I couldn't find his owner and the diner wouldn't take him, so I had to bring him home. Maybe we can take him to the dog home tomorrow. What do you think?" enquired Ed.

"Well, let's see. What we need to do now is feed him. I wonder what he eats. Let's take him to the kitchen and see what he likes," replied Abella, as she stood up, gently clasped the dog and headed through the room and downstairs, giving her husband a big kiss on the way.

Ed, the dog, was astounded to be back home. He loved Abella such a lot and was so happy and relieved to realise he had successfully steered his larger alter ego away from his fateful appointment. It was a little odd being a 'fly on the wall' in their lives, but he felt complete and satisfied being home. Soon they had all moved down to the kitchen and were looking into the fridge for likely dog food. The hound held his paw out and eagerly gesticulated towards the packs of prosciutto and sliced honey roast ham.

"He can't be for real, Ed, he's pointing towards the ham as if he knows what it is. That's crazy," exclaimed Abella, a little aghast.

"I told you he was extraordinary. It wouldn't surprise me if he could open it," replied Ed, as he flicked on the TV with the remote and tuned in to live premiership football.

"Well I'll put some down on a plate for him on the floor and see how he gets on. How was your day anyway, did the meetings go well?"

"Yes, all good. The meetings went well but I was being bombarded all day with other bullshit. I really think some good opportunities are opening up though. I think we might be poised to go to the next level with the company. Let's see," replied Ed, as the TV blurted out irrelevant comments on footballers with two good feet and powerful heads.

"Oh Ed, look, he's eaten the Italian ham and the sliced ham and now he's pointing to your case of beer on the floor."

"Don't give him beer for Chrissakes, Abella, are you nuts?"

"Why not? A little won't hurt," replied his wife heading over to the case.

"Because!"

"Oh, too late. I've just poured him some in a little bowl. Look, he loves it. This dog is mad."

Ed jumped up and ran out to the kitchen, perplexed to see the hound gulping down the beer.

"I think I've seen it all now," exclaimed Ed in disbelief as the dog brushed past him and jumped up into his arm chair, arranged a pillow and settled down for a nap.

"He's in my fucking chair now, can you believe it. Are you sure he's not me?"

"I'm not. He's as affectionate as you, Ed. I love him, he's really cute. Can we keep him?"

"Let's see in the morning. We can't have a dog. How will we ever be able to leave the house?" replied Ed, not so keen.

"Oh, we'll find a way somehow, baby," replied Abella seductively.

"Let's talk about it tomorrow. One thing's for sure, he's not having my fucking arm chair," exclaimed Ed, as he lifted the dog from his chair and plonked him down on the sofa. Abella soon followed in quick succession with a small blanket and Ed the dog settled down for the night. He was so tired yet so happy to be home amongst everything familiar that he loved, the sights, the smells and the people. In no time at all he went straight off into a deep and comfortable sleep.

The silence of the morning was sliced apart by the penetrating tones of the alarm clock, fervent beeping in 7/8. It didn't disturb Abella though. She was already awake and sat upright looking at Ed as his helpless arm strayed out aimlessly from under the covers to assault the offending clock. The dog sat calmly on her lap, wide awake, enjoying the stroking being lavished upon the top of his head and back.

"Oh, Ed, can we keep him, please? Please?"

"Oh, Christ, I've only just woken up, give me a chance," replied Ed as he became conscious.

"Please, Ed, please, he is gorgeous."

"What would we do with him when we go on holiday? We'd be tied to the house."

"Let's cross that bridge when we come to it. There will be a way."

"Oh blimey. You're aggravating me first thing in the morning. Please give it a rest," barked Ed, still caught in the atmosphere of a dream. The dog remained silent, trying to be as endearing and cute as possible, staring at Abella with his head on one side and his panting mouth slightly open.

"Can you believe it I even had a dream that I was the

fucking dog? Is he taking me over or what? It was the most realistic dream I have ever had. I was really a dog but I could speak and act like a human. How strange."

"It's a sign, Ed. It means we must keep the dog. Please, please, Ed," pleaded Abella.

"Oh for Chrissake, if it keeps you quiet, we'll keep the dog. Does that make you happy?"

With this, Abella jumped out of bed, flinging the dog across upwards and onto Ed's lap. He barked excitedly as Abella jumped for joy, unable to contain her excitement. She leapt back onto the bed and kissed Ed over and over like an excited child.

"What shall we call him, Ed? What shall we call him?"

"I don't know, how about Fido?"

"Don't be silly. That's a dog's name. What about Little Ed, Little Ed will be perfect."

"Okay, Little Ed it is. Anything for some peace. Welcome to the family, Little Ed. I hope you don't eat too much."

Ed picked the dog up and handed it to Abella.

"We'll need to get a basket and some dog stuff I suppose. Let's have breakfast and go down to the pet store."

"Okay, baby. Let's do that, yippee, yippee," replied Abella, as she plopped Little Ed down on the floor and went off into the bathroom to shower. Knowing that this would be a clear hour of bathroom activity and grooming, Ed turned himself back over, pulling the covers over his shoulders. It was Saturday. Why shouldn't he have a lie-in? Little Ed jumped up on the bed and took up position outside the covers with his head resting on Ed's legs.

He knew he only had a couple of days of consciousness before he'd dissolve into the animal but was happy to let that happen. He was where he wanted to be and one way or another, big Ed had been saved and was back with his wife, ready for his dreams, happiness and success. Little Ed meanwhile had learnt so much about life, history and people in his time as a Transient. He'd come to a much deeper understanding of existence and what it could mean without ambition, possessions and greed. He'd heard stories of survival in the most extreme of circumstances, battling with compassion and understanding against the tyranny of bigotry, fascism and persecution. He'd also learnt the value of what he had right there in his own life in the present, right here and now, there and then. That place of security and familiarity was where he decided to settle. The grass was not always greener.

Printed by BoD™in Norderstedt, Germany

9 781910 104118